High Five
In
Jerusalem

Tony Barnard

ISBN: 978-1-326-86760-7

PublishNation
www.publishnation.co.uk

*This book is dedicated
to the citizens of Sarajevo
who for 1,425 days
simply refused to give in
to tyranny.*

'The Only Thing Necessary for the Triumph of Evil is that
Good Men Do Nothing'

Edmund Burke

Author's Note

"High Five in Jerusalem" is a story set against a factual historical background. The information and dates are as accurate as possible but on occasions slight alterations have been made to suit the narrative.

All of the characters in the book, other than the mention of names of actual political and military figures, are entirely fictitious. None of the characters in the story are based on any individual either alive or dead and their actions are entirely figments of the author's imagination.

The Siege of Sarajevo and the massacre at Srebrenica were war crimes that I never believed I would witness in the second half of the twentieth century in Europe, and I had hoped that mankind would learn the lessons of history and they would never be repeated. Unfortunately, the events in Daraya and Aleppo in Syria over the last few months would indicate that these lessons may yet take some time to learn.

Tony Barnard

October 2016

Acknowledgments

I would like to thank the members of my family and friends for their support and encouragement during the writing of this book, particularly during those long sessions sitting at my table in front of the laptop by the window in Portugal.

I would also like to thank the following people / organisations for the permission to use their material:

Gary Kemp / Reformation Music Ltd for the permission to use the lyrics from the Spandau Ballet song *"Through the Barricades"* in Chapter Six

U2/Blue Mountain Music for the permission to use lyrics from the U2 song *"Miss Sarajevo"* in Chapter Seven

Barry Moore / DSM Design Ltd for the Book cover design

Shutterstock (UK) Ltd for the use of the photographic images on the book cover.

Prologue

Tarik Tanović pulled back the heavy, dark curtain and lifted the wool blanket that had also been hung in front of it, just a fraction so he could see through the crack that he had created. He looked up at the sky. It was as he had feared. A full moon was beaming back at him. He lowered his gaze and he could see the streets below bathed in a soft illuminating glow. Tarik hated the moonlight.

He turned back to see his father getting ready for the routine he had carried out many times before. His face was smudged with black ash from the improvised cooking stove and he had a black woollen hat pulled right down over his forehead. His clothes were all dark and on his feet he wore some very battered black training shoes which at one time he had used to play his beloved baseball for the Dan Sarajevo Baseball Kluba.

Sejo Tanović grasped the large plastic containers that his wife passed to him. He checked them thoroughly for any signs of damage where the precious water might leak out from on his hazardous return journey. He embraced her warmly and their eyes met briefly in a moment of mutual understanding and shared concern. Then turning on his heels, he tussled the teenager's hair as he made for the front door.

"Don't go tonight papa" Tarik said in desperation *"It's too light outside"*

But he knew that his words were in vain as he heard the gentle 'click' of the front door closing very quietly.

Like all Sarajevans, the Tanović family had long become accustomed to outages of electricity and gas – in fact there had been a regular occurrence since the start of the war. At first when the light bulbs dimmed and went out they thought that the power lines had

1

been hit by shells but it soon become clear that their utilities had become a weapon of war.

The main power plant supplying Sarajevo was in Vogošća – a suburb now occupied by the Serb rebels. With a simple flick of the switch they were able to cut the power to Sarajevo whose citizens then had to make do with candles, torches and gas lamps in their bomb shelters. Daily life revolved around the availability of electricity. As soon as the power went on, word would spread like wild fire through the streets and people would start hoovering manically or boiling water, washing clothes or ironing. All of the domestic chores that one took for granted in everyday normal life. But normal life, whatever that was, had long been a thing of the past for the besieged citizens of Sarajevo. Their normality was now defined by others who were trying to control their destiny.

However even more critically, this blackout also affected the pumping station for the Sarajevo reservoir at Bacevo so no electricity meant no running water. The citizens of Sarajevo had quickly learnt that they could survive in the dark but they could not survive without water. The shortages of water were becoming more and more acute and the Tanović family like every one else in the besieged city had done their best to preserve their precious small supplies. If someone did not finish a glass of water then Tarik's mother, Jasmina would wet a sponge with it and wipe down the kitchen table and the kitchen tops. She would wash the dishes over a bucket instead of the sink so that the rinse water was not wasted as this was then used to flush the toilet. This was now their normality.

However, the supply of water was becoming scarcer and scarcer and they had not had any for a very long time now and so his father was once again performing the night ritual of running the gauntlet to the brewery which he had to do every few days even though they eked out their meagre supplies as best as they could. Initially he had collected water at night from an old well about a half mile away but recently he had been advised that the water was probably contaminated which was not surprising given that the city no longer had a functioning sewage system and a number of people had

2

become seriously ill. So the only option left, unless another more local reliable and safe source became available was the brewery. The brewery which was no longer functioning and had been badly shelled, drew its water from deep underground springs and was known to be pure. Many people did this in the day time but Jasmina had insisted that Sejo go at night which made the return journey take many times longer because of the very poor visibility but she believed that he would have a better chance of survival. The Serbs had regularly attacked the brewery building with mortar shells and the long queues of people waiting for their turn to get water were easy targets for the snipers up in the hills above the city as the brewery was situated in a vulnerable position quite close to were they were located.

Once outside the apartment block Sejo could make out a number of other similarly clad, black silhouetted figures who were also sprinting across the open ground and then diving for the shadows close to the walls of the apartment blocks on the same mission as himself in some kind of macabre dance or sinister and twisted game of hide and seek. It was insanity. There was no other word to describe it.

"How had things come to this" Sejo had often asked himself but he repeated it as he passed by the remains of the Vjenica which had been constructed in 1892-94 and was built to house the city's local officials and administrative staff and at the end of World War Two it was turned into the National Library. Prior to its destruction on 25th August 1992 by Serbian forces it had held one and a half million books and over one hundred and fifty five thousand rare manuscripts and it was the largest and most representative building from the Austro-Hungarian period in Sarajevo. Although the infrastructure was still standing the interior was completely and utterly destroyed. The fire had blackened the window spaces and the splendid glass domed ceiling that had stood majestically for over a hundred years lay shattered on the ground amongst the ash of hundreds of thousands of books. Sejo had never been an academic or an avid reader but he had loved to visit the Library as it provided a place of peace and tranquillity and a sense of magnificence and achievement.

It had been an icon of what Sarajevo had once stood for – tolerance, enlightenment and the opportunity to learn that was open to all its citizens. It was not a surprise, therefore, that it had been a primary target for the Serb artillery as part of their campaign of 'memoricide' which sought to destroy the cultural history of Sarajevo with incendiary shells. It was an iconic moment in this devastating war. It was to become a symbol of not only an assault on a city and its people but on its culture, dialogue, subtlety, multiplicity and language.

After about two hours of zigzagging and darting in and out of doorways he reached the bottom of the hill that led up to the brewery. The bright red structure of the brewery building was now clearly visible and he felt relieved at reaching his destination but very apprehensive about the long trip back when he would be hampered by the heavy and bulky water containers. He rested for a few moments against the wall of a half destroyed building with gaping shell holes in its upper floors. His heart was beating wildly, thumping in his chest and his face taut with anxiety and strain and he looked down at the stream of water that was coming down the hill from the permanently open water taps of the brewery. He took two deep breaths taking care not to exhale the air in a stream of tell-tale vapour. The air smelt bad with the acrid odour emanating from dozens of domestic stoves that were consuming shoes, plastic and other random objects that were being burnt by his fellow Sarajevans just to try and keep warm.

Steadying himself Sejo moved up the hill as fast as he could. There were about fifty people in front of him which was not many as he knew that about twenty at a time could fill their containers from the branch network of small hoses that fed off the main pipeline so he knew that he could get this done quite quickly and get back on his way home. He took his turn carefully filling all of the containers and then he strapped one once again onto his back. It was heavy and uncomfortable and every time he moved it banged against him so that when he got home he was always covered in bruises. He turned away from filling the containers and immediately his place was taken by another. Sejo did his best to smile at the old man who was holding

4

two small pathetic one litre plastic bottles which was all that he could carry,

Sejo moved quickly down the hill steeling himself for the return journey back to the relative safety of home. Suddenly there was an enormous explosion just behind him and the force threw him forwards and his face hit the cobble-stoned road hard. He lay there sucking in deep breaths, his ears ringing and he felt pinned down by the weight of the water on his back. Finally he pushed himself up into a sitting position, he felt completely numb and could not hear anything of the commotion and chaos going on behind him about twenty five metres up the hill. In the poor light he instinctively ran his hands over his body searching for any signs of blood seeping from hidden wounds. He sensed that all was ok and he managed to stand and he saw that both of his water containers were intact and he picked them up and feeling guilty that he was not returning to the carnage nearer the brewery, he automatically began to move further down the hill. He glanced back just as another shell exploded not far from the scene of devastation caused by the first.

"I need to help. You cannot just stay here and not get involved. Have you lost your humanity Sejo otherwise you will have become like them and they will have won?" he said to himself out loud not knowing what he could do but that he needed to be back there and not running away.

"But this is the reality of Sarajevo as it is now. We must survive any way we can and my obligation is to my family"

His mind was wrestling with so many conflicting emotions, his desire to remain, even after everything he had endured, a civilised human being and his refusal to be brought down to the grotesque depths of depravity of his enemies in the hills but at the same time reconcile his overwhelming natural drive to protect the ones that he loved the most Suddenly in those few seconds of confusion and deliberation he was hit in the neck by a high velocity round fired by a Serbian sniper using a Yugoslavian-made sniper M76 rifle with night-vision optics, from the ridge above the brewery. He dropped

5

the plastic canisters as he collapsed into the road and one split sending water gushing onto the cobbled stones which quickly mixed with his flowing blood to make a crimson froth on the moonlit stones as the crisp crack of the rifle rolled down from the hills.

As Sejo lay dying face down with the water canister still strapped to his back a soldier on the ridge rested his rifle and turned to his colleague next to him with a broad smile on his face and raised his hand in a high five and then held out the other hand in an expectant gesture The other sniper reluctantly delved into the pocket of his camouflage jacket and pulled out a packet of unopened American Marlboro cigarettes which he then handed over with the universal grimace of someone who had just lost a bet. It was 23.33 on 25th November 1994.

Chapter One

Sarajevo. The name is a slavicised word based on *saray*, the Turkish word for palace and the *evo* portion may have come from the tem *saray ovasi* meaning 'the plains around the palace.' It had always been a mosaic city that had been able to create a powerful image to both people who know it and to those who have never seen it. The mosaic city concept gives Sarajevo an appearance of a place that has always involved the coexistence of different religions, without building ghettos, giving the city a special cultural identity and cosmopolitan charm. For centuries Muslims, Christians, Serbs, Croats and Jews had lived easily together in close proximity sharing an identity as Bosnians and forging the culture of a city that became known as the *'Jerusalem of Europe.'*

There are a number of places that claim to be 'the crossroads of Europe' or 'where east meets west' and cultures collide but in Sarajevo they do not confront one another but genuinely intermingled. Sarajevo had been an Ottoman city, an Austro-Hungarian city, a socialist city, an Olympic city and was now to become a war city. It is surrounded by hills and mountains and sits in the middle of the valley of the Miljacka River. Like many cities it has a very complex urban identity and throughout history it has been often partially destroyed and then rebuilt. This complexity is demonstrated by the fact that the business sector alone contains a mosque, administrative court, Orthodox and Catholic churches, Jewish synagogue, caravanserais – places for travellers to stay, public baths, public dining halls workshops, besistans – shopping centres, clock towers, warehouses and military barracks. It is from this early, small Ottoman nucleus that the city had gradually developed and expanded.

Pre-war tourist brochures boasted of Sarajevo's historic mosques, Roman Catholic cathedrals and Serbian Orthodox churches with the same multicultural pride that the residents of New York or London apply to the plethora of their ethnic restaurants. The Sarajevans' traditions of religious tolerance were deep rooted dating back over five hundred years to the late fifteenth century when they welcomed the influx of Sephardic Jews who were fleeing the Spanish Inquisition.

The Tanović family lived in a second floor apartment in an old Yugoslav Communist-style non-descript concrete block. Sejo Tanović was a third generation Bosnian and a printer by trade and his wife Jasmina was a part time nurse at the local hospital. They had two children, thirteen year old Tarik and his eleven year old sister, Minka.

Before the war religion had never been an issue. Nobody really knew who was a Serb, who was a Croat or who a Muslim and nobody really cared. In pre-war Sarajevo, twenty eight per cent of the population were Serb, forty nine per cent were Muslim and sixteen per cent Croatian. There certainly were prejudices and unspoken tensions that exist in all societies. For example, Muslims thought the Serbs were not fastidious enough about taking their shoes off before entering a house as is the Muslim custom and there was a lingering jealousy from the Communist years, when Serbs had held a disproportionate share of the senior government posts but neighbours were neighbours and that was more important than anything else.

Pasan, a Serb who lived in the apartment on one side of the Tanović's said to Sejo one Saturday morning a few weeks before the breakout of war as they passed on the stairwell of their apartment block:

"All this nonsense about Greater Serbia being spouted by Radovan Karadzic – we have lived with Muslims all our lives as we have done for generations."

Six months earlier, before the start of the war they had both viewed with incredulity the speech made by Radovan Karadzic to the Bosnian parliament which was being shown on television as they drank coffee on 15th October 1991 when he had stated:

"The path along which you wish to take Bosnia-Herzegovina is a highway to the hell and suffering that Slovenia and Croatia have already experienced. Don't think that you are not taking Bosnia-Herzegovina to hell and the Muslim people maybe into annihilation."'

8

"There is no hiding it" said Pasan *"What this crazy man is predicting and forecasting is not just a bloodbath but genocide. I thought that Europe had left this behind nearly fifty years ago."*

Sejo turned and looked at his friend:

"I just cannot believe that I am hearing this that in 1992 in a modern European country we can witness on television someone threatening that forces under his command would turn Sarajevo into a 'black cauldron' and that a large section of the Bosnian population would 'disappear from the face of the earth' unless the will of the majority is rejected."

Sejo poured his friend another cup of coffee and said:

"The world has seen and will no doubt continue to see demagogues who play on false patriotism and people's fears for their future and their status in society by targeting a common enemy who can be blamed for all of their perceived ills. This is a populist and dangerous mix but I genuinely believe that modern Europe has no appetite for a return to the nightmares that were witnessed in the 1930's and 1940's by our parents and that history has taught us all lessons about tolerance and inclusion."

The cosmopolitan residents of Sarajevo had always thought of themselves as just like other Europeans, it was the war that was to make them acutely conscious of their differences. As Jasmina was to say to Sejo one night in the first year of the war as they sat huddled together in the basement of their apartment block watching the shadows on the damp walls caused by the flickering of the candlelight:

"I do not think that we really knew that we were Muslims before. It is the Serbs who have forced that distinction on us, so now I will make sure that Tarik and Minka never forget who they are."

9

Chapter Two

Thirteen year-old Tarik's world changed forever on Monday 6th April 1992.

At 7.00am his mother raced into his bedroom and closed the curtains that Tarik had already half opened.
"You are not going to school today," she exclaimed breathlessly.
"Why?' he replied.
"Because you are just not! Now get yourself dressed and join your father and sister and me for breakfast."

And with that she closed the door and Tarik could then hear the banging of pots and pans in the kitchen and then the noise of the television being switched on which drowned out everything else.

Tarik washed and dressed quickly, things were not right and he needed to know what was going on. He entered the lounge where the rest of his family were huddled on the sofa staring at the television set. The TV was tuned to the local Sarajevo news channel RTVSA and the presenter was talking furiously at the camera.

"Oh my God it really is happening here. I just cannot believe it," said his father out loud.

Behind the presenter, Tarik could see footage of groups of armed men in stocking masks setting up barricades and standing menacingly behind them throughout the city.

"I never thought it would come to this," his father said as he turned to face his wife sitting next to him. *"Not here. Not in Sarajevo."* He added incredulously.

It had only been a few weeks earlier over the weekend of 29th February to 1st March that voters in Bosnia had answered a referendum *question:*

'Are you in favour of a sovereign and independent Bosnia-Herzogovina, a state of equal citizens ...of Muslims, Serbs, Croats and others who live in it?'

The response to the referendum had delivered a unanimous 'yes' although only sixty four percent of the eligible voters had participated. Things had then escalated at a gathering pace. The leader of the Bosnian Serbs, Radovan Karadžić had declared a boycott of the election and in many Serb-controlled districts voting had not been permitted to take place. Despite this a clear mandate had been delivered to the government by the majority of the population.

A few days after the referendum, Serb militants had blocked the roads in and out of Sarajevo and five student demonstrators had been killed trying to remove the barricades. However, Sejo, Tarik's father had believed that that would be the end of the violence. Tarik had remembered overhearing his father saying to his friend who had been having coffee with him in the kitchen of their flat:

"I have a very positive feeling about the cohesion of the people in Sarajevo Pasan. We have always lived together and always will. I am certain that this trouble will not happen here."

"I am not so sure" his friend replied *"I know many families who are preparing to leave as they fear that war is coming to our city but I shall not go. Sarajevo is my home and was the home of my parents and theirs before them."*

However, what Sejo and Pasan had not realised was that unknown to them and many of the citizens of Sarajevo was that the Serbs were undertaking a huge military build-up in the mountains with the aim of choking off Sarajevo from the outside world. They had commandeered much of the arms and heavy weaponry from the disbanding National Yugoslav Army and had established a formidable force. The previous year they had already declared large chunks of Bosnia as 'Serb Autonomous Regions' and had set up their own parliament and finally on 27th March 1992 they declared a Serb Republic – *Republika Srpska* which would have the city of Banja Luka as its capital. The Serbs had effectively created the situation of a state within a state which was to be defined not just by geography but by the ethnicity of its inhabitants.

It was only later when Sejo could look back and see that the signs had all been there. At the time he had just thought it was odd that a number of his Serb colleagues at the large printing works where he was employed had unexpectedly just left the city claiming the visiting of relatives or the death of a family friend or a variety of other reasons why they would have to leave for a while and at such short notice.

The family watched the TV in silence as the events unfolded before them and it was immediately clear to Sejo that this was the start of something very serious indeed and that their lives may never be the same again and inside he was very frightened but he kept those thoughts to himself.

The optimism of the people of Sarajevo so clearly demonstrated the day before was now evaporating. Just yesterday an impromptu march for peace had made its way to the front of the Bosnian Parliament building. There had been a peaceful almost carnival atmosphere among the broad swathe of tens of thousands of Sarajevans as they chanted:

'We can live together' and 'Mi smo za mir' – we are for peace'

The Tanović family sat glued to the television for hours drinking coffee but saying little – each deep in their own thoughts wondering what all this meant. Tarik did not know but he was thinking whether it would be possible to go to school tomorrow because it was the day that they played football and he really didn't want to miss that. During the afternoon they were joined by some of their neighbours all wanting to know and understand what was happening in their city. A tense atmosphere of apprehension and disbelief had been pervading the occupants of the apartment block all day and they were all having tense, guarded conversations searching for answers and reassurance. The prospect of war was on everyone's frightened lips.

The peace demonstrations of the day before had carried on and now the TV was showing scenes of a vast heaving crowd that had swollen to about a hundred thousand people, about twenty per cent of the entire population of Sarajevo, in a great outpouring of support for ethnic unity and the maintenance of their way of life that had existed for centuries. They wanted peace. This mass of people was not led or coordinated by anyone, but they all chanted the same slogans. This was one hundred thousand people speaking with one voice. They had lost confidence in their politicians and they wanted wholesale resignations and a new government that would listen to their demands.

Suddenly Jasmina shrieked *"Oh my God"* and she brought her hand up to cover her mouth.

There had been a sudden confusion and disruption in the crowd and there was pushing and shoving and people were being trampled upon as they tried to disperse quickly and above it all were the unmistakable sounds of gunshots ringing out – *crack, crack, crack-crack.*
The TV reporter on the screen suddenly shouted to his camera man:

'Gore, snajper! – Above a sniper!'

The camera panned around and up and focused on the upper floors of the Holiday Inn behind them. The reporter didn't need to say it because everyone watching new that the upper floors of the hotel had been rented by Karadžić for the headquarters of his Serb Democratic Party. By the end of the day the TV news channel was reporting that fourteen people had been killed in Sarajevo. Things would never be the same for the next three and a half war torn years and perhaps for ever.

The following day the thunder of explosions and the whistle of bullets frightened the Tanović family and many of their neighbours and forced them to take shelter in the basement of their apartment block taking with them blankets, food and bottles of water. They were cramped into these small, dirty rooms breathing stale air as they all listened in terror as the explosions outside made the ceiling shake and dust and debris rained down on them continuously. They had already been reports of ethnically motivated murders, expulsions, and robberies which were pouring in to Radio TV Sarajevo (RTVSA). The city was on a knife-edge: there was sporadic gunfire at night, reports of snipers, multiple roadblocks, and paramilitary-run checkpoints. The residents of Tarik's apartment block huddled together for comfort and mutual reassurance.

Day by day the situation continued to deteriorate at an alarming rate. Residents started to stockpile food and supplies but no one knew how long this terrifying situation would continue. The whole city was in a complete state of flux. The days turned into weeks and the weeks into months and slowly and steadily the siege mentality settled onto the inhabitants of Sarajevo.

Tarik had always looked up to his father. He was in awe of him. As head of the family he was firm but fair and above all loving to his mother, his sister and himself. He was a good sportsman and was a member of the top baseball team in Sarajevo, Dan Sarajevo Baseball Kluba, often taking the young Tarik along to watch matches from the position of a privileged seat. Six months ago Tarik had been selected to play football for the school under thirteen football team. He was tall and strong for his age and had made a natural attacking forward. He had modelled his style on the great Dutch player, Johan Cruyff watching hours of videos of the player in action for Ajax, Barcelona and his national team and there was a large poster of him stuck up on the wall of his bedroom and underneath it had one of his best quotes:

"Don't run so much. Football is a game you play with your brains"

Sejo had always liked Johan Cruyff too because before his football career had taken off he had been a talented baseball player showing great ability both on the mound pitching as well as behind the plate as a catcher.

On only his first game for the team, Tarik had leapt high to meet an in swinging corner and the ball had soared into the roof of the gaping net passing the outstretched hands of the goalkeeper. Sejo had whooped in delight from his place on the sideline and as a treat they had all gone out for a meal to his favourite restaurant to celebrate – the *'All American Diner'*. Tarik had ordered his favourite a huge juicy cheeseburger with salty fries and a cold strawberry milkshake. Since that time his Sejo had never missed Tarik playing in a match on a Saturday morning, standing on the sidelines cheering and waving him on and encouraging him when they spoke at the half time interval.

However what frightened Tarik most in the those first dreadful days cooped up in the basement, even more than the relentless explosions that shook the building and the nervous toxic silence between them, was that for the first time he had witnessed his mother and even his father starting to feel hopeless and discouraged. All of his life he had looked to them for advice, comfort and security but now in this damp and dirty basement these initial days of war had already started to transform his parents. Even his once bubbly and effervescent sister had retreated within herself clutching her favourite doll under her arm she spent the day clinging to her mother's side.

Sejo sensed his son staring at him through the half light and turned and smiled trying to reassure him by saying:

"Don't worry Tarik this will all be over soon and the football season is not over yet"

Tarik smiled weakly back but said nothing. He could plainly see the fear in his father's eyes that he just could not hide.

"So the war has turned us all into frightened children"
he thought to himself and stared up at the ceiling as a massive explosion caused it to shake once again and the light from the single hanging naked light bulb swung and flickered causing shadows to race up and down the damp and mouldy basement walls. He also had noticed that his sister, Minka had withdrawn more and more into herself and like other children in the city she had started to imitate the aberrant lifestyle of war. Tarik had seen her shouting at her doll mimicking their mother by saying:

"Hurry up! We have to go to the bomb shelter in the basement now. No you cannot go outside to play today."

The first few days of the war turned into months and a regular unnatural and distorted pattern of life had emerged. The families in Tarik's block all moved relentlessly between their apartments and the basement depending upon the situation outside in the city. No one slept in their beds. Sleeping in a bed particularly next to a window was considered to be too dangerous because the window could be shattered by an explosion at any time and without warning.

As the supply of electricity became more and more infrequent, the television became redundant and the radio became their lifeline. It provided them with a connection to the outside world and kept them informed of what was happening in other parts of the city and in the rest of the country but Sejo knew that soon batteries would become scarce and expensive to buy or trade.

After nearly sixteen months of war on 30th July 1993 it was the radio that brought some terrifying news to the Tanović family. At about noon a large number of citizens on Miskin Street in the suburb of Alipashino Polje were waiting in a long queue for bread when a mortar shell was launched from the mountains into the crowd killing eight people and wounding more than fifty. From where the Serbs were positioned a 120mm mortar shell could find its target in about thirty seconds with devastating accuracy. A chunk of fast, hot metal that splintered into thousands of shards of sharp metal and shrapnel on impact and explosion which could shred anyone unlucky enough to be within a fifty yard radius.

"This cannot go on." Sejo had said to his neighbour later that evening as they sat smoking a cigarette in the basement:

"We are Europeans, a modern country in a modern continent. Our neighbouring countries will not allow this slaughter to continue."

However, as he had said it he didn't feel confident in his own words. So far the outside world had shown no appetite for intervention in the conflict beyond making statements and platitudes that he knew full well that the Serbs would just smirk and sneer at and then completely ignore them. This was all too evident when The UN Secretary-General, Boutros Boutros-Ghali had made a one day visit to their city on 30th December 1992, nearly nine months after the start of the war supposedly to show solidarity with the besieged citizens, he instead infuriated them, Sejo and Pasan among them, when he dismissed the conflict as *'a rich man's war'* and went on to say that:

'I can give you a list of ten places where you have more problems than in Sarajevo.'

A few days after the visit a group of Sarajevo intellectuals issued a statement bitterly condemning the Secretary-General as having signed *'a great number of futile UN Resolutions which were used to shamelessly deceive Sarajevo and Bosnia-Herzegovina for nine long months.'* The intellectuals went on to characterise his visit as *'an attack on the only thing we still have after nine months of suffering – our dignity.'*

One of the injured in the devastating attack on the people queuing for bread was a five year old girl called Irma Hadzimuratovic who suffered severe injuries to her spine, head and abdomen. She had been in the queue with her mother who was killed outright. Sarajevo's overstretched hospital was unable to provide the specialist treatment that she needed for her injuries and so the surgeon treating her started to distribute her photograph among foreign journalists at the Holiday Inn. From 6th April 1992 onward, the Holiday Inn with its distinctive yellow-coloured exterior had become the surrogate home for news crews from around the world as they reported on the events taking place within Sarajevo. BBC correspondent, Martin Bell, described the Holiday Inn during the siege as *"ground zero"*. *"From there,"* he said, *"you didn't go out to the war, the war came in to you."* And the war did come to the building because it was located on the most dangerous street within the city at the time, Ullica Zmajja od Borne or Dragon of Bosnia Street which had earned the sobriquet, *'Sniper Alley'*.

Several of the journalists picked up the story including the BBC which led with coverage of Irma's injuries on its nightly news broadcast on 8th August. The following day the British Prime Minister, John Major personally intervened and an RAF Hercules aircraft was despatched to airlift Irma to London's Great Ormond Street Hospital.

In the following days and months dozens more Bosnians were evacuated under a programme the British media called *'Operation Irma'* but it was a small response to a massive problem. Although the British press storm had prompted offers of one thousand two hundred and fifty hospital beds in seventeen countries by 15th August which was a significant increase on previous offers of help, it was dwarfed by the estimated thirty nine thousand children that were requiring hospital treatment throughout Bosnia.

"If they can organise this support why can't the British and other leading European nations mobilise the large resources that they undoubtedly have to help us and all our wounded children and adults and intervene to stop this genocide"
stated an exasperated Sejo when the heard news of the airlift on the radio.

18

"The slaughter goes on here every day and not just when the foreign press decide to focus on it"

As he said this he slumped back in his chair and covered his face with his hands. When he removed them Jasmina could see the face of a beaten man, a face of despondency and despair and his eyes were moist and grey. She moved across the room and stood over him and he buried his face in her chest and she cradled his head, gently stroking his hair with her fingers. They stayed still like this for a few moments in complete silence with just the radio in the background. Eventually Sejo stood with a huge sigh and walked out of the room.

So this surreal scary life continued for Tarik and his family without abating. In daylight it was too dangerous to go outside within view of the snipers and school had now been cancelled for months. At night, with no streetlights the city became a void of darkness pierced by streaks of tracer bullets and a glow from the frequently erupting fires.

As usual, that year winter descended with speed and ferocity in Sarajevo. The snow started falling in October and lasted well into March. In the early months of the siege Sarajevans could not contemplate spending a winter without heating oil or coal. But as the winter started in the first year of the war there were fewer and fewer trees visible in the city as they were all being cut down for firewood and people were forced to burn their cupboards and bookshelves and eventually the clothes and books that they contained. The previous weekend Sejo had chopped up the large wooden table in the kitchen to feed the stove. The familiar table that had the unsaid designated set places, his father at the head, Tarik at the other end facing him, his sister on his right and his mother on his left. The table that had seen so many happy times sharing a meal with family and friends was now gone and the bare open space in the kitchen was a constant reminder to Tarik of the war and a life that would never be the same again like an open sore that would not heal.

Wherever the stove was, that was where the Sarajevo families slept, cooked and bathed unless they were taking refuge in the basement as no matter how large their apartment or house as the other rooms were effectively refrigerators at an average temperature of only forty degrees Fahrenheit. Tarik tried to maintain his lessons which were often delivered on the radio and for hours he would read and study but found it difficult to concentrate in the smoky 'safe room' around the stove with the noise of explosions outside and the flickering of shadows on the walls cast by the flame of a lamp that his father had made from an empty tuna fish tin that was burning vegetable oil.

As the war dragged on, life for Tarik seemed very much the same on the surface but in reality it was slowly getting worse and worse. The days went by each like the last with no electricity, no gas, no water, no firewood, no bread, no food, no friends and no hope as the outside world seemed to be indifferent to their fate. Every day life was a grind and a fight for survival for the Tanovic family as it was for everyone else in the city. Water the essence and basis of life had become so precious. Each bucketful served many purposes – drinking, rinsing soap off dishes, then used for cleaning and finally flushing the toilet. Rice, beans and stale bread became their staple diet and Jasmina used all her creativity to try and keep the family fed but Tarik had noticed how his once athletic – looking father was now pale and thin and looking older and more haggard. He had become used to going to sleep still feeling hungry and sleep was often fitful punctuated by loud explosions and the wail of sirens.

As the war entered its third year and all of the citizens of Sarajevo became more and more miserable with the city being shelled constantly and around five to ten civilians dying daily, Tarik witnessed his parents becoming more and more despondent. He had heard his mother crying softly in the night when she thought that he was asleep and she had begun to lose all hope for the future. The Serb strategy was to obviously starve the city into submission but it seemed that the war had become a long and bloody stalemate with no end in sight. Most people in Sarajevo believed that the Serbs would continue to pound the city to rubble but that they could not get past the Bosnian defenders dug into their trenches often perilously close to the Serb front lines where they exchanged curses with people who

20

may have been school friends or work colleagues before the conflict. It had therefore become an endurance test – a battle of wills and determination.

Sarajevo was however, not well suited for defence. Splayed out along the Miljacka River the city was an easy target for the Serb artillery entrenched in the mountains. There was hardly any area that the Serbs could not see from their elevated fortified positions and with only a handful of access routes for roads and rail lines it took relatively few soldiers with their tanks strategically placed to seal off the city. To make matters worse for the citizens of the city the enemy was not only surrounding them but also lurked within. Some Serbs sympathetic to Karadžić's separatist vision remained in the city. Tarik remembered a couple of months ago when a sniper who only lived around the corner from them was caught after a chase which only added to the overall sense of confusion and panic that was endemic throughout the city.

If things had been bad so far then the third year of the war saw things deteriorate further to unbearable tragedy and pain in three separate and devastating incidents that affected Tarik and the Tanović family. At 12.37pm on Saturday 5th February 1994 a 120mm mortar shell ripped through the Markela marketplace. It had been a sunny winter's day which had persuaded many Sarajevans to shed their heavy coats and hats and pour onto the streets and try and forget that staring down at them from the hillsides there were those waiting to do them harm. It was the bright warming sunshine that had encouraged and enticed many people to venture outside and leave the relative safety of their homes. The mortar shell had plunged in a perfect trajectory straight through the market's ramshackle roof and exploded. Its five pounds of high explosive spewed out red hot shrapnel and sent corrugated metal shards slicing through the crowd. In the blink of an eye a gathering of chattering and bartering people had been mercilessly cut down.

The market was crammed full when the shell hit and the scene of utter devastation was one from hell. Indistinguishable body parts and severed limbs and pools of crimson blood were mixed with the leeks, potatoes and other vegetables that had been on sale. Everybody in the city knew somebody who worked or shopped at the market. Sixty eight people died that day and over two hundred were injured. One of the fatalities was Jasmina's sister, Jela who had gone out in search of some fresh vegetables. From a very young age Jasmina had always looked up to her elder sister for advice and support. She had never got married but had dedicated her life to teaching and had become a very accomplished mathematician. For Jasmina who had never quite mastered even simple algebra, she could not comprehend the complexity of the long and detailed formulae and equations that her sister could write out easily in front of them. In the early years of Jasmina's marriage Jela had helped support her financially and with offers of doing housework as she tried to cope with the young children and now she was lost forever.

For the surviving citizens of Sarajevo the 'Marketplace Massacre' as it quickly became known locally was their nadir. The Serbs had shelled Sarajevo for two years, they had destroyed the National Library and destroyed thousands of books and they had methodically reduced to ruins many of the city's other cultural treasures. They had cut off their water and electricity and forced them to place themselves in the sniper's telescopic sights as they chopped down every tree in every park in search of firewood or stood in line filling plastic bottles from outdoor water spigots. They had killed or wounded thousands from the safety of their bunkers in the hills and from their vantage points in the burnt-out high rise buildings that lined 'sniper's alley.' But now after two years of siege they had struck at the very heart and soul of Sarajevo. The constant relentless daily slaughter just continued and not even something on the scale of the Markela Market tragedy could make the headline *'Massacre'* in the newspapers and media of New York, London or Paris.

Moreover, Radovan Karadžić continued to deliver with great sincerity grotesque falsifications and distortions of the truth by stating that the Muslims had tried to gain the sympathy of the world by *'shelling themselves.'* These absurd statements were creating doubt in the world's media when they should not have been any and it perpetuated a situation where the outsiders could continue to stay on the sidelines.

For the next few weeks Jasmina was inconsolable. Whilst the presence of death was a daily occurrence in the city, it was still possible to remain slightly detached from it when the victims were people that you didn't know. But death had now penetrated her inner circle and it was impossible to escape from. It was just there all the time and she started to sleep even more fitfully than before with her mind continually reflecting back to her childhood when she had played carefree with both of her sisters in the garden of her parents home. She was silent for long periods of the day and sat quietly deep within herself often just pulling Tarik and Minka close to her, hugging them and refusing to let them go.

After one such occasion when the children had eventually left the room she looked up at Sejo, She could see that he was deeply worried about her and shared her sorrow but she could also see his complete sense of helplessness. After a few moments she said quietly:

"Sejo we must find a way to get our children out of this city and to safety."

"I know" he replied *"I just don't know how."*

The following month Sejo's best friend Pasan just disappeared. According to his wife he had gone out to try and collect some firewood but he had never returned and she had no idea of what had happened to him. Sejo took the loss of his friend and neighbour very badly indeed. He had looked forward to the daily conversations with his friend over a cup of coffee and a couple of cigarettes. They had helped to keep him sane and maintain some sense of normality as insanity raged all around him. Even when the price of coffee had soared to a stratospheric level on the black market they had maintained their daily ritual by substituting coffee beans for lentils. They would blacken them by frying them in oil and then ground them in a Balkan coffee grinder which resembled a pepper mill. The grounds were then boiled like Turkish coffee and then served in small cups. Whilst it looked authentic when Tarik tried it he thought it neither tasted like coffee nor lentil soup but more like muddy water. The loss of his best friend caused Sejo to become more and more depressed and indifferent to his fate but at the same time increasingly defiant and determined that he and his family would survive and in doing so defy the murderous and barbaric aggressors hidden from view in the mountains above the city.

The third winter of the war was a very harsh one. For most Sarajevans the household items that were easiest to burn had gone up in smoke a long time ago and they were now resorting to burning anything and everything. The family's supply of water had run out and their plastic containers were dry. For the last few weeks Sejo had made frequent sorties to a nearby well which had been brought into use but that had now been deemed unsafe and dangerous due to contamination. So the only option was to now make the long and perilous journey to the brewery building where natural spring water was available but this meant running the gauntlet of the Serb snipers and therefore could only be done at night but the danger was still ever present particularly on the return journey as he endeavoured to stay concealed and then run to the next nook or cranny to find some protection without spilling the precious water that he was risking his life for.

Sejo came into the room where the rest of the family were huddled round the stove and Jasmina was ripping up a cushion from the sofa to feed the stove and keep it going. His face was covered with black soot from the stove and a black hat was pulled down over his face and he was carrying two empty large plastic water containers – one in each hand and a third strapped with makeshift handles to his back. Sejo, like many of his fellow citizens had learnt that he had to juggle the complexities of his mission each time before he went out. If you carried too little water then you had to repeat the trip and run the gauntlet dicing with death form the men in the hills more often but carrying too much meant that you lost the ability to run, duck and weave to shield yourself from the very real unseen danger that was ever present.

He went over to Jasmina and took her in his arms and as they gently embraced Tarik ran to the window and heaved aside the heavy blanket and curtain that was covering it just a little to provide a crack through which he could see out. He shouted over his shoulder:

"Papa don't go tonight it's a full moon and it's too light."

But as he turned his father was already going through the door and he heard the click of the latch as it closed behind him. It was the last time he would ever see his father alive and his life would be changed forever.

Chapter Three

The death of his father hit Tarik very hard. His mother was inconsolable and just clung to his sister, Minka. Jasmina's younger sister Lejla, Tariks's aunt, who was also not married had moved into the apartment to help with the funeral arrangements which had been very simple and quick. Sejo was buried in a small cemetery in the hillside above the city that faced away from Mount Trebevic and the Serbian snipers so as to provide some limited protection for the funeral party. It was a desperately sad and sombre affair. In accordance with Muslim tradition Sejo was buried within twenty four hours of his death in a grave that had been dug by his neighbours – both Muslim and Serb alike. The formalities of the traditional funeral prayer had been considered to be too dangerous as it would expose the attendees to danger for far too long so before the interment just a few simple prayers were said by the Imam of the local mosque and the group gathered around the grave in silence.

As the small party filed away Tarik remained at the grave side, knelt and closed his eyes. In accordance with Muslim etiquette the female members of the family did not attend the funeral which only added to the loneliness and burden that Tarik now felt. A dark shadow had descended over him. He just felt numb and insensitive to all feelings and a coldness he had never known before seemed to have penetrated his heart and soul. As he knelt there, tears streamed down his face leaving it streaked with the dust that was blowing up from the open ground. He slowly unzipped his jacket and took out his father's baseball shoes that he had concealed there. He had been surprised to find them still in the apartment and that they had not yet been burnt in the stove. He kissed each one in turn and then gently tossed them into the open grave.

"I will never forget you papa"
he whispered as another explosion rocked the city not that far from where he was kneeling. Two neighbours who had acted as the

gravediggers then approached him with spades and shovels in their hands:

"You must leave now Tarik" one said *"It is not safe here"*

He turned and slowly walked back down the hillside and as he did so the two men started to hurriedly fill in the open grave which was marked for the time being with just a simple pile of stones.

The Tanović family whilst Muslim had never been overly devout restricting their attendance at the Mosque to one day a week and the observance of the most important religious festivals but even the young Tarik was aware that in Islam, family responsibility is a highly esteemed value. Although all members of the family are charged with taking care of one another, in some contexts, it is culturally appropriate for certain responsibilities to fall on the eldest son. The most important of which was the care and protection of female siblings.

As Tarik turned away from the makeshift grave and towards the relative safety of the apartment block he straightened his shoulders and looked defiantly towards the surrounding city skyline and said quietly out loud:

"We will survive papa. I will look after the family. The monsters in the hills will not win and I will make you proud of me."

The following day he fetched his school bag out of the cupboard which had not now been used for nearly three years. It was an old black rucksack and he took it to his mother:

"Why have you given me this Tarik" she said

"Because I want you to modify it to carry this" and he produced *a large, empty sealed plastic container which had once contained dried herbs in one of the local shops.*
"Why"

"So that I can fetch water and run back quickly with agility and guile without my arms and hands being encumbered. I am fast and strong and can hide in the shadows and sprint quickly without being seen by those murderers in the mountains. We have to have water mother and I have promised papa that we will survive. We will beat them"

Jasmina looked up at her son with tears in her eyes. Despite the harsh conditions of nearly one thousand days of war and deprivation, he had grown physically and matured into the sixteen year old young man that he now was. She nodded her head slowly and with great reluctance she asked him to find her sewing box.

Over the next few weeks Tarik made regular nightly runs to find water and what ever else he could scavenge. As he left the apartment block each time he took two deep breaths and felt the numbness descend over him but with it some form of inner calm and steely purpose. He became an alley cat, a master of the shadows, sprinting quickly across open ground and then flattening himself against a wall or squeezing into a nook or cranny making sure that his mouth and nose were covered with one of his sister's head scarves, a dark navy blue hijab so that as he regained his breath he did not exhale air into the cold night air which might betray his position.

Over the next few weeks as his confidence gained he ventured further and further away from the apartment block and eventually on one occasion he went passed the brewery building and found himself at the entrance to one of the Bosnian Army's defending trenches. He could see figures moved silently in the dark occasionally whispering to one another as the flash of tracer fire flashed over their heads. Here and there were camouflaged figures – he could not tell if they were male or female and they were absolutely motionless but kneeling or lying down with their face pressed against a large scope on a rifle. As he stared into the darkness a hand touched his shoulder:

"What are you doing here? Go home it is not safe here as you in sight of the snipers"
"I have come to see if I can help" replied Tarik.

"How old are you son"
"Sixteen"
"You are too young to join the army and fight" came the gruff reply *"Now go home"*

But Tarik just stood there not moving and said firmly:

"My father was killed by those bastards in the hills two months ago and I just cannot sit by trapped in our apartment day after day because if I do they have won and my father's death was for nothing"

The man in front of Tarik said nothing and then pulled a cigarette from his top pocket and cupped his hands as the match flared to conceal the light and then inhaled deeply. Tarik could see that he was in army uniform and could see the Bosnian flag emblem sewn onto his jacket and he must have been some officer rank because he had other insignia which he did not recognise.

"Where do you live" he asked Tarik

When Tarik replied he moved closer.
"Are you scared easily?" he asked casually exhaling a plume of smoke into the air.

"No – if I was I wouldn't be here now. I would be cowering in the basement of my apartment block with many of my neighbours" replied Tarik as a huge explosion lit up the night sky about four hundred metres away. A huge orange fireball then erupted and Tarik could hear further smaller explosions and the crack of automatic weapons piercing the previously still and quiet night air. The officer standing in front of Tarik did not flinch and said briskly:

"OK we do need logistical support. Three nights on and two nights off. You will be acting as a runner between the trench lines and also carrying materiel to appropriate locations. It will be hard and dangerous work because you are on the front line. There will be no pay but you will get some bread and maybe some other items to

29

take back to your family when they are available. Report here the night after tomorrow at 20.00 and wear dark clothing."

Bosnia had no army of its own having only become an independent nation only a few days before it found itself in Europe's worst hostilities since the Second World War. When the war erupted in April 1992 Bosnia had to cobble together a military from scratch with no organised defence in Sarajevo whatsoever. When the Serbs opened fire on Sarajevo there were hardly any Bosnian soldiers to return it and those that had a gun hardly had any ammunition for it. The Bosnian Army quickly assembled a pitiful arsenal of weapons by requisitioning hunting rifles and re-commissioning antiques and World War One and Two weaponry and the city's criminal underworld and gangsters were enlisted to help supply guns and other weaponry. The United Nations had placed an arms embargo on all of the former Yugoslavia in 1991 which basically sealed the disparity between the two opposing sides because the Serbs had access to all of the previous Yugoslav army's resources. Whilst the Bosnians were receiving some arms support from Iran and some other Muslim countries which eased the situation slightly, the sides were always going to be unevenly balanced.

Volunteers from all districts around the city started to come together and with often homemade weapons and little ammunition marched off to strategic points around Sarajevo where the Serbs were trying to penetrate. Starving, exhausted, in rags, they battled on the frontline for six days and returned to the city to protect and be with their families for two. Sarajevo, however was naturally difficult to defend. Strung out along the Miljacka River, the city was an easy target for the Serb artillery entrenched in the mountains. There was hardly anywhere that they couldn't see and attack with precision from their elevated positions.

By the time that Tarik was now joining the defence forces in the city, the war had rumbled on for nearly three years and despite the ferocity of the daily bombardment by the Serb artillery and some medieval tactics that they employed like filling barrels with high explosive and rolling them down the hills, the siege had become a long and bloody stalemate. The Serbs continually tried to carve the city in half by attacking the strategically important Bridge of Brotherhood and Unity, west of the Holiday Inn where the foreign media were encamped, which connected Sarajevo with the Serb-held district of Grbavica. The Bosnian Army defended the bridge and the twenty square mile enclave of besieged Sarajevo that the government controlled. As Tarik was to discover however, the Bosnians made up for their lack of firepower with their manpower, zeal and conviction.

"This is a fight to the death" one soldier said to Tarik one night
"We are fighting to defend our lives, our homes and our families and they are just up there in the hills staring down at us"

He sat smoking a cigarette and clutching an old AK47 assault rifle with only three bullets in it when the magazine took thirty. He, like many others had been instructed not to shoot unless he was sure that his opponent would kill you unless you killed him first. For three months Tarik tirelessly ran the trenches carrying and fetching materials and ammunition and dodging sniper's bullets He made good friends with a teenager called Faris Sidran who had lost his entire family in a direct hit on their apartment block by an artillery shell a few months before. He had only survived because he was out looking for firewood at the time.

Unable to advance or unwilling to retreat, the Bosnian soldiers spent their time trading curses with the enemy who were close enough to shout at. Probably many on the other side were former work colleagues, people they had sat next to on the tram or in a cafe or school pupils. Sometimes even the Serb troops would shout at the defenders to see if they wanted to buy something or even to have coffee with them. Many of the attackers were irregulars and often didn't wear uniforms and some were clearly bored and tired of the relentless siege and the conditions that they too were living in.

To Tarik it was a truly bizarre and surreal situation and reminded him of an early history lesson at school when he had learnt that the British and German troops had fought ferociously across the trenches in the First World War and then men from both sides had wandered into what was called 'no man's land' and played football together and engaged in conversation or bartering for cigarettes or other small-scale fraternisation during a Christmas truce on the Western Front in 1914 before they carried on the slaughter as soon as the truce came to an end.

Then one bitterly cold night in February, Tarik was on the front line in the north of the city delivering a box of bullets to a counter-sniper who had taken up a forward position because there were sightings of a senior Serbian officer in the vicinity. Tarik said nothing as he approached stealthily but as he bent down to place the box on the ground he heard the sharp crack of a rifle very close by which penetrated the night air and the Bosnian sniper crumpled to a heap beside him,. Blood was pumping from a wound at the front of his head and much of the back of his head was now just a mush of blood, bone and brain matter. Tarik looked away and found himself retching in the trench. Instinctively he thought of his father – is this how he died just like this? The anger welled up inside him and he knelt in the bottom of the trench careful to keep his head down low. He reached beside him and grabbed the rifle that had fallen from the grip of the fallen counter sniper. In an act of rage and undoubted stupidity he stood, mounted the rifle into his shoulder and hard against his cheek as he had seen the others do and fired a shot into the darkness above him. The recoil of the rifle almost knocked him flat on his back but almost immediately there was a scream from a man he could not see but must have been very close by. His friend Faris came running up to him as he lay on the ground:

"Are you ok Tarik? Have you been hit? I heard a gun shot' he asked urgently as he gasped for breath from the sprint he had just made.

"Yes I am ok. I just fired this rifle and it knocked me over."

He was later to learn that there had been a Serb raiding party on the way down the hill to attack that forward position

Meanwhile life just ground on for the besieged citizens who surprisingly seemed to be getting more stubborn by the day:

'We've survived so far and suffered so much that there is no way that we can give in now'

seemed to be the popular mantra present in almost all daily conversations. This stubbornness demonstrated itself in a number of ways. They opened schools in basements ensuring that that the teachers came to the children and not vice versa as it seemed more acceptable for one teacher to die getting to school rather than ten children. Desperately hungry people risked death gathering humanitarian aid dropped in the dead of the night as they were often crushed by crates that fell from the sky or picked off by Serbian snipers. Blood was in constant demand in the hospitals but an effective scheme of blood for food became popular giving donors a tin of beef in exchange for a transfusion.

However, despite these stoical efforts, inevitably in the closed cauldron that was war-torn Sarajevo, constant rumours and counter rumours constantly swirled round and round the city but in the last few days one in particular had refused to go away. When Jasmina first heard this from her neighbour sitting in the cellar one night she was paralysed with fear and she just cried out involuntarily:

'My God. Is there no end to their savagery?'

According to her neighbour, Natlija, the missing Pasan's wife, she had heard from a number of sources that the Serbs were preparing to fire poison gas artillery shells into the city to force the end of the siege. It was a well known fact by Western intelligence agencies that the former Yugolsavia had been developing Sarin and other agents at four chemical complexes, Prva Iskra in Baric, Miloje Blagojevic in Lucani, Miloje Zakic and Merima. All of these sites and the substantial chemical stockpiles were now known to be in the possession of the Serbian army. A fact that was acknowledged by the residents of Sarajevo but rarely discussed because of the incomprehensible and potentially catastrophic consequences.

Sarin gas was discovered in 1938 by scientists at the German company of I G Farben who were researching into developing stronger pesticides. The discovery was passed to The German Army Weapons Office which ordered that it should be brought into mass production for war time use. It was incorporated into artillery shells but was never used against Allied targets during the Second World War probably because they understood its potential and feared retaliation in kind.

Sarin had become infamous when in 1988 around five thousand Kurds died at Halahbja after Saddam Hussein's Iraqi used both Sarin and other chemical agents. Jasmina, like many others around the world had seen reports and graphic images which had been taken by Iranian journalists, in the newspapers and footage taken by a British ITN camera crew, airlifted out by the Iranians and spread around the globe via news programmes at the time. She, like others was now well aware that since Sarin has no smell or taste, she and her fellow citizens may very well have no idea what is going on until it is too late. The chest tightens, vision blurs and if the exposure is great enough, then this can progress to convulsions, paralysis, and death within one to ten minutes.

"I know it is just unbelievable" said Natlaija *"This is 1995. Not 1914. Surely the world has moved on and learnt from the terrible experiences of the trenches. The international community simply cannot just let this happen to us. "Just what will it take for them to sit up and take notice and intervene to stop this murder?"*

Jasmina just sat in silence. Her hands gripped into tight balls as she recalled the nightmare images that she had seen on historical programmes on the television years before, of the First World War raced through her mind. After an hour or so she just knelt and prayed quietly the light from the make shift old fish can lamp flickering off the bare brick walls and piercing both the darkness of the space and her mind. She stared at the brightness in the centre of the small flame and for five minutes she just focused on it with an intensity that she had never felt before. This small bright light burning in the darkness provided a crumb of comfort:

"Where there is light there is hope" she thought. *"Sejo I must save our children. I must get them out somehow no matter what it takes"* she whispered.

Two weeks later she was back in the basement and she and her sister Lejia were joined by Fahreta, a friend from the hospital where she worked.

"There is a way" Fahreta announced suddenly.
"To do what" Jasmina enquired
"To get the children out"
"How?" she demanded quickly
"Through the tunnel" replied Fahreta

Everyone in Sarajevo knew about the tunnel. It was an open secret although it was never publicised and no foreign journalists were ever allowed to enter it. The tunnel was dubbed *'The Tunnel of Hope'* and the building had begun in secret on 1st March 1993 under the codename *'Objekt BD.'* Nedzad Brankovic. A Bosnian civil engineer, created the plans for the tunnel's construction which connected two suburbs, Dobrinja on the northeastern side of the airport and inside the Serb siege lines and Butmir another Bosnian-held suburb on the south western side outside of the siege lines. Both entrances were heavily guarded by Bosnian troops and although the Serbs had bombed Dobrinja heavily, they had not got close enough to threaten the tunnel. It was constructed at an average height of one and a half metres and average width of only one metre. In total some two thousand eight hundred square metres of soil were removed from beneath the airport's runway whilst the tunnel was constructed.

The construction took time though, owing to a lack of skilled manpower, tools, and material to complete the task. Consequently, the tunnel was dug around the clock by hand, with a pick and shovel and wheelbarrow. – an enormous physical task comparable to the building of the Egyptian pyramids in ancient times. The diggers would work relentlessly in eight-hour shifts digging from opposite ends, and would be paid for their efforts in cigarettes rather than money as they had become the most common form of currency during the siege.

The tunnel was completed on 30th June 1993 when the two tunnels met in the middle. Use of the tunnel began the following day on 1st July 1993 and from that point onward between three and four thousand Bosniak and UN soldiers (as well as civilians) and thirty tons of various goods passed through the tunnel each day. The primary use of the tunnel was to transport aid, rations and weaponry into and out of the city. Of course, it was necessary for someone to carry all of these items through the tunnel though, and that responsibility fell not only to the male parties travelling the eight hundred metres from one side of the airport runway to the other. Women and young girls were also made to carry their share of goods through the tunnel, and most were said to be given bags/sacks weighing in excess of thirty kilos to transport whilst the men carried fifty to sixty kilos. This was no easy task. On entering the tunnel the air and the smell both changed and the walls hugged at the elbows. The iron reinforcements above preventing the roof from falling in dripped with moisture which meant that sometimes the travellers were sometimes knee high in water. It was not possible to stand up straight whilst walking in the tunnel which meant that it was necessary to literally bend in half to either walk or waddle and the banging of heads on the roof was a constant threat. It was a very unpleasant experience with the only light coming from torches that were being carried and because there was no ventilation, the air was sparse and fetid forcing everybody who entered it to wear a mask.

It was a chaotic experience for all those involved with many thin and pale people standing over small fires waiting to be told that the tunnel was now open from whichever side they were waiting on. Small trolleys were built on rail bars to move ammunition and humanitarian aid back and forth. Badly wounded civilians and soldiers were occasionally carted through the passageway but they took up valuable time and resources so it was not a frequent occurrence.

"Many have tried to get through the tunnel" replied Jasmina to her friend *"But you need a special pass as it is restricted for military and government personnel and their priorities."*

"I know" replied Fahreta *"But I have heard there is a man, a government official who for special favours will issue an occasional permit or two"*
"But I have no money" replied Jasmina solemnly
"That is not the payment that he seeks"

The consequence of the answer suddenly dawned on Jasmina and she felt sick in the pit of her stomach. She had been a virgin when she had married Sejo and he was the only man that she had ever made love to. She hung her head in despair. She was a good person, had been a loyal and supportive wife and a caring mother and she had always done her best to follow the ways and teachings of her religion and to encourage her children to do so too. But she knew that at forty two years of age that despite the ravages of nearly three years of war she was still an attractive woman and would be very desirable to any man.

She lifted her head slowly and her eyes once again focused on the small flame burning from the lamp by the wall. She stared almost hypnotically at the small flickering light at the end of the wick which was sitting in a pool of vegetable oil in the discarded fish can.

"Where there was light there was hope. Was Sejo speaking to her? They cannot extinguish the light. The light will always find a way to pierce the darkness"

She turned away and faced the darkness of the basement her face set like stone. In many ways her life too had ended the night last November when Sejo had been shot by that sniper. He had not only killed her husband but he had extinguished the flame of life and love that had burned within her. She would do whatever she had to do to save Tarik and his sister Minka. It was their lives that mattered now.

She slowly turned to face Fahreta and said softly:
"Please can you make some discreet enquiries?"

Chapter Four

It was now April 1995 and the war had been going on for exactly three years. Tarik had been supporting the city's defenders night after night and he had matured and grown up fast .There simply was no room or time for sentiment of any kind even for a sixteen year old. Tarik did not experience any excitement or adrenaline rush like he had the first few times when he had made the journey at night to the brewery to get water after the death of his father. He just now felt flat, emotionless and cold. He was just functioning and doing whatever tasks he was asked to carry out. At least he wasn't in the basement of the apartment block staring at the candlelight flickering off the bare brick walls breathing in the stale air made far worse by the cigarette smoke of frightened neighbours.

He could not be sure that he had killed anyone that bitterly cold night two months ago when he had picked up the dead Bosnian counter sniper's rifle and fired up at the hill but he suspected that he had. At least the soldier would have been seriously wounded. He had decided not to relate the incident to his family as it would only cause distress and bring back unpleasant memories of his father's death or it would plainly demonstrate to his mother that he was very much placing himself in harm's way. No, he would be judged when his time came and he was sure that he had done the right thing probably saving his own life and those of his fellow citizens and defenders around him.

Initially Tarik had been surprised that the defenders came from all the ethnic groups that had inhabited the city before the war. But later giving it some thought he was not surprised at all. Not everyone was like the men in the hills. Unfortunately they had fallen victim of a distorted and vile ideology spread by propaganda that preyed on concerns over the survival of identity and way of life when the complete opposite was true if viewed objectively. For centuries Sarajevo due to its geographical position at the crossroads of Europe, where east meets west had been a melting pot of nationalities and religions. The central mosque, the synagogue and the cathedrals of the Serbian Orthodox and Catholic faiths grew up within a few hundred metres of one another. The city often referred to as 'The Jerusalem of Europe' was the great trading point between Italian merchants and silk road caravanserai. So why should Tarik be surprised that many citizens did not want these centuries old traditions to be trampled over and crushed by a belligerent force motivated by a warped popular nationalistic agenda. They wanted to preserve the way of life into which they had been born and their fathers before them and their fathers before them. Sarajevan men had never been defined by their creed or nationality but by their openness, accommodation of differing views and by their civic pride and companionship which is why it was so sad and alien to Tarik that one of the most frequently asked questions now was:

"Sta je tvoje ime?" meaning 'what is your name'

because your name was a significant clue to your ethnicity. Before the war one's name was one's name. It was a personal definition of you as an individual not as part of an ethnic group. This once innocent question now took on a far darker implication.

Tarik had met many Serbs fighting in the Sarajevo defence units and as one said to him on one occasion when the topic of conversation amongst a group of defenders had drifted on to what they had done before the war and where they came from:

"We are all just ordinary Sarajevo guys defending our homes, our families and our city. Those artillery shells aren't discriminating which house they will destroy and which people they will kill and which they won't."

Similarly, the Sarajevan Jewish community who had decided to stay firmly neutral in the war was also determined to demonstrate that Sarajevo was and would continue to be a model for living together. Benevolencija had been an old Jewish cultural and welfare organisation and it was re-established in Sarajevo just before the war and the subsequent siege had begun. They had started to stockpile medicines and tinned food, pasta, rice and oil, enough to last the first winter. When the first shots of the war were fired they immediately organised the first evacuation of children and the elderly. Half of the one thousand four hundred strong Jewish community left the city but many refused to leave saying *'that they would not run again'* for these were the survivors of the Sephardic Jews who settled in Sarajevo in the mid sixteenth century and were some of the few who had survived the persecution of the Nazis in the Second World War.

In the opening months of the siege Benevolencija had spearheaded the early efforts to get medical supplies to the population and it eventually became the only local organisation delivering humanitarian relief on a non-sectarian basis. As half of their elders had fled the city they had more drugs than the community needed and in a clear demonstration about the importance of living together as one community they opened a free pharmacy which eventually supplied more than forty per cent of the medical needs of the population and the citizens would say to one another:

'If it isn't in the Jewish pharmacy then it isn't in Sarajevo.'

It was a bright sunny afternoon at about three o'clock and Minka had been at a friend's house, only a couple of streets away and was walking back to their apartment when the grenade landed. She had never seen it or heard it coming but the blast knocked her off her feet and embedded shrapnel deep into her arm, knee, leg, back and her neck but it was her left leg that was the worst affected. She collapsed unconscious in the street and woke up in hospital nearly four weeks later after being in a shock-induced coma. She spent almost three months in hospital and eventually the doctors told Jasmina that they could not do much more for her and that she really needed specialist treatment in a foreign hospital. They promised to do all that they could to help.

Jasmina made numerous desperate attempts to plead for assistance at the Presidential Palace and contacted every person she could think of who might be able to help. However she made no progress and became more and more despondent. That evening she sat in the cold, dark apartment suddenly feeling more alone and more desperate than ever before. She had lost her beloved husband, Sejo five months ago and although she visited his grave and prayed regularly he had not even had the decency of a proper funeral although she knew that Tarik at just sixteen years old had done his best in the very challenging circumstances.

Now her son Tarik was out on the edge of the city on the front lines somewhere, she did not know exactly what he was doing and she didn't want to but she was certain that he was in constant danger. However, she had decided some time ago that Tarik would have to cope with the loss of his father in his own way and she was sure that this was part of the healing process although she trembled every time he left the apartment and then returned maybe a day or two later, Her younger sister, Jela had been blown to pieces in the Markela market just trying to buy a few vegetables. And now Minka. Beautiful, sensitive Minka had been lying in a hospital bed for three months, her slender body blighted by terrible scars and wounds that were struggling to heal. How much more punishment must her family take she thought? Then almost immediately she remonstrated with herself for these selfish thoughts. How many families across the city had suffered loss on a far greater scale? Did the aggressors in the hills have any compassion or feelings at all? What could possibly be worth the violence, deprivation and cruelty of this magnitude? What was so wrong with the way that the citizens of Sarajevo had lived together for hundreds of years that it should be so brutally blown apart in this protracted way? She just could not understand how this could have happened or been allowed to happen in the twentieth century.

She covered her face with her hands and fell to her knees and just let the tears stream down her face. She sobbed pitifully until she didn't even have the strength to cry any more. Just at that moment her sister, Lejla opened the front door of the apartment and seeing Jasmina on the floor she ran to her distraught sister cradling her in her arms:

"Lejla I have to do something for Minka' Jasmina sobbed *"If I don't she will be maimed for life."*

41

"Then you must do whatever you possibly can or you will never be able to forgive yourself" her sister replied.

So Jasmina got up and wiped the tears away from her face with an already stained handkerchief and went to one of the remaining pieces of furniture left in the room and opened a drawer. She scrabbled through the assortment of items that had been thrust in there until she found what she was looking for. It was a folded piece of paper. She opened it and written in handwriting by her friend Fahreta was one name – the corrupt government official who could provide two tunnel passes for a special price. Jasmina just stared at it and all the hurt and anger in her heart welled up inside her but she did not cry again. Instead her face hardened and she clenched her teeth and her hands and then whispered, *"So be it."*

However, miraculously the following day fortunes changed for both Jasmina and Minka. On arrival at the hospital to visit Minka she was told by an extremely enthusiastic doctor that Minka had been selected to participate in '*Operation Second Chance,*' an airlift organised by an American group of hospital administrators in conjunction with the United Nations, The US Air Force and a Swiss-based relief organisation named the International Organisation for Migration. The airlift was due to take place in five days time and Minka could be accompanied to America by her mother. Jasmina just stared at the doctor in disbelief and then she flung her arms around his neck and embraced him warmly:

"Thank you for everything that you have done for Minka."

However, later that evening Jasmina was alone in the apartment and once again thoughts had been racing through her brain and after about an hour she had reached a conclusion. She could not accompany Minka to America as much as she knew that her daughter needed her support but she could not leave Tarik on his own. Without her guidance she was convinced that he would put himself more and more in harm's way and she would end up loosing both male members of her family.

"No," she said out loud *"Tarik must go and look after Minka and at the same time protect himself – he is only sixteen years old and has*

already lost his father. Besides I will not leave Sarajevo, the aggressors in the hills will not drive me out. I will not give them that victory and satisfaction. This is my city and I belong here with my sister, my friends and with Sejo"

Surprisingly her argument was accepted by the authorities and it was agreed that Tarik, although not injured and in need of evacuation and hospital treatment abroad could have a place on the '*Second Chance*' programme because of their unique circumstances. However, when Jasmina tried to explain this to Tarik that evening he would not have any of it and stated adamantly:

"My responsibility is here In Sarajevo to defend our city against this brutal aggression and stop people being killed. This is what my father would have wanted me to do."

Jasmina looked at her son who, even with the meagre diet on which he like everyone else had been subjected to for the last three years, now towered over her. She smiled at him with an expression of enormous pride and then the smile quickly faded and Tarik saw that her whole body suddenly stiffened in front of him, her face became taut and as she spoke her voice was steely and firm. He had never seen his mother like this before:

"No Tarik! Despite your noble and honourable aims, your responsibility is to help me care for your younger sister. We are Muslims and you are now the head of the family and you must protect your sister in a foreign land where she will be frightened and scared. This is your responsibility. Look after Minka, survive, get educated and then return to help rebuild Sarajevo when all of this insanity is over. This is what your father would have wanted from you. Do this in his name and in his memory."

Tarik's shoulders slumped and a wave of tiredness and exhaustion swept over his young body. He knew that she was right. He would not defy her and by doing so stain the memory of his beloved father. He stepped forward and held her tightly in his arms:

43

"Stay safe mother."

On the morning they were to leave Bosnia Tarik, his friend Faris and Minka, leaning heavily on a crutch under her left arm, with just a few belongings, stood at the entrance to the hospital. They were flanked by Jasmina and Jela and the doctor who had secured the place for Minka on the programme. They were collected in an armoured car and after embracing their mother who told them to hurry they sped through the city to the airport where they joined others who were about to board a US Air Force Hercules C-130 Jet.

As the armoured car roared away Jasmina just turned to Lejla and without any words being exchanged they just embraced and as they hugged each other closely and then made their way back to the apartment, Jasmina felt a huge weight lifted from her shoulders and she exhaled a long breath through her mouth. Explosions rocked another part of the city but she did not hear them.

She was certain that she had done the right thing. She was not abandoning her children, far from it. No she firmly believed that sending them away maybe the only way to save their lives. For three long years now Sejo and herself and for the last six months just herself, despite being trapped in a bombarded apartment building for months on end, having no winter clothes, limited water, no electricity, no vegetables or meat and in the midst of all this misery they had still held their children close, consoling them; and attending to their needs. Despite all of the shelling, bombing, fear, shortages, misery, cold, hunger and deprivation they had striven to provide love, security, understanding and the best protection that they possibly could in the circumstances.

She felt lighter and more content than she had done in a very long time. It was if a very dark cloud had partially lifted itself from surrounding her and as she once again stared at the centre of the flickering candle she whispered to herself:

"They cannot hurt me now Sejo."

Chapter Five

After a long flight Tarik, Minka and the other evacuees arrived at Andrews Air Force base in the United States near Washington D.C via a brief stopover at Ramstein Air Base in Germany. Tarik had never flown in an airplane before let alone in a huge military aircraft and when they landed he was just in awe at the size of the sprawling complex and the noise of military jets landing and taking off all of the time. As they disembarked he just stared around him in amazement but he did not have time to take it all in as he and the others that could walk unaided were ushered into a bus that took them to a special reception centre that had been prepared for them.

They were met by a smiling group of people - doctors, nurses, translators, hospital administrators, charity workers and a host of others who enveloped them with a warmth that Tarik had not experienced in a very long time. After a hot shower, a luxury he had long forgotten about and a change of clothes he sat down with the others to perhaps what he thought at the time was the best meal of his life – real American burgers and fries with a large Coca-Cola. But the best of it was that he was allowed to go for a second helping. After years of deprivation and living on a meagre basic diet, Tarik just could not believe it. Although overjoyed he felt an enormous sense of guilt for those they had left behind. He thought of Faris who once again tonight would be running the trenches and if he was lucky he would get a little bread and maybe some cheese. Tarik decided not to take the option of a second helping.

They spent the night at the Andrews Base and the following day the whole of the group underwent an immediate preliminary medical examination and assessment. They were eventually segmented into smaller groups and were then due to be distributed to hospitals across the United States. Tarik and Minka were scheduled to leave for Chicago the following day. For the remainder of the day they were recommended just to rest. They could watch the TV but there were no sub titles but cartoons provided an excellent diversion for many of them who were injured and scared and very unsure of themselves in a land far away from home but at least they could sleep without the noise of explosions and they were not cowering in a dark and damp cellar or basement.

The flight to Chicago took about an hour and a half the following morning. On arrival at Chicago's O'Hare International airport Minka was taken straight to the Rush University Medical Centre in the city where its Children's Hospital had a renowned international expertise in a wide range of paediatric specialities for infants, children, adolescents and teenagers. She looked frail, gaunt and scared. She had hardly let go of Tarik's hand for the whole of the journey that morning but he persuaded her that she would be alright and he would be able to see her later in the day and she reluctantly left with her carers and travelled to the hospital in a medical car.

Tarik accompanied by a charity worker and a translator was taken to his new home in the Lincoln Park neighbourhood in the north side of the city in the care of two very experienced foster parents. Paul Stanton and his wife Christine were in their late sixties. Paul was a retired insurance executive and had specialised in marine insurance and was one of the minority of Americans who had travelled extensively internationally. They had had one son, Joel who had unfortunately been killed in Vietnam in February 1968 in the Battle of Hué in the fight back by the South Vietnamese and American forces against the Tet Offensive launched by the North Vietnamese the previous month. Paul and Christine had been left devastated after the loss of Joel and had decided that they would help foster disadvantaged teenagers as part of his memory.

Minka need not have been scared as she was overwhelmed by the warmth of the welcome on arrival at the Rush medical Centre. She had her own room off a main ward and it had been decorated with roses and balloons saying 'get well soon' and she smiled broadly as this was translated for her. She had the services of a female translator (a language teacher at the university) for a few hours each day who also served as a rudimentary English teacher who had been provided by the Illinois State Department of Public Aid. During their conversations the following day Minka turned to her and said:

"It is incredible to know that there is still humanity – that there are people who still care"

The language teacher said nothing and just turned away to face the window and bit her lip hard to stop herself bursting into tears.

The following day the charity organisation had set up a small local press conference such was the interest in the city in her story and that of her brother. The session opened with the orthopaedic surgeon who was looking after Minka stating that she had been evacuated from Sarajevo because of the severity of her injuries and that the bones in her leg and knee joint had not healed and there was a lot of infection and she would need a minimum of two months of surgery and rehabilitation. During the half hour session Minka was asked by a journalist for the *Chicago Tribune* newspaper through the translator what life was like back in Sarajevo. Without hesitating she stared back at him and said:

"Sarajevo used to be a beautiful city, a cultural centre and place of friendship and community but now it is hell on earth. The snipers killed my father and many others who were just queuing for water or bread or just trying to buy vegetables in the market. They don't care if they are shooting at armed soldiers, men, women, old or young or children it is just a target to them. They do not care about the death or injury of their target or whether it has ended or blighted a life. They do not care about the effect that will have on the people around them. They have absolutely no humanity or conscience whatsoever. To them we are not fellow human beings we are not the people they may have passed in the street, sat down next to at a café or worked with. To them we have now just become something that must either be killed or driven out of the city by fear and intimidation."

When she had finished speaking the journalist who had stopped taking notes half way through just stared at the expressionless fourteen year old girl, closed his notebook, turned and walked silently out of the room unable to speak.

Whilst Tarik had settled in quickly to his new environment, Minka was never happy in America. She was homesick and constantly missed her mother and friends terribly. She struggled to learn English and was dependent on the services of a translator for conversations of more than a few words. This inevitably left her in a state of isolation and loneliness despite all the best efforts of the nursing staff. Her first spell in hospital lasted three months during which time she underwent numerous operations on her left leg. Fortunately her other injuries had healed well but her leg was to prove problematic. Tarik visited her as often as he could to try and lift her spirits and every time that it was time for him to leave she clung desperately to him; her eyes wet with tears.

After three months Minka was discharged from the main hospital and placed in a specialist recovery and rehabilitation unit in the hospital grounds which she attended as an outpatient. Paul and Christine Stanton had offered their home for Minka to stay in so that she could be with Tarik. But Minka had decided that as soon as he was fit enough and there was no more that could be done to help her she wanted to return home at the earliest opportunity provided that it was safe to do so. After some lengthy interviews and conversations the hospital offered her the opportunity to stay as a guest boarder in a furnished apartment usually reserved for visiting medical staff because the senior administrators believed that they now had an obligation to Minka. They had helped bring her to the States and had offered her the medical attention that she urgently needed and they now needed to finish the job properly and not 'drop the ball' as the Senior Vice President and Chief Operating Officer had stated in a press release to the media. Minka was delighted to accept their kind and generous offer and was happy to pose for photographs next to the senior hospital executive whilst supporting herself with a pair of crutches.

As Tarik was to discover over the next few months, many Bosnian refugees decided to Americanise their names as their original ones were hard for Americans to pronounce. They also believed that it would help them to integrate quicker onto their new communities and aid them in their search for higher education and better employment opportunities. Tarik however, was adamant that he would not do this. He would not become 'Tad Tanon' or something similar. He was proud of his ethnicity and identity and would always retain his Tanović surname in honour and respect of his father and their heritage.

In their different ways and different circumstances the Tanović siblings were adapting to their changed circumstances and to life in America. Sarajevo was five thousand miles away but it might have been in another solar system so different was their life. It was something that both of them found difficult to comprehend and come to terms with on a daily basis. They had been lucky enough to have been give this opportunity through the 'Operation Second Chance' programme and they realised how fortunate they were as the TV news channels continued to broadcast footage of the war and things were no better at home in fact they were probably a whole lot worse.

Minka stared at the TV in her room and said to herself:

"How many people are still in Sarajevo who are severely injured? Why was I so lucky to be able to escape?"

She thought of her mother and her aunt trying to survive in their apartment and in the basement and now dependent on the generosity of their neighbours for water and food:

'How would they manage to cope?'

She rolled into her pillow and just wept.

Fortunately for Minka the nursing staff had recognised the symptoms of 'Survivor's Guilt' or 'Survivor Syndrome' which can occur when a person perceives themselves to have done wrong by surviving a traumatic event when others did not and over the next few weeks she was provided with careful counselling just through casual conversation.

Chapter Six

It was the early summer of 1995 and whilst Minka was recovering back in hospital from her final correctional operation on her left leg. Tarik was settling in at school and working hard on his English lessons both at school and outside of it as he had enrolled in 'English as a second language' course at night school which he attended three times a week. Tarik and Minka had managed to speak to their mother twice in the last few months as telephone lines had now been installed through the tunnel and they had been able to have two brief but very emotional conversations which Minka had been able to clutch on to as if it was a physical lifeline.

Tarik regularly watched the reports coming out of Bosnia and Sarajevo on CNN on the TV in his foster parent's lounge. The face of the correspondent Christiane Amanpour became very familiar to him often reporting wearing combat boots and a flak jacket and Tarik liked her matter-of-fact, frank and strident style of reporting often laced with emotion. At times it seemed that she was the only person telling the outside world the truth about what was really going on in Bosnia. CNN's reach to sixty nine million households in the United States and one hundred and ten million worldwide ensured that her reports were sometimes uncomfortable viewing for policy makers in western capitals who all watched her transmissions and eventually she was undoubtedly able to make an impact on policy towards the Balkan conflict.

Whilst he couldn't understand all of the commentary the striking images and videos told him everything he needed to know and had tried to forget but nothing could prepare him for the reports of what had happened at the Muslim enclave of Srebrenica on 14th -16th July. At first his foster parents had tried to shield him from the horrendous images but he had insisted and they reluctantly relented and what he saw was beyond anything he had experienced in Sarajevo. It was just beyond the comprehension of even him who had seen and witnessed so much horror and brutality. As the reports unfolded he constantly looked over at his foster father who was just shaking his head in disbelief and shock. After they had watched the first report he rose out of his chair and turned the sound down on the TV with the remote control and just came and sat next to Tarik on the sofa and put his arm round his shoulders. A fatherly and comforting gesture that Tarik had not received in a long time and he said quietly:

"Tarik I am very sorry to say but I think that we may be witnessing the single worst war crime that has occurred in Europe since the Second World War. This is pure genocide. There is simply no other word for it. I am very sorry that you should have to see this and thank God that you are here and not there.'

'But how can this happen? Tarik asked almost rhetorically *'Srebrenica is supposed to be a United Nations dedicated 'safe haven' protected and monitored by UN troops. I just cannot understand how this could be allowed to happen in front of the eyes of the world.'*

Paul just shook his head in despair and disbelief *'I just don't know what to say Tarik. I am starting to lose faith in all of our politicians and leaders. They all seem to like to talk the talk but are afraid to walk the walk."*

The unfolding massacre and undoubted war crime continued to receive enormous international media coverage not just because of what happened but why it happened and why it was allowed to happen by the international community in what was supposed to be a United Nations 'safe haven.'

Previously, except for a few days in April 1992, Muslims had remained in control of Srebrenica through three years of war. It had become a symbol of Bosnian resistance and was even featured in Bosnian pop songs. But on 11th July 1995 the existence of Muslim Srebrenica came to an abrupt end. On that day Bosnian Serb television broadcast an announcement by General Ratko Mladić, the commander of the Bosnian Serb Army that:

51

"The moment for revenge had finally come.'

With the takeover of Srebrenica and one week later, Žepa, the Serbs controlled a large swathe of 'ethnically clean' land in eastern Bosnia, even though between January 1993 and July 1995 successive failed peace plans had always envisaged that Srebrenica and Žepa would remain Muslim towns.

The massacre that followed the Serb takeover of Srebrenica was unprecedented in European history of the last fifty years. Between 6th and 16th July the Serbs seized and expelled twenty three thousand Bosnian Muslim women and children and executed more than eight thousand Muslim men and boys. The killing fields of Srebrenica were not the usual battlefield - a pretty Alpine valley, seven miles long and a half-mile wide, with a fast-flowing stream running through it. The hillsides were green pastures dotted by whitewashed farmhouses that gradually transformed in the higher reaches, to thick evergreen forest. At the southern end of the valley was the small town of Srebrenica. At the other end, where the land opened up and the stream joined the much broader Drina River basin, lay the town of Bratunac. Roughly halfway between these two settlements was the village of Potocari, where the United Nations military compound was located during the war.

As the details of the tragic massacre continued to unfold in the American media, Tarik recalled a conversation that his father had had with his neighbour and Serbian friend Pasan just before war had broken out:

"I have a very positive feeling about the cohesion of the people in Sarajevo Pasan. We have always lived together and always will. I am certain that this trouble will not happen here."
'You were wrong Papa' Tarik thought *'the whole world has underestimated our enemy's fanaticism and their capacity for doing evil deeds.'*

A couple of week later he saw an article in the Chicago Tribune that had been reprinted from the British Sunday Times of 23rd July:

52

which related to comments made by a Dutch peacekeeper who had spoken to some Serb military police whom he had witnessed leaving the area in the morning and returning in the evening exhausted:

'They bragged about how they had murdered people and raped women. They were proud of what they had been doing. I didn't get the feeling they were doing it out of anger or revenge, more for fun.'

Tarik threw the newspaper on the floor in disgust and just sat staring into space feeling sick in the pit of his stomach and he said to himself:

"Even here five thousand miles away I cannot escape the impact of these evil men.'

However, six months later the war in Bosnia had finally ended. Minka had recovered well from her final operation and for the last few months had been working as a volunteer in the hospital and in the rehabilitation unit by carrying out a supporting role to the nursing staff doing any duties that she was permitted to do as some way of trying to repay the enormous debt of gratitude that she felt towards the medical institution.

On 29th February 1996 she had watched on the television with Tarik and others from the hospital staff as the Muslim-led Bosnian government declared the Serb siege of Sarajevo to be officially at an end yesterday after taking control of the suburb of Ilijas and a vital road connecting the capital to the rest of Bosnia:

"The siege of Sarajevo is now officially over."

said the Bosnian Interior Minister, Avdo Hebib, after he and other government officials arrived in Ilijas in a convoy of bullet-proof cars, police vehicles and fire engines. Minka turned towards Tarik and embraced him tightly and said:

"Now I can go home"

53

Two weeks later Minka was back in Sarajevo. She was met at the airport by an over emotional Jasmina and her aunt Lejla. She had been away for nearly twelve months but to all of them it seemed far longer than that. Jasmina was overwhelmed to have her daughter back safe and sound and looking so healthy. Her leg was as good as it was going to be and any lingering doubts that she may have had about sending her children away melted away in an instant.

"Let's go home Minka and tell me all about what has happened to you and tell me how your brother is doing."

Tarik had developed into a tall and physically strong teenager and was readily accepted into the High School baseball team which he was absolutely delighted with so that he could follow in his father's footsteps. He had initially wanted to continue playing football because he had been so successful in the school youth team in Sarajevo before the war but the Americans were just waking up to the opportunities of playing 'soccer' as they called it and it was not yet an option at the High School which Tarik now attended.

He became a prolific 'pitcher' and after his first season was a regular in the first team. His height of six foot one inch gave him a huge natural advantage and enabled him to project the ball with enormous power and accuracy from his position on the mound. Tarik was later to discover that this ability was due to what became known as the 'constructal law' theory of sports as devised by Professor Adrian Bejan of Duke University in the USA. Basically the theory goes as explained to him by the first team coach when he was eighteen and now at College, is that the advantage comes from the 'falling forward motion of the athletic task.' In other words the taller the athlete, the more force they can put behind either themselves or an object that they want to propel forward. More than once as Tarik stood on the mound ready to pitch he thought of his father and how proud he knew that he would be if he could see him now.

Tarik became a very popular figure on the college campus because of his sporting prowess and the success of the high school team both regionally and nationally. Eventually after months of interview after interview, he was offered official refugee status in the United States helped by the fact that his application was sponsored by the college that he was attending. They had found themselves the best baseball pitcher that they had had in the last few seasons and were not going to lose him because of some bureaucrat in the Department of Immigration.

Tarik, however, was very modest about his sporting abilities and was a generally quiet, reserved student who worked hard and diligently at both his studies and his English language skills. He had chosen a one year intensive course in Information Technology. Despite having a very dysfunctional and interrupted early education, he had an innate ability for mathematics, equations and logic. He picked up the basics of personal computing very quickly indeed at High School and moved on to advanced computing and programming. His foster parents had bought him an IBM machine to have at home and had installed the internet through a telephone dialup service so that he could continue his studies whilst at home. Tarik was so grateful promising that one day he would pay them back for all their kindness and generosity but Mr and Mrs Stanton would have nothing of it:

"It's our pleasure" they would say *"It is what we would have liked to have done for our own son."*

He received a long letter from his mother. His sister had settled back into life in Sarajevo well and was walking with only a slight limp now. Her experiences in the last few months at the Rush University Medical Center in Chicago had encouraged her to take up nursing and through her mother's contacts in Sarajevo she had recently been accepted as a trainee nurse.

During the start of the Summer semester at college however, something changed within him. Looking back Tarik could never put his finger on the exact moment that it happened but a shift in mood and outlook seemed to envelop him during the first semester. He was sitting in the changing room before an inter college match when his mind suddenly flashed back involuntarily and he was back in

Sarajevo sprinting across the Sěher Ćehaja Bridge with two large water canisters hanging from a homemade yolk over his shoulders. He zigzagged and then sprinted in a straight line to make his passage as random as possible and not easy to predict for the snipers in the hills.

Initially, when Tarik had begun the trips to the brewery to fetch water for his family after the death of his father he was fearless and even derived a sort of thrill of crossing a road or a bridge where a sniper was known to be operating. Amongst his fellow young Sarajevan teenage boys it became a new bizarre sport, a Sarajevan version of Russian roulette but this initial adrenaline rush and bravado soon started to fade and anxiety, fatigue, depression and a feeling of hopelessness replaced it. This was reinforced the morning that Tarik saw a teenage boy he knew well called Afan, sprint before him from the shelter of a building to cross a road on the way to the old brewery. Suddenly his head seemed to explode in a red spray that shot upwards and Afan collapsed in the middle of the road and then came the familiar rolling 'crack' of the sound of a rifle from up in the hills.

It was this memory of just over three years before that Tarik was suddenly reliving in the changing room. He started to sweat profusely and he felt his heart rate increase dramatically and his stomach tighten involuntarily in a vice-like grip. A wave of anxiety and confusion just swept over him with a strength that just floored him and he felt himself start to shake. He felt like he was just falling through space and losing control. It was a frightening experience. Moments later there was a hand on his shoulder. It was the captain, Mitch Corrigan, a good friend and team mate:

'Are you ok Tarik?' he enquired.

"I am not sure. I think I may have eaten something that did not agree with me last night" Tarik replied hurriedly trying to recover his composure. *"I think I may have to sit this match out."*

Following this incident Tarik started to withdraw more within himself for the next few weeks and sought solace in a growing friendship with Peter who was the college 'geek' whom he started to sit next to in lectures and seminars. Peter Soberg was thin and gangly with large rimmed spectacles and unkempt long black hair. He wore T shirts and jeans that were at least a size too big for him but he never noticed or cared. Peter found it difficult to socialise and avoided any of the locations where fellow students would congregate both during the day and in the evenings. He preferred to stay in his room reading books and spending an increasing amount of time often throughout the whole night on his personal computer doing what he explained as 'surfing the internet.'

Fortunately these dark mood swings did not last long, maybe a few weeks, sometimes longer and then he would be back where he was before. It was a strange cycle that he could not understand or predict but he decided to keep it all to himself rather than seeking any help from the campus medical staff or telling his foster parents. If what he was experiencing was as a result of the terrible things he had seen and witnessed in Sarajevo then so be it but he was not going to let 'the bastards in the hills' continue to instill fear and control him half way across the world. He was free of them now. Even back in Sarajevo they were no longer perched above the city thinking that they could shell and bomb and shoot innocent men, women and children with impunity. Their time would come. Justice would prevail.

He learnt that if he felt that an episode was about to start he would make an excuse and retire to bed early hoping that his mind would 'reboot' itself like his IBM computer when occasionally it 'froze' and would not allow him to navigate around freely. So he became more adept at managing the situation and no one really noticed that sometimes there was turmoil going on within him because he maintained a confident external posture that betrayed nothing not even to his foster parents.

Following the initial traumatic months in the second year, he was much more able to control his anxieties and mood swings and prevent himself from descending into a spiral of flashbacks and depression. But although he was better at managing it he could not make it disappear. All he was achieving was to suppress it for that moment in time and hope that it would not resurface any time soon but it always did. He continued to always sit next to Peter Soberg in both lectures and seminars. Tarik was probably the only person who Peter ever talked to and when Tarik did persuade him to go to the social area for coffee between lectures he did not integrate with other students. Instead he would take great delight in relaying to him what he had discovered on the internet and the latest programmes he had managed to download or which bulletin boards he was reading and interacting with.

It was one such afternoon between lectures that Tarik and Peter were sitting in one of the coffee bars on the campus. Peter had been boring Tarik for ten minutes now about the new cyber café called *Screenz* at which he was a regular visitor along with other computer nerds from the college and elsewhere in the city, when Mitch the captain of the baseball team called to him from where he was playing table soccer. Most people did not know that the game was actually developed in the United States by a man called Louis P.Thornton who had been visiting his nephew, Harold in 1922 in London who had created the concept. The inspiration came from a box of matches: and by laying the matches across the box he had formed the basis of his game. Louis took the inspiration back to Oregon where he patented it. However, he didn't see a lot of success with the game and let his patent expire. It wasn't until decades later that the game took off in the USA.

"Tarik. I need you to play offence for me. I'll play defence" Mitch shouted once more.

"OK" said Tarik and he was glad of the break from Peter's boring monologue.

"I don't know why you associate with that geek" Mitch said as Tarik grasped the two front handles of one side of the table football table:

"Oh he's ok" Tarik replied *"Just a bit intense sometimes"*
"Weird if you ask me". Right let's beat these guys."

Tarik and Mitch were playing the blue team and two other guys the red team.

"Best of five and loosing team buys pizza later" said Mitch confidently.

The red team won the toss and put in the quarter coin and released the balls and inserted the first one to kick off. Soon there was a crowd gathered around the football table cheering on both of the teams but Tarik noticed that Peter had wandered off and not stayed to watch the game or get involved. After about half an hour it was two games all and the growing crowd were cheering and urging on the respective teams. Two girls had arrived about five minutes earlier and had now started a small 'cheer leading' session leaning against the coffee bar and waving their hands in the air and they were quickly joined by others.

Tarik looked up from the table. He immediately made eye contact with one of them. He had not seen her before. She was quite tall with long blonde hair, blue eyes and was wearing tight faded Levi jeans. She caught Tarik's eye and smiled:

"Go blue team" She shouted *"Go blue offence!"*

It was six goals all with one ball to play – it could not have been tighter or more even. The atmosphere in the coffee bar was tense.

*"Come on bud. Let's do it "*shouted Mitch as he slapped Tarik's left shoulder.

Tarik inserted the last ball in the hole in the side of the table but unfortunately it veered towards the red team forwards and his opponent swung at it and it rocketed straight into Mitch's goal without touching another figure.

"Foul;" Mitch shouted *"You spun the rod"*

Just then the buzzer sounded announcing that the next series of lectures would start in five minutes. Tarik walked back to where he had been sitting with Peter to collect his bag which had fallen off the chair on to the floor when everyone had pushed forward to get a better view of the football game being played on the table. Tarik leant down to pick up the books which had fallen out of the bag and when he looked up a smiling face was looking down at him:

"Sorry you didn't win" She said *"I was cheering for you"*
"I heard you"
"Hi I'm Kimberley and I am studying modern languages"
"Hi I'm Tarik and I am studying Information Technology"
"You have a strong distinctive accent. Where are you from" she enquired
"Bosnia" said Tarik as he stood up and put his bag over his shoulder.
"Will you buy me a coffee tomorrow" she ventured with another confident smile.
"You bet" replied Tarik and he watched her leave the coffee bar and head for the bank of elevators to the lecture rooms.

Over the next few weeks Tarik spent a lot of time with Kimberley at the expense of his friend Peter who decided to avoid the coffee bar area completely and other places where Tarik and Kimberley met. Tarik explained to her how he and his sister had come to be in America but that she had eventually recovered well and was now living back with their mother in Sarajevo.

"Do you miss them" Kimberley had asked one day
"Yes of course I do" he replied *"But I owe it to the memory of my father and to the suffering that my mother has gone through to make the most of my chance to be in America and to learn as much as I can so that I can return one day to support my family properly and be part of the reconstruction of my city and country."*
"Tell me what happened to your father" Kimberley said quietly.

60

So Tarik told her everything that had happened, about their family life before the war and then how it had all changed so dramatically and gone from worse to worse until the death of his father and then the serious injury to his sister.

Kimberley listened intently. She had obviously seen the images of the war on the television but she couldn't really engage with the enormity of the experiences that Tarik had already been through at such a young age. It had all been such a long way away and had not penetrated the immunity of her world. She had been born and brought up in a rural community near the city of Cedar Rapids in the county of Linn in Iowa. Iowa was a Midwestern state that was located between the Missouri and Mississippi rivers and was known for its landscape of rolling plains and cornfields and it bore no resemblance to the battlefield of Sarajevo and other areas of the Balkans.

It was a Friday evening and Tarik and Kimberley had been at a college dance but had decided to leave early as they did not like the band. The music was too loud and they just weren't that good. As they crossed the college campus they could see a scuffle between three guys up in front of them. Two bigger guys were pushing and shoving a smaller and much thinner one who eventually fell to the ground and dropped a bunch of books and magazines that he was carrying, The two assailants then started laughing and kicking the magazines around the floor and when the one on the ground started to protest they both laid into him with hard kicks to the body and head. Tarik felt a strong anger well up inside him and said:

'Wait here Kimberley' and ran towards the evolving scene in front of them
'No Tarik. Come back. It is not our fight' Kimberley shouted after him but Tarik paid her no attention.

As he neared the others he could see the thin guy on the ground curled into a ball with his hands covering his head trying to protect himself as the blows and kicks rained in on him from the two laughing assailants. It was only then that he recognised the victim.

61

He could not see his face but he recognised the T shirt. It was Peter Soberg. Tarik just launched himself at the two attackers.

'Heh what the hell' one said but then Tarik grabbed them both with each arm and with a huge force banged their heads together twice and they fell to the ground with one clutching at a split and bleeding nose and the other holding the side of his head:

'Now clear off before I really sort you out' Tarik shouted at them and the two guys picked themselves up muttering and swearing revenge and staggered away and Tarik shouted after them:

'If you hassle him again it wont be my fists that you will be facing but my baseball bat.'

Tarik looked down at his friend Peter. His face was cut and bleeding and there were two or three large red swellings coming up fast on his cheeks and forehead. He suspected that his ribs were hurting like hell too. He helped him to his feet and just then Kimberley arrived and started to pick up the magazines and books that had been scattered on the ground. She took out some tissues that she had in the bag she was carrying and passed them to Peter.

'Thanks' he said with a forced smile.
'What was all that about?' Tarik asked a few moments later.
'I don't know' Peter replied. 'They just came up to me and asked me for some cigarettes and when I said that I didn't have any left, one just said:
'Let's just bash the geek anyway. I think that they were high on drugs or something.'
'Come home with us and we'll get you sorted out' Kimberley then said with a genuine compassion in her voice.
"We'll pick up a Chinese take-out and watch a movie"

and the three of them walked slowly back across the campus together.

A few weeks later Tarik and Kimberley were sitting in the new Comiskey Park Stadium watching the Chicago White Sox play the Detroit Tigers. They had just had two burgers and two large Cokes delivered to their seats. Suddenly Tarik's hand started shaking uncontrollably and his heart started racing and he spilt some of the Coke on his jeans, Kimberley glanced at him:

"Are you ok," she enquired genuinely concerned.

For a moment Tarik said nothing. In his mind he was suddenly back once again in Sarajevo sheltering behind a building and peering round the corner when he saw his friend Afan suddenly shot and his head exploding with a red spray that sprung upwards as he collapsed on the floor and the distinctive sound of a high powered rifle ringing in his ears.

Kimberley grasped Tarik's left hand. His palm was sweaty and moist. Tarik still said nothing but placed the Coke on the floor under his seat. He took three deep breaths, held them for a moment and then exhaled each one through his mouth slowly.

"I am ok Kimberley, Honestly I am. I am sorry. Sometimes I remember things. Horrible things that I saw and happened to me back in Sarajevo during the war. They just come into my mind involuntarily and I cannot stop them."
"Have you told anyone about this" Kimberley replied
"No. I am afraid to. To be honest I really don't want to relive it all. I thought that it would all just go away."
"Is it to do with the death of your father?"
"I don't know. It might be but I really don't know. There were so many really bad things that you wouldn't believe"
"Tell me" Kimberley replied gently but somehow now a little unconvincingly. She had never experienced anything like this before.
"May be I will but not yet" Tarik replied now calm and relaxed again. He lent sideways and kissed her on the cheek. She squeezed his hand tighter and noticed that his palm was no longer sweating.

63

Five minutes later she leant towards him and whispered in his ear:

"Let's be together tonight"
"We are together" he replied.
"No! Properly together silly" she said with some amusement in her voice.

For a moment Tarik did not understand what she meant and he just stared straight ahead at the players on the pitch crashing into one another with colossal force and then it dawned on him in a flash and he just felt stupid. He was not in any way prudish it was just that he simply was not used to this level of assertiveness and confidence in a female companion. He had been brought up in a culture with a religious patriarchal tradition according to which women were expected to be submissive to men. The social norm was for women to perform most of the housework duties including cooking, cleaning and child rearing and certainly not to take the lead in such a demonstrative way in personal relationships.

The following morning he awoke as the sunlight streamed through the skylight set in the sloping ceiling of Kimberley's room. He lay on his back and stared upwards to the light. Kimberley was still asleep next to him and some of her long blonde hair lay across his bare chest. A myriad of thoughts raced through his mind. He had been clumsy and awkward in the bed the night before whilst Kimberley was at complete ease. It was obviously not her first time as it had been his.

"What would mother say," he thought.

They had never been an exceptionally religious family mostly just observing the most important days of the Islamic year but they were never fervent and as Tarik lay here in his girlfriend's bed he felt a very long way from Sarajevo and the local mosque that he had attended as a boy. No, the religious element did not concern him but there was something else and he just couldn't realise what it was but he forgot about it as Kimberley stirred beside him and lifted her face towards him and said with a mischievous grin:

"Shall we see if you learnt anything from last night"

Over the next few weeks Tarik saw a lot of Kimberley and he stayed often at her place which was a rented apartment which she shared with two other college girls. It didn't happen at any one time but gradually Tarik began to tire of Kimberley. He enjoyed her company and the physical side of their relationship was great but gradually he started to find that she just lacked any depth and her conversation would be very insular concerning music and sport and social occasions. She had little or no grasp of international events or what was happening outside of the United States. So he decided he would cool the relationship a little and see how he felt about it. He deliberately avoided places where he knew she would be and he spent more time in the library studying or practising with the baseball team.

Six weeks quickly passed and he realised that they had not been out together at all, in fact he had not even seen her in the college for a couple of weeks. Later that day he bumped into one of the girls with whom she shared her apartment only to be told that Kimberley had dropped out of college and returned home to Cedar Rapids in Iowa. For a few days Tarik had felt sad and kept wondering if he had done the right thing. The sexual adventure had been fun and exciting and he had enjoyed her company but the final exams were only a few weeks away and it was time to really buckle down and work so that he had something to show for all his efforts and pay back all those who had given him this opportunity and supported and invested in him.

Tarik needn't have worried as he finished his second semester in the early summer of 1997 graduating with very good grades. He said goodbye to his friends at college and a very emotional farewell to his foster parents promising to stay in touch and visit them whenever he was able to do so. The College had facilitated him in obtaining a temporary contract at the huge American company, Qualcomm that employed seven and a half thousand people based in San Diego, California. It was not in the heart of what had become known as

'Silicon Valley' being a few hundred miles away but it was a very good placement indeed.

Qualcomm developed, manufactured, marketed and licensed advanced communications systems. They welcomed Tarik not only because of his proven educational and technical ability but also because the company had just won in February of that year, the prestigious 'Annual National University Multicultural Heritage Award' in the technology category of companies. Tarik's offer and welcome letter included a statement from Dan Sullivan, the company's senior vice president for Human Resources which said:

"Bringing employees together from diverse backgrounds has given us a better understanding of our customers in a more global and competitive marketplace."

He quickly found himself a condo to rent not far from his place of work at a reasonable rent which also had a parking lot for the car that he planned to buy himself soon.

After a few weeks at the company he was invited by a group of colleagues to attend a party one weekend. Whilst chatting with his friends, Tarik saw a group of three girls standing in the corner of the room. As he looked across one of the girls saw him and called him over to join them. Tarik recognised her as Anna, a work colleague that he had talked to occasionally whilst taking lunch breaks in the company cafeteria. As he approached the group he saw that one of the other girls was a red head with vibrant flowing curly hair whilst the other had blonde hair and appeared to him to be somehow familiar.

"Hi Tarik. Come and meet my friends. They both work for the company."
"Hi. I'm Alice Gregory' said the red head with a broad smile somehow shaking her head so that her hair seemed to swish at the same time.
"And I'm Jelena Petrović said the other girl. Her English tinged with an accent that sounded eastern European.

And then Tarik knew why she had looked vaguely familiar. She was Serbian. His stomach tightened a little but he forced a smile. Once again one's name now revealed where you were from and to what ethnic group you belonged stereotyping you without any reference to individuality and personality. Without even thinking Tarik regarded Jelena as the enemy and a representative of those that had oppressed him and his family without mercy. After five minutes Tarik broke away and joined another group of guys who were discussing baseball and the coming season.

A week later Anna who was carrying her lunch on a tray came and sat next to Tarik in the cafeteria:

"I'm slimming this week" she said as Tarik looked down at her tray of three small bowls of different salads.

"Jelena really liked you" Anna said whilst eating a large forkful of carrot and raisin salad *"She's asked me to ask you if you'd like to go out on a date"*

Tarik felt his stomach tighten once again.

"I'll think about it" he replied quickly without really thinking. To be honest he was lost for words. This was a complication he probably did not need in his life right now:
"I am really busy at the moment. I have just joined a new club and the baseball season is just about to start."

And with that he made his excuses placed his tray with the dirty plates in a stacking trolley in the corner of the cafeteria and returned to his desk.

A few days later Tarik was queuing at the coffee cart outside the entrance to the huge white and blue headquarters office building where he worked which he tended to do most mornings. As he turned away after paying the coffee vendor, Jelena was the next in line but he had not noticed her.

"Hello" she said *"I thought that you might be ignoring me."*
"No sorry – I just didn't see you" Tarik replied hastily
"Let's walk round the block together?" she said quietly *"We're early and work is not due to start for twenty minutes"*

Tarik did not know what to say. His stomach had tightened up once again and he felt slightly annoyed at her intrusion. But he couldn't deny that she was pretty. Tall and slim with long blonde hair with an oval face and high eyebrows over her deep brown eyes accentuated by some dark eyeliner make up and a line of glossy red lipstick on her thin lips. Tarik's eyes took in the curves of her body and her slim waist and then he quickly looked away disgusted with himself.

"But she's Serbian!" he said to himself *"She's related to those bastards who murdered my father"*

He said nothing and reluctantly followed her as they crossed the road and entered into a park that was opposite the towering glass and concrete office block where they both worked albeit on different floors and in different departments. They sat on a bench in silence and Tarik took large sips of his coffee through the opening in the styrene lid but he was not concentrating and he spilt some of the coffee down the front of his jacket.

"Don't worry I have got a Kleenex" Jelena replied and searched in the hand bag that she was carrying.
"Thank you" Tarik replied as he brushed the front of his jacket with the tissue soaking up the spilt coffee.

A few minutes passed in total silence and awkwardness as they sipped at their hot coffees and watched as people passed on their way to work and pigeons came and went from the expanse of grass in front of them.
"We are not all evil Tarik" she suddenly said breaking the silence between them.
"What do you mean" he replied nervously

68

"I know that you knew that I was Serbian from my name the minute we were introduced by Anna at that party"

"Yes I did" Tarik said quietly looking down at the coffee cup in his right hand feeling a little ashamed.

"Anna told me where you are from and what happened to you and why you are here in America. We are perhaps not as different as you think we are. I am from Belgrade, my father is head of the Politics and Modern History Faculty at the University of Belgrade and when all this nationalistic nonsense started he could see that it could only end in disaster. I am an only child and my parents are quite well off so they sent me to America to get a broader education and escape the insane wave of nationalistic fervour that was sweeping our country. My father said over and over again do these people never learn anything from history?"

After a few moments Tarik said quietly *"Your countrymen killed my father"*

"Not in my name or those of my family" Jelena replied quietly but firmly and her head sunk on her chest despondently.

"Thank God the war is over Tarik. We must all get on with our lives and hopefully move on from this period of utter madness and brutality. Do you think that things will ever be the same again?" She asked without lifting her head off her chest.

Tarik thought for a while and then said *"Come on or we will be late for work"* in an effort to break the continuing awkward silence that had developed between them.

With that they rose off the bench and threw the empty coffee cups into the trash can and crossed the road into the office building without another word being spoken between them.

Two days later Tarik arrived at his desk and immediately he noticed that there was a small parcel, gift wrapped with a bow sitting on the keyboard of his computer. It had no tag on it or any other form of identification and just as he picked it up to examine it his section leader appeared and said:

"Tarik. Can you come with me I want you to look at this new development"

Tarik shoved the small carefully wrapped package into the pocket of his jacket and followed his boss into one of the conference rooms. He was not feeling that well this morning because he had experienced another bad episode the previous evening which had resulted in a fitful sleep and he felt exhausted and what was worse was that he had not had time to purchase a coffee from the vendor cart outside the office like he did on most mornings.

Later that evening he arrived home and eat supper with his foster parents but after thanking them he said that it had been a really tiring day and that he was going to retire to his room and listen to some music before going to sleep early. It was only when he was hanging up his jacket in the wardrobe that he remembered the small packet. He reached inside the inside pocket where he had placed it earlier that morning and brought it out.

He turned it in his hands. It had been very carefully wrapped and there was a small neat bow on the front. He ripped at the wrapping, throwing it on the floor and was left with what was obviously a music cassette tape box in his hand. He looked at it, *"Through the Barricades"* by *Spandau Ballet."*

"Never heard of them" he thought.

But he took out the cassette and inserted it into the machine by his bed side but as he did so he noticed that there was a handwritten capital 'J' and a small 'x' on the label of the tape. He lay on the bed and listened. When it had finished he listened to it again and then again and then again letting the haunting melody wash over him:

"Born on different sides of life
But we feel the same

70

And feel all of this strife
So come to me when I'm asleep
And we'll cross the line
And dance upon the street"

Tarik was exhausted after the day's work and the lack of sleep and the physical and mental exertion of the torment that he had experienced the night before and here was the enemy reaching out to him. He closed his eyes and listened to the music and suddenly there she was at the end of the bridge shouting at him, willing him to run faster to safety, her arms open ready to embrace him.

He closed his eyes and drifted off into a deep sleep.

Chapter Seven

It was now September 1997 and Tarik had been in America for nearly two and a half years. His grasp of the English language was now excellent and though still nearly twenty years old so much had happened and changed in his life since the death of his father nearly five years earlier. Like his sister previously he also had experienced repeated episodes of 'Survivor's Guilt.'

"Why had he been allowed to take a place on the 'Operation Second Chance' programme? Minka could have gone to the States for treatment on her own. He had taken a valuable place that could have been used by another seriously injured Sarajevan. Why had he been so lucky? He should have stayed to look after his mother and aunt. He should have stayed to support his friend Faris on his nightly errands. Where was Faris now?"

A myriad of thoughts raced through his brain when he allowed them to and all he could do was to say to himself:

"I didn't engineer those things to happen. They just happened. All I can do is make the most of the opportunities that I have been given and to not squander any chances that I have to use my newly acquired skills to help others. I will return to Sarajeo when the time is right to be part of the future of the city and not to dwell on the past."

He worked diligently at Qualcomm and he started to make a name for himself. His work experience was supposed to only be for an initial three month period but his section leader had been so impressed with his development and his contribution that he was persuaded to accept an offer of an additional six months contract with an option to extend to a further six months and on a salaried pay scale. He had started to specialise in the development of new communication software which was Qualcomm's core competence.

It was only four years earlier that Qualcomm had established its leadership by demonstrating that basic packet data services could be sent using code division multiple access or CDMA. CDMA was an example of multiple access where several transmitters could send information over a single communication channel which therefore allowed several users to share a band of frequencies. To permit this without undue interference between the users, CDMA employed spread spectrum technology and a special coding system where each transmitter is assigned a code. The US Telecommunications Industry Association adopted CDMA as a cellular standard in 1993 and Qualcomm was at the centre of the international proliferation of advanced digital wireless technology.

In the previous twelve months CDMA had gone global and there were now more than one million subscribers and Tarik was working as part of the huge project team that was developing the first commercial CDMA smartphone which was due to be launched by the company in the following year. It was exciting and pioneering work and Tarik loved it

With his increase in pay he was able to send more money back home to his mother and Minka and to start saving. He also bought a second hand car, a blue Toyota Corolla and learnt to drive. He bought some new clothes, Levi jeans, Reebok trainers and a leather jacket and a pair of aviator sunglasses. Looking at himself in the mirror of his rented condo he remarked to himself with a big smile:

"Now I am in America I can be like Tom Cruise in the film 'Top Gun"

It had been his friend Anna who had set up the 'date' with Jelena two months earlier. It was supposed to have been a foursome with Anna and her boyfriend, Rick. They had all bought tickets for a concert by the phenomenally successful Irish band U2 who were undertaking their 'PopMart Tour' across the USA and it had come to San Diego.

Tarik had turned up at the agreed time at the McDonalds just outside the Jack Murphy stadium the home of the San Diego Chargers NFL team and he sat on the bench outside the restaurant sipping a coke through a straw watching the people all arrive. Ten minutes later Jelena arrived and Tarik bought her a strawberry milkshake which she had asked for. Fifteen minutes went by as they talked nervously mostly about work and what was happening in the company. The concert was due to start in about five minutes and it quickly dawned on Tarik that he and Jelena had been 'set up' but they made their way into the stadium anyway and took their seats waiting for the show to start.

Towards the end of the concert, Bono, the lead singer of the band stepped into a single spotlight at the front of the stage which was clearly visible on the giant video screens either side of the main stage and sang the song *'Miss Sarajevo'* there was a sudden and complete mood change in the huge audience and a sort of hush descended around the stadium. The song was inspired by the film-maker Bill Carter's 1994 documentary of the same name about a beauty pageant staged in the Bosnian capital depicting that in the midst of brutality, aggression and deprivation, the citizens of Sarajevo could pretend to carry on a normal life. Gone were the piercing guitar riffs and soaring vocals of previous songs and replacing it was the slow melodic guitar rhythm and measured haunting lyrics:

"Is there a time for keeping a distance
A time to turn your eyes away
Is there a time for keeping your head down
For getting on with your day"

Tarik had been aware of the incredible event that had been held in Sarajevo in May 1993 during the siege called the 'Miss Sarajevo Beauty Pageant' which had to be staged in a cellar to avoid becoming a target for snipers. The event was won by seventeen year old Inela Nogić who with fellow contestants had held up a banner that read *'Don't let them kill us.'* For many girls from Sarajevo – fashion and beauty were a matter of pride and they grew into a symbol of resistance to the bloody siege. Fashion designers like

74

Amna Kunovac-Zekic worked on such a project with models who wore her creations. Photos of these models were taken in the destroyed buildings, next to UN soldiers and tanks. The girls were making their own make-up, it was DIY fashion – they tried their best to live a normal life and not let the oppressors kill their spirit and love for fashion and freedom of expression.

As the song was sung Tarik felt a lump develop in his throat and his eyes misted over as he thought of his parents and his sister huddling around the makeshift stove or spending the endless hours in the basement feeling hungry, lonely and forgotten watching the shadows dancing on the walls caused by the flickering light of the candles. He turned to look at Jelena and there were tears streaming down her cheeks, her face set in a twisted contortion as the video of Pavarotti played with his penetrating emotional, sad and sombre vocals. Without thinking Tarik placed his arms around Jelena and rested his head on her shoulders and as he smelt the sweetness of her hair he let his own emotions just flow and he didn't release her for some minutes but when he did their red, wet eyes met and he held her face in his hands and kissed her gently on the mouth. She held out her hand and they watched the rest of the concert without speaking but without ever letting go of each others hand.

For the next two months their relationship developed and they became inseparable. Every morning before work they met at the coffee cart and sat in the park opposite the large glass office building where they both worked and every lunchtime they sat together in the staff restaurant, huddled in a corner talking quietly to each other and hardly noticing anyone else in the cafeteria and barely acknowledging friends when they came over to say hello.

Jelena was a year older than Tarik and ever since she had been in America she had watched the news avidly as to what was happening back home and her weekly telephone conversations with her parents had also filled in more details and she could tell from her father's voice his deepening despair and despondency that the situation was deteriorating all the time:

"Our politicians are criminals" he would say knowing that these thoughts if known publicly could be very dangerous to himself and his family and would certainly cost him his job and probably imprisonment.

"Slobodan Milosovic is a megalomaniac and Radovan Karadzic is just a psychopath. Can they learn nothing from recent European history? Their world views are distorted and anachronistic and the rest of the world seems happy to let them peddle this poisonous philosophy and carry out continuous atrocities without any serious intervention or repercussions."

It was not however, until Tarik had relayed to her his experiences and those of his family, friends and neighbours that she started to fully understand the gravity and desperation that the people of Sarajevo had been subjected to. Often she would break down in tears and ask Tarik to stop and talk about something else because she just could not bear to hear any more. The hardest part was that these were her people. She could not believe that in the twentieth century neighbour could turn on neighbour and after years of peaceful coexistence. How could neighbours, friend and work colleagues suddenly become the bitterest of enemies?

"Will there ever be a reconciliation" she had asked many times *"Can people ever forgive and can life ever return to what it was before"*

Tarik had never answered those questions because he simply did not know and had not thought about it. Here in America he had become somewhat immune to what was happening and had happened back in the Balkans. The letters and phone calls from Minka and his mother however, had been more upbeat of late. Reconstruction was taking place rapidly in Sarajevo but signs of any reconciliation were a long way off. There was a peace in the sense that the city was no longer under siege and people were no longer dying and being shot at but this peace had only been achieved at the cost of segregation. Sarajevo was no longer the 'Jerusalem of the

East,' the multicultural melting pot of religions and races that had coexisted side by side for centuries.

Jelena had come to America in early 1992 just before the war started. Her father had had contacts in the American education sector and managed to get her a place at a very good boarding school, Asheville School in the Blue Ridge Mountain city of Asheville, North Carolina. It was a private coeducational school founded in 1900 where students could challenge themselves both academically and personally. She had then gone on to do a degree in Human Resource Management at the University of North Carolina in Asheville. The university was known for providing students with an intellectual rigorous education that builds critical thinking and workforce skills that would last a lifetime. Jelena with her excellent English language skills had thrived academically in the small class size, award-winning faculty.

She was an only child, the daughter of Dr. Pavle and Adrijana Petrović. Her father was a head of faculty at Belgrade University and her mother was a high school teacher. They were both middle class liberal-minded academics. Completely at odds with the surging wave of nationalism that was rising in their country they had opted to send their daughter away at great expense so that she could receive a broad education and not be subjected to the narrow-minded thinking and populism that was now becoming so prevalent at home.

President Milosovic and his supporters had appealed to nationalist and populist passion by speaking of Serbia's importance in the world and using aggressive and violent political rhetoric. In a speech in Belgrade on 19th November 1988 he had stated:

"At home and abroad, Serbia's enemies are massing against us. We say to them 'We are not afraid'. We will not flinch from battle."

and on another occasion:

"We Serbs will act in the interest of Serbia whether we do it in compliance with the constitution or not, whether we do in

compliance with the law or not, whether we do it in compliance with party statutes or not"

Serbian media then began to speak of 'the alleged imperilment of the Serbs of Bosnia and Herzegovina', as tensions between Serbs and Bosnian Muslims and Croats increased over the Serbs' support for Milosovic. In 1991 Milosovic rejected the independence of Croatia and the seeds of destruction for Bosnia and Sarajevo were sown. This was enough for Pavle Petrović. He had studied the impact of Serbian nationalism in overthrowing the Ottoman rule, its role in the First and Second World wars and now its resurgence and its role in the dissolution of the centralised state of Yugoslavia. His daughter, Jelena would not have any part in this. He wanted his only child to have an international, liberal and tolerant outlook that reflected the views of himself and his wife and so they agreed that at great expense they would ensure that she had no experience of this part of their country's history which might distort her views and personality for life.

The one thing that Tarik had never mentioned to Jelena in their conversations was his recurring nightmares, sudden fits of anxiety and deep depression. These he kept to inside well hidden behind the mask that he had now perfected to protect himself and portray a confident image to the outside world.

"I am hiding it deliberately form her or am I?" he would ask himself often and then comfort himself by saying: *"No she just doesn't need to know right now."*
But main reason that he had not confided in her was obvious. He did not know what was wrong with him. So he could not explain it properly and deep down he was now frightened that it might put her off him. So he just left it at that even though he felt very alone at times and desperately wanted to reach out and share his problems.

Then one night towards the end of August they had been out to an Italian restaurant with Anna and Rick and some other colleagues from Qualcomm. It was late as Tarik dropped Jelena off at the apartment that she shared with two other girls and as he turned to kiss her good night she said softly:

"Stay with me tonight Tarik" she said softly *"I need you to be with me"*

An hour later they lay in her bed in her bedroom of the apartment. Jelena had lit a scented candle and put a CD on quietly on the stereo system. It was one of her favourites, by Lionel Ritchie. Tarik turned to look at Jelena as she lay with her head on the pillow and he saw that she was smiling and her eyes were lit up in the candlelight. He kissed her gently and then she placed her arms around his neck and kissed him long and passionately. He let his hands trace the contours of her body, marvelling at her soft, smooth skin and as they kissed he felt her breathing increase and her ample breasts rose and fell beneath his chest. He entered her gently and she winced but then smiled and held him firmer in her arms as she whispered:

"Be gentle darling as you are my first. I wanted to wait till I found the right one"

Later Tarik lay on his back staring at the ceiling, letting the scent of the lavender from the candle and the soft lyrical music wash over him. Jelena lay with her eyes closed, cradled up next to him with his arm firmly around her. He had never known such peace and contentedness. It was only two and a half years since he had left Sarajevo but it felt like a very long time ago but he also knew that it would be time to return home soon. His contract at Qualcomm would not be extended again in the autumn but they had assisted him greatly in developing his CV and personal portfolio and had sent his details to recruitment agents in his home country and elsewhere. Only last week he had had initial contact with an agency in Bosnia who were working with the Civil Service Agency of Bosnia to staff up state institutions and who were looking particularly to recruit IT specialists.

Six weeks later following a series of interviews, Tarik had been offered and had accepted a job with the Civil Service Agency in

Sarajevo and was due to start work at the beginning of January 1999. His mother and sister were absolutely delighted that he would be coming home in a few weeks time. Tarik was not so sure. Everything had changed. He wasn't even sure that Sarajevo was home any more. There were so many ghosts back there which he had tried to turn his back on. He loved the American way of life and had really adapted to living here and if it hadn't been for the recurring visions and frequent flashbacks he had almost forgotten life beforehand, And now there was a huge complication in his life - Jelena.

Since that night in August they had been inseparable. He had moved into her apartment sharing her bedroom which her flatmates had said was perfectly ok with them as they liked him a lot and were more than delighted that Jelena had at last got herself a proper boyfriend. When he told her of his decision to accept the offer, tears welled up in her eyes and she looked up at him saying:

"Does that mean the end for us?"
"No Jelena it is most certainly not but we must accept that it will be difficult. Sarajevo is not the place it used to be. Bosnia is not the place it used to be. There may be a kind of peace and no war but there is no integration any more. There are now two entities, Republika Srpska and the Muslim-Croat Federation and to the eyes of the outside world we are on opposite sides."

Tarik sat on the sofa next to Jelena and tried to comfort her. They said nothing but just embraced each other tightly. Tarik had no idea of how difficult it would be, he only knew what his family had told him but he knew one thing for sure. He would never be able to visit Jelena on a regular basis if she returned to her family in Belgrade.

There was another problem. Both of them knew this and had put it out of their minds but it was now 'the elephant in the room' – neither of them had told their families about their relationship. It was Jelena who broke the silence:

"We could go to Belgrade together. My parents won't mind – I know them."

"Jelena you know that is just not possible. I would never be able to get a job and I would only bring trouble and difficulties to your family. No I must return to Sarajevo now, I owe it to my mother and to my sister. They both need me there. My mother has failing health and my sister has her own health problems to deal with and I cannot leave it all to her. I also have some money now and they need my support. I have no choice. It is what my father would expect of me."

There were a few moments of silence once again between them, each deep in their own thoughts. It was Jelena who eventually broke it again by saying:

"I could come and join you. We could live in Sarajevo together and start a new life there."

Tarik looked at her and kissed her passionately on the mouth smudging the red glossy lipstick that she always had on her thin lips:

"I was hoping you would say that Jelena. But we both must not underestimate the difficulties. It will not be easy for us."

"I know but we will have each other."

Jelena was contracted with Qualcomm until the end of March so the plan was that she would join Tarik a few months later the following year as Tarik was planning to return home to Sarajevo in December so that he could re-orientate himself and acclimatise before starting work at the beginning of the new-year.

Before returning to Sarajevo, Tarik and Jelena had flown up to Chicago to spend a weekend with his foster parents in an emotional reunion and farewell meeting. They were delighted to see him again and so pleased that he now had such a beautiful girlfriend. Tarik had bought gifts and insisted on taking the Stantons out to dinner to an Italian restaurant in the neighbourhood which he knew was a particular favourite of theirs. On the ten minute walk back to the house Paul Stanton walked with Tarik whilst his wife, Christine walked a little behind with Jelena both in deep conversation. Paul turned to Tarik as they strolled along the sidewalk and said quietly:

"Things will be very difficult for you in Sarajevo if you return with Jelana and you must be very careful. I have heard that there is a lot of reconstruction of the city going on now that the war has been over for two years but reconciliation will take a very much longer time. Your country is now divided into three ethno-national groups – Serb, Croat and Muslim which unfortunately as you know was the result rather than the cause of the war."

"Yes I know. I am under no illusions about the challenges that we face if we are to remain together and try to build a life together back home. Many people just will not be able to forget and forgive and in many ways I would prefer to stay here. Thanks to you and many people like you I have been welcomed and I have done well here – far better than I ever thought I would be able to do with the stop-start education that I have had. My English is good and I have computer skills which I never imagined that I would be able to obtain but I owe it to my family and the memory of my father to return and support them. They have suffered so much and they need me and deep in my heart I want to play a part in the future of a new Bosnia whatever that may mean. Remember it was never my decision to leave in the first place. I would feel enormous guilt if I stayed here enjoying an easy life and not contributing to try and build a positive future for my country and also I would be saddled with very negative memories of home which I don't want to be burdened with for the rest of my life."

"You are a good man Tarik and it has been our pleasure to have you in our family for a while and stay in touch."

As they rounded the corner and entered the street where the Stanton's house was located Tarik suddenly stopped and said softly with a real sadness in his voice:

"Paul, there is something I want to tell you that I have not told anyone and have had to keep to myself. For the last two years I have

been having regular nightmares and flashbacks and I suddenly get gripped by fear, anxiety and panic. It lasts for a while and then passes but it leaves me exhausted and in a deep depression. Often the images or incidents are the same. There is one particularly that I witnessed of the death of a friend that keeps reoccurring over and over again."

and he told Paul what had happened to Afan as he had sprinted from the shelter of a building to cross the road to get to the old brewery building and as he relayed the story Tarik closed his eyes and once again he could see his friend's head explode in a red spray that shot upwards and then he collapsed on the floor.

Paul turned towards him and put a comforting arm around his shoulder as he had done many times previously:

"Tarik with what you have been through, seen and witnessed at such a young age I am not surprised that this has had an effect on you. After our son Joel was killed in Vietnam many of his old army buddies used to call in on us from time to time and some of them took a long time to adjust back into normal life, they just couldn't forget, let go and move on but time is a great healer. You will be ok."

The following morning after breakfast Tarik and Jelena embraced the Stantons warmly and made their way back to Chicago airport in a taxi and waited for the flight back down to San Diego.

"You were very lucky Tarik" Jelena said to him as they sipped coffee at a stall in the terminal *"They are really lovely, caring and sincere people. It must have been devastating for them when they lost their only son."*

"I know" Tarik replied as they walked towards the departure gate that had just been announced over the tannoy system:

"I owe them a huge debt which I can only repay by never losing contact with them"

Chapter Eight

Tarik really did not know what to expect when the plane landed at Sarajevo airport. He felt tense and apprehensive but at the same time excited to be seeing his mother and sister again after nearly three years. He was certainly arriving back in very different circumstances to those in which he had left.

He was not prepared however, for what hit him when he exited the airport terminal. He got into a red taxi to take him to his mother's apartment and he noticed immediately that the streets were busy with people and traffic. The trams were running and people were walking freely in the open and not cowering behind walls or running from shelter to shelter. The signs of the war were everywhere. Bombed out buildings, rubble and wreckage, barren recreational sites and parks that had been stripped of all of their trees but there were also giant cranes, boarded off building sites and change was everywhere. It was obvious that Sarajevo was being reconstructed with incredible speed and determination.

Coming out of the war, as both a post-socialist and post-conflict society, Sarajevo was a city undergoing dramatic transitions. In the initial months after the war, Sarajevo faced the physical and infrastructure dilemmas of a city overcoming nearly four years of chaos. The frontline around the city was riddled with mines, explosions were common as gas lines were reconnected and mechanical parts of all kinds failed through the lack of maintenance and damage. The international community had pledged substantial funds to Bosnia, of which Sarajevo received a considerable portion to aid the reconstruction process. Many Islamic countries contributed generously to the rebuilding of mosques and other Islamic structures. Many foreign countries chose to reconstruct pre-existing buildings to house their new embassies to the independent country of Bosnia.

Most of Sarajevo's factories were heavily damaged and many had been gutted by retreating Serb forces and their machinery sent to Republika Srpska. The machinery that remained was for the most part out dated or beyond repair. As a consequence most of the city's factories never reopened and those built after the war were being located outside of the city in places like Zenica. Unemployment in Sarajevo had hovered around the forty per cent mark after the war and the city transformed from having an overwhelming majority of the population as middle class to a polarised society with virtually no middle class at all. Most of the city's middle class citizens had managed to flee the city during the war and now lived in Europe, North America or Australia. The city's new elite was now composed of politicians that had grown wealthy by taking bribes and powerful by entrenching nationalistic divides and of people who had profited enormously from activities like smuggling during the war.

The peace agreement that had ended the war had also dictated a very complex government structure. Businesses had to now deal with several layers of government, each of which had complicated and in some cases nonsensical legislation. New businesses were faced with a government that only provided additional problems rather than solutions and support in return for its company taxation. The only companies that seemed to be benefiting from the government, in the form of receiving subsidies, were the public companies of the past. Many of these businesses without this support would not have been able to survive but they had now become uncompetitive and bureaucratic and were led by people chosen for their political affiliation rather than their technical expertise.

What struck Tarik so forcibly after just a few weeks back in his home city was the way that society had changed and was continuing to change. After the war many older people including his mother, Jasmina referred to the 'Spirit of Sarajevo 'having been lost. Neighbourhoods had provided a support system that created and reinforced the shared values of the time. There was an unstated but understood bond between neighbours which underpinned Sarajevan society before the war. Neighbours were family so neighbours should always be there to help you and you should be closer to your neighbour than to your own family because if something happens, the neighbour is the one who would come to your house first.

Tarik could sense that even now, two years after the war had ended; the people of Sarajevo could not believe what had happened to them. How could so many people with so many shared values suddenly be caught up in such a horrible and vicious war with one another? It was a question that many Bosnians had asked themselves every day for the last five years.

It quickly became clear to Tarik that there were significant differences in the experiences between those who had stayed in the city and those like him who had left and then returned. He realised that even though he had been out of the country for a number of years now and been in the States as a student, there was no hiding from the fact that you are a survivor of something that is overwhelmingly horrible, actually, a war and genocidal violence. Tarik did not believe that this was suffering from survivor guilt, after all he had lost both family and friends but he had been able to leave whilst others had had to stay and many had perished or been terribly injured.

For those who stayed it was simply that one day the shells started falling and from then on and it was just a daily struggle to survive and life was never the same again and for those that left they went through a longer process of introspective whilst in exile but most felt homesick and their minds were always back with their city.

For Tarik, the biggest change was demographc, the majority of Serbs had now moved out of the city. Jasmina still did not know many of her neighbours that now shared her apartment block where as before the war they had lived in close proximity sharing one another's lives whether Muslim, Serb, Croat or Jew. Her husband's best friend, their neighbour, Pasan had been a Serb. It just had not mattered. What mattered was simply being neighbours. There had been a major influx of people from the rural countryside and Tarik noted that just calling out a non-Bosniak name in a public place would now attract attention and the turning of heads. He and Jelena would have to be very careful.

Tarik's taxi pulled up outside the concrete block that housed his family's apartment. He paid the driver and took out his bags and looked up at the drab grey building. He thought that it had survived the war comparatively unscathed to many others that he had seen on his journey from the airport. There had been many windows that had been blown out by blasts but these had been replaced long ago but a few still had bullet holes remaining. The exterior walls showed the tell tale signs of conflict with small craters and holes created by bullets or shell fragments and black scorch marks but somehow miraculously the old concrete building had not taken a direct hit from an artillery shell.

Tarik placed his bags in the lobby and then immediately went out the rear exit. A whirlwind of emotions were swirling through his mind and momentarily he just lost control and broke down in tears as he looked around at the ground that he knew so well. After a few minutes he wiped the evidence of any tears from his face and re-entered the building. He picked up his bags and noticing that the lift was still out of action he took the stairs and climbed to the second floor. He waited for a few seconds outside of the front door to the apartment and then knocked twice. The door opened quickly and there was his mother who just stared open mouthed up at her tall, muscular and mature son.

"Oh Tarik I have waited so long for this moment" and she embraced him tightly and refused to let go until Minka appeared behind her and started to embrace him too.

Ten minutes later they were seated in the lounge drinking coffee and Minka and his mother were opening the presents that he had bought for them. Tarik looked over at his mother as she was unwrapping the gifts. She had aged a lot in the last few years. There were some lines under her eyes where previously there had been none and there were flecks of grey in her dark hair and she seemed to be more diminutive in stature. His sister, however, had regained much of her effervescence that she had had before the war. Her physical injuries had healed well and despite a pronounced limp she was back to how she once had been.

A while later Tarik noticed his mother staring at him:

"Are you alright son" she said *"Your eyes look troubled"*
"I am fine mother. I am just tired from the transatlantic flight"

Inside however, he hoped that his mother had not known he had been crying earlier and during the night flight he had experienced a minor panic attack:

"Would his mask deceive his own mother? He thought.

He really did not want to explain all of this to his mother as it would only upset her and she would not let it go. No, it was far better to keep it all inside and portray the strong, confident persona that he had been doing for quite a while now.

A few days after Tarik's return to Sarajevo Tarik, Minka and Jasmina had all gone together to one of the many small Muslim cemeteries that were dotted around in the hills above Sarajevo to visit Sejo's grave that was situated amongst those of many other victims of the siege. His mother had paid for a new white stone stele, the traditional Bosnian Muslim headstone and there was already a small posy of flowers in a bowl on the grave. Tarik stayed for a while longer than his mother and Minka and knelt and prayed:

"I miss you Papa. I have worked hard whilst I have been away and I will make you proud of me.
No matter what happens in the future I will never forget you."

After the visit that had taken place mostly in silence they were back in the city sitting outside a café enjoying a coffee with the winter sun on their faces.

"There is something that I want to tell you both" Tarik suddenly said. *"I have found someone that I really care about and has become very special to me."*

Both Jasmina and Minka looked at Tarik inquisitively and with a smile on their faces. Tarik took a deep breath and said:

"Her name is Jelena Petrović "

For a few moments there was a silence and the smile had dropped from the faces of his mother and sister.

"But she is a Serb Tarik"

Minka said reactively with her mouth slightly open *more* as a rhetorical statement and not as a question. Once again thought Tarik one's identity has been revealed by one's name and then automatically classified into an ethnic or social grouping with preconceived perceptions without any reference to their individuality and personality. Jasmina sat there and said nothing lost in thought and then she reached to take a large sip of her coffee and looked intently at her son.

"Yes she was born in Belgrade. But she is different. She was not of a family that supported those barbarians who killed Papa and injured you Minka"

and for the next hour Tarik related Jelena's story and how they had met and then he described how beautiful he thought that she was. Jasmina looked at her son and reached out her hand to touch his and said:

"I think that you are in love Tarik and I am pleased and so would your father have been. You are a man now and old enough to make your own decisions and evaluations of people. You have grown up sharing the values of your father and I. One's ethnicity was irrelevant to us and still is to me. It was only the Serbs who made it an issue and created a division that never existed and it is very

important to remember that it was not all of the Serbian people. Many stayed in Sarajevo and were killed and suffered as well as us Bosniaks. It is what is in one's own individual heart that matters. There is the potential for good in every one. You must follow your own heart and your own conscience and I am delighted for you Tarik" and she squeezed his hand tighter and leant forward and kissed him on the cheek.

"I am very pleased for you Tarik" Minka said and also kissed him and smiled.

Tarik blew out a breath of relief and searched in his pocket for his wallet and pulled out a photograph of himself and Jelena taken on a night out in a restaurant in San Diego and he passed it across the table to Minka who picked it up and said:

"She is very beautiful and you look great together."

That night Tarik, delighted and relieved telephoned Jelena who was still in San Diego:

"You are welcomed into my family"

he said with a broad smile on his face.
Six thousand miles away an emotional Jelena listened in silence and just let the tears roll down her cheeks in happiness.

A few months later Jelena who had now joined Tarik in Sarajevo was walking slowly arm in arm with Minka through the Sarajevo city centre district when she suddenly pointed at the ground and said:

"What are all these red patches in the roads and on the pavements"

"They are Sarajevo Roses" replied Minka *"During the siege an average of three hundred and thirty shells a day fell on the city and every shell that exploded on a road or a paved area left a crater.*

These craters were often in the shape of a flower so they were filled in with red resin after the war as small monuments to the suffering."

Jelena just stared in silence at the red marks on the ground and now that she had noticed them she could see them everywhere she looked. She shuddered as she realised that on those spots people had died and out of nowhere everything had ended for them. She could not think of a suitable response to Minka who had just explained their existence and horrific significance in such a matter-of-fact voice so she just continued walking but drew the slightly limping Minka closer to her and they walked on in silence.

Chapter Nine

Tarik's government job had allowed him and Jelena to move up the priority list for accommodation and they were now settled into an apartment that had been left relatively unscathed by the war and had been recently re-modernised and decorated so that it could house key government employees. Tarik had joined a local gym and also the same baseball club that his father had once belonged to who had welcomed him with open arms. They had just finished renovating their ground and the grass was looking green and lush again. The Captain of Dan Sarajevo Baseball Kluba just could not believe his luck when this tall, very skilled and experienced pitcher asked to join their ranks which had been seriously depleted as a result of the war.

It was April 1999 and in the midst of the NATO bombing campaign in Belgrade, Slobodan Milosovic, the President of the Republic of Serbia, was charged by the International Criminal Tribunal for the former Yugoslavia with war crimes, including genocide and crimes against humanity in connection with the wars in Bosnia, Croatia and Kosovo.

"They are going to nail that mad man"

Jelena's father Pavle said later reading the headline in the morning's edition of Oslobodenje, the popular newspaper in Sarajevo over breakfast in Tarik and Jelena's apartment. The newspaper whose title means 'Freedom' had continued to print in Sarajevo throughout the war without missing a single edition and had been a significant symbol of defiance and freedom. Jelena's parents were staying with Tarik and Jelena for a few weeks whilst the NATO bombing campaign was under way and there was a resolution to the crisis.

There had always been simmering tensions between the Albanian and Serb communities in Kosovo throughout the twentieth century but with the rise of Milosovic to power the continuing repression convinced many Albanians that only armed resistance would change the situation. On 22 April 1996, four attacks on Serbian security personnel were carried out almost simultaneously in several parts of Kosovo. A hitherto-unknown organisation calling itself the "Kosovo Liberation Army' (KLA) subsequently claimed responsibility and these attacks continued and the slide to war had begun. Over the next few months fighting intensified and claims of atrocities were made by both sides and the international community demanded that the Yugoslavian Federation (Serbia and Montenegro) should show restraint and that peace talks should commence. However on 23rd March 1999 NATO announced in Brussels that all peace talks had failed and hours before the announcement, Yugoslavia announced on national television it had declared a state of emergency citing an imminent threat of war and began a huge mobilisation of troops and resources.

The proclaimed goal of the NATO operation was summed up by its spokesman as:

"Serbs out, peacekeepers in, refugees back".

That is, Yugoslav troops would have to leave Kosovo and be replaced by international peacekeepers to ensure that the Albanian refugees could return to their homes. NATO's bombing campaign started the following day and involved up to one thousand aircraft operating mainly from bases in Italy and aircraft carriers stationed in the Adriatic, Tomahawk cruise missiles were also extensively used, fired from aircraft, ships, and submarines. Life started to get very uncomfortable in Belgrade both because of the bombing campaign and also because of the atmosphere amongst its citizens and Pavle decided that it was just better to leave with his wife Adrijana until the crisis was over.

"It is a shame that they cannot reach many of the others who committed horrible crimes" Jelena added *"It always seems just a token gesture but what about all the others. I am sure that they would argue that they were 'just carrying out orders' but I don't really*

know who really is to blame. Is it the person who gives the order or the one who carries them out? In my view it is equal guilt."

"An interesting moral point" her father added and he continued:

'*The question of how much responsibility ordinary Germans had for Nazi atrocities has haunted Germany since 1945. It has raised questions such as whether there should be such a thing as collective guilt for Germans and prompted a great deal of soul-searching over how much Germans knew about the death camps and massacres on the Eastern front. It is difficult to distinguish clearly between perpetrators, fellow travellers and bystanders – and assess their responsibility. These categories are not as clear-cut as they might appear and they reflect our own moral standards on human behaviour.'*

Pavle had the attention of all the family now. He was a real academic and a deep thinker but he always spoke with clarity and perception which is why all of his students liked him and his lectures and seminars were always well attended. For a moment Pavle forgot where he was and thought he was back in the university conducting a seminar with a group of students:

The distinction between four types of guilt offered by the German philosopher Karl Jaspers in 1946, though flawed, is still instructive. First, there is criminal guilt of those individuals who committed crimes. Second, political guilt refers to the responsibility of ordinary citizens for the actions of the government that they had supported or tolerated. Moral guilt, by contrast, means that individuals have to examine their own conscience for having taken part in crimes, no matter whether they did so voluntarily or by obeying orders. Finally, metaphysical guilt relates to the lack of human solidarity shown by perpetrators and bystanders with the victims as fellow human beings by not preventing crimes against humanity. Oh I am sorry I have been rambling on a bit' he said

'*No that is fine Pavle. I find it very interesting and I think that it is right that we should have these types of discussions and debates.'*

Tarik replied and Adrijana just smiled.. She was well used to her husband's proclamations and detailed historical analysis which he often came out with at dinner parties and other social occasions.

Tarik got up from the table and kissed his wife and said goodbye to the in-laws and walked to the tram stop to travel to his office. During his lunch break he reflected back on the discussion that they had had during breakfast. He had heard of the concept of 'Universal Justice' but wasn't sure what it meant or how it was applied so when he got back to his desk he typed the words into Google the search engine that he preferred to Yahoo which many of his colleagues used. He read to himself what he found:

'The term universal justice or universal jurisdiction refers to the idea that a national court may prosecute individuals against international law – such as crimes against humanity, war crimes, genocide and torture – based on the principle that such crimes harm the international community or international order itself which individual states may protect.'

He leaned back in his chair and took a large sip of the cup of coffee that he had just helped himself to from the vending machine at the other side of the office. He was tired today. He had not slept that well last night having woken once again soaking in sweat having suffered another nightmare. Jelena had woken too and asked him if he was feeling ill but he had just put it down to 'stress at work' over a new programme that he was working on at the moment.

Tarik had been brought up from an early age to believe in the Islamic 'Six Articles of Faith', he had learned these at school and from his parents and belief in the 'Day of Judgement' was a key tenet of that. He believed that every human, Muslim and non-Muslim alike, will be held accountable for their deeds and will be judged by God accordingly. He knew that the Christian faith also professed a similar belief about "the Day of Reckoning' and Jews believed in the 'Last Day of Judgement' so why did he not leave it at that:

'Who was he to pass judgement? This was in the hands of the Almighty who after death would ensure that everyone's actions were called to account'

But he couldn't just leave it at that and just accept that whoever this person was who murdered his father he would get his comeuppance at the time of his death. Although he realised that Divine Justice was a far higher standard than human justice surely human justice was also relevant? Both the Old Testament and the Qu'ran mentioned the *'eye for an eye'* concept but Tarik had read somewhere that in the Sermon on the Mount, Jesus had urged his followers to turn the other cheek rather than to seek legal or other retaliatory steps for any compensation that corresponds in kind to the injury.

During his time at college in American in order to improve his English, Tarik had taken to borrowing books from the campus library to read in the evenings. For some unknown reason he had become fascinated with the Civil Rights Movement and the struggle of black Americans to end racial segregation and discrimination. Maybe it was because he could ally himself with those who were oppressed by others and just at that moment he recollected a speech made by Martin Luther King jr which he had said the powerful words:

"The old law of an eye for an eye leaves everyone blind."

He wrestled with these thoughts constantly for a few weeks off and on and gradually came to realise that in the end it was all about compassion and charity and he just had not arrived at that point in his life or had the capacity in his heart to sacrifice his own desires and wishes - maybe he would in time. However, right now he concluded:

"I am not a philosopher" he told himself *"I am just someone who is seeking closure so that I can get on with my life and like everyone else I will be judged by my own actions"*

Suddenly a thought came to him:

"Would it be possible for the person who murdered his unarmed father in cold blood ever be brought to justice? To face a criminal court?"

He then dismissed the thought as fanciful however desirable that outcome would be. There had been eleven thousand, five hundred and forty one people killed in Sarajevo during the war – many in similar circumstances to that of his father. The allocation of justice on such a scale was a simple impossibility.

For the next few months hardly a day went by when Tarik was not thinking about the person who murdered his father: The thoughts had become stubbornly lodged in his head. Maybe it was because he was now back in Sarajevo that it had all come back to him with such strength and persistence:

"That murdering bastard saw him simply collecting water. He knew he was not armed and was not wearing a uniform and clearly was not a soldier but he put his gun sight on him and shot him. Cold blooded murder. For what? "

He kept trying to imagine what the man looked like, how old he was and what he thought after he had killed his father. Round and round these thoughts and questions went in his brain. A few times he had mentioned it to Jelena but she had simply said:

"Tarik it is time to put this behind you now. There is nothing you can do and it is time to move on. You and your family have grieved for your father and now it is about your life with me. It is time to look forwards with positivity and not backwards with negativity and hatred in your heart."

So Tarik did not raise the subject at home again. But he simply could not forget. He could not get it out of his mind. In some way these thoughts, obsessive as they may be, were linked to his nightmares and all his repeated anxieties. He had to find a way to exorcise them one way or another for good.

He had been working for the Bosnian government for just over six months now and he was due for a performance appraisal which he sailed through. They were extremely pleased with his aptitude to the tasks set and his abilities which had far surpassed their expectations. He was immediately moved up a pay grade which Jelena was absolutely delighted with as she could now afford some more furniture for the apartment. His promotion also meant he was assigned to more important tasks and was moved to a different department with much more sophisticated IT equipment than he had been working with previously. One afternoon he found that he had completed his tasks quicker than he anticipated so he had a couple of hours to spare till he had a meeting to report on the progress of his project to date. He found himself *'surfing the net'* initially looking up results for baseball teams back in the USA and then moving on to international news and what was happening in the wider world. Although he had been around computers for a few years now both at college and in his working life, he simply could not believe what the internet had achieved. The linking of millions of computers and their networks worldwide had changed everything forever. In just twenty years the internet had moved from a high-tech curiosity to a basic element of modern life transforming the sourcing of information and research from a famine to a feast.

Looking back Tarik didn't know why he did it. It just seemed an automatic action but he found that he had typed *'Siege of Sarajevo'* into Google and then *'Serbian involvement'* and so on and so on. The amount of detail astonished him and all this was free public access, available to anyone around the world at any time. He carried on looking for *'Bosnian Serbian army'*, *'Bosnian Serbian regiments involved in the siege of Sarajevo.'*

He had a number of advantages to aid his search. Language. He now spoke and could read fluent English. The pre-war language of the former Yugoslavia was Serbo-Croat; a term which was virtually extinct now. In post war Bosnia there were now three 'official' languages with different names to which local people ascribe great importance. In reality, these languages are practically the same. The differences being similar to those between American and British English. The only exception being that Bosnians and Croats used the Latin alphabet whilst Serbians used some Cyrillic. *'It was ludicrous'* Tarik thought but often consumable items that he purchased in local shops had the same thing written three times on the packet – all of which were virtually the same.

Over the next few weeks and months Tarik continued his quest whenever he had any spare time available searching with words and phrases or derivatives of them that were linked to the Serbian siege of Sarajevo and in particular anything that he could find using the word *snajper* or *sniper.*

What was amazing about searching on the internet, Tarik thought was that it was almost like the child's game of 'hopscotch' which was called *školica*, in Bosnian, meaning *little school* where one step would lead on to another. Links provided additional links and so deeper and deeper into research you went. This kind of research and analysis would have taken years in a library if it would have been possible at all. He didn't know how he had found the site but he had been searching for over an hour that day and suddenly he arrived at a web site that detailed Bosnian Serbian Army records.

Tarik was fairly sure that any details or records of individual soldiers would be at least password protected and probably hidden behind some other layers of security only available to those given access in the hierarchy of users but to his amazement he was able to enter the site at level one at least. There were sections on history, structure, regiments, actions and general propaganda. Sections on health and re-employment advice for veterans and then there were navigational sub-headings that led to sections on various parts of the army and then there it was – there was a section on sniper troops. The introduction of the section detailed the 'heroic' role these highly trained and skilled individuals had played in the Siege of Sarajevo and elsewhere during the war.

Tarik returned time and again to the site. He was convinced that within here somewhere they would be a hidden clue that could inadvertently and unintentionally link him to the murderer of his father in some way:

'Or was he just being hopelessly optimistic? Was he being blinded by an obsession that was completely unrealistic?

He considered these thoughts every day to and from his journey to work, Careful to keep them to himself and never discuss them at home with Jelena or with anyone else. He was careful always to delete his browsing history and clear out any cookies that may have been automatically downloaded on to his machine. A cookie was a simple text file that was stored on your computer by a web site's server and only that server will be able to retrieve or read the contents of that cookie. Each cookie was unique to someone's web browser and will contain information such as a unique identifier and the site name. The one thing he could not be sure about was whether his IP address would leave a footprint that could be traceable. An IP address or Internet Protocol Address is a numerical label assigned to every computer that uses the Internet Protocol for communication and would therefore leave a direct trail back to the computer sitting on his office desk. But these were issues which were outside of his knowledge sphere and he would just have to take a chance and bluff his way out of it as 'idle curiosity' if anyone raised any questions about it..

Then a few days later he found what he was looking for or at least he thought he had. It was his sixth or seventh return visit to the site:

"How did I not spot that before?"

he said under his breath at his desk one lunchtime. Under each army section at the bottom of the page there was a hyperlink which opened in a new window:

Log in to access your individual pay and pension records

That was as far as Tarik could get. The log in required three fields of information:

- User name
- Service number
- Password

none of which he had in his possession. So disappointed he closed the session and once again erased his records and went back to work.

For a few days Tarik forgot about the web site and what he had found mainly for two reasons. One, he wasn't sure what he had found and what information lay behind the security protection and whether any of that information would be of any use in identifying an unknown individual who possibly may have been an irregular and not in the army records anyway. Secondly he couldn't get passed the security protection anyway.

Sitting on the tram one morning on the way to his office Tarik found himself staring out of the window and he looked up at Mount Trebevic and his mind wandered:

"I wonder where that bastard was located"

Then as he descended from the tram back on to the street for the short walk to work a thought occurred to him. If he could access the portal through the log in process on the web site that he had found then maybe there would be service records of individual soldiers. It was just possible that pay records would relate to actual service dates and places of action. It may even reveal personal details like names and addresses. It was a long shot but it was possible. Then just as he was about to enter the building he chastised himself for very wishful thinking because he knew that there was no way that he could break through that security protection. He knew nothing about 'hacking' as he knew it was called and the private world that those shadowy people existed in.

But just as he pushed open the large glass office main front door he broke into a wide smile and he stepped into the lift to take him to the floor where his office was located. He was the only person in the lift and he turned to look at himself in the mirror that was located on the back wall of the lift and said:

"I may not have the skills that are necessary but I know a man who has!"

Chapter Ten

The last twelve months had been very busy for Tarik. In June he had announced his engagement to Jelena after visiting her parents in Belgrade. It had not been an easy trip for Tarik and one that he had not been looking forward to despite the assurances that Jelena had given him. She had spoken to her mother in confidence and she was convinced everything would be perfectly alright.

There was a time in the former Yugoslavia when the notion of a "mixed marriage" causing a problem would have seemed far-fetched. Indeed, according to the 1991 census, every fifth marriage involved partners from different ethnic backgrounds. The intermarriage rate was highest in Sarajevo itself at 34.1 percent.

However, the war changed all of that perhaps forever. The divisions now were not just geographical but religious and cultural. To those who subscribed to the current mood of extreme ethnic politics, mixed marriages were a direct threat to their ideology that Serbs, Croats and Muslims cannot live together in a multi ethnic society.

'Ethnic intolerance was not a precursor to the war but its consequence' Jelena's father had said to them over dinner that evening. *'You are brave and courageous. You must follow your hearts and not your collective identity but it will not be easy for you. You will have to pick your friends and where you socialise carefully.*

The war created an atmosphere of fear and that the only way to survive was to stick to your own flock but when someone decides to live with someone of another flock this undermines that concept and some will lash out because of fear.'

Tarik and Jelena listened carefully without interrupting and when her father had finished Jelena simply looked up and said very quietly:

'So do we have your approval father?'

Pavle Petrović looked across the table at his wife Adrijana who just smiled and then said;

'Of course you do Jelena. You must follow your heart and Tarik is a fine man but it will not be easy for you. Both of your experiences in America have taught you that the real world is made up of a whole variety of differing cultures, religions and influences and unfortunately what we have witnessed here in the former Yugoslavia is an anachronism, a throwback to a fascist ideology which has no place in a modern world. Hopefully over time, that fear I spoke about earlier will gradually fade and then marriages like yours will not be unusual again and a matter of freedom of choice and not a burden that might stem that choice.'

With that he rose from the table and outstretched his hand to Tarik who also stood and shook it firmly. Jelena walked round the table and kissed her parents in turn with a tear of joy in her eye.

Apart from his personal life things were also busy at work for Tarik as well. The new government supported by international aid was pushing through a number of new programmes related to both reconstruction of the physical infrastructure and introducing new computer technologies for the various departments of state to both act more effectively and efficiently. Consequently he had not given his internet search much thought recently as the wedding that was now planned for the following July was occupying much of both his and Jelena's time

Then out of the blue one morning that autumn he received an airmail letter from America. It was an invitation to an Alumni gathering of his college year group but in addition to make Tarik even more excited he had been invited to play in the alumni baseball team against a rival college in the neighbouring state of Wisconsin in the annual competition. So important was this game for his old college for the annual 'bragging rights' that Tarik had been offered an economy return airfare free of charge to ensure that their former prolific pitcher would once again perform his magic in their colours.

At first Tarik was reluctant to accept the invitation as it would be very unfair on Jelena as only one air fare had been offered and they did not have the spare money for another as they were saving hard for the wedding the following year.

"You must go Tarik" Jelena implored him one night *"I will be absolutely fine. You can take some holiday from work and I have lots to do. I am sure that my mother would be itching to come to stay to discuss the wedding – you will never know the burden of being an only child! But that is fine because I know she only has my best interests at heart and I know that my father will be very generous towards us."*

So Tarik replied saying that he would be delighted to accept the kind invitation. He also mentioned that he had joined a local gym and was keeping himself in shape and that he was also playing for the Sarajevo baseball team which whilst it might not be up to USA college standard it was still keeping him from going 'rusty.'

Six weeks later he was saying goodbye to Jelena at Sarajevo airport for the flight back to America that he had left less than two years before. His foster parents had been delighted to hear from him and absolutely insisted that he came a day early and stay with them before he 'checked in' with his team buddies and started the pre-match final training and briefing from the coach.

Unknown to Jelena however, Tarik had also contacted someone else in the States. Someone he had not seen for quite a long time and he was, therefore, delighted that he received a return email to say that he would be most welcome to call in and catch up and so the arrangements were made.

Tarik bent down and kissed his fiancé goodbye promising that he would call as soon as he was able and the time zones would permit and with that he picked up his luggage and turned to go through the check in security.

Chapter Eleven

Tarik made the three and a half hour flight to Los Angeles International Airport from Chicago's O'Hare International Airport and then hired a car from the Avis desk in the terminal and drove into the city stopping at a diner on the side of the road. He was heading for the city of La Habra which lies about twenty eight miles south of Los Angeles. He got on to the US-101 south from North Main Street and then joined I-5 South for about 13 miles and then took exit 124.

As he was driving along in the slow moving traffic his mind went back to Sarajevo ten years before when he would go with his father to the American burger restaurant that was brightly lit with flashing neon signs after he had watched his father playing in the baseball team. It was his highlight of the week as a young twelve year old boy. Now older and after spending time in the States he had come to realise that perhaps the food did not match up to everything the advertising said it should be and it was a far cry from his mother's home cooking before the war when food supplies had been plentiful.

After about forty five minute's drive Tarik arrived in the outskirts of the city of La Habra. He pulled the car over to the edge of the road and took a street map out of the glovebox. He was relieved to just stop driving for a moment:

"How did the citizens of this city commute in this madness every day,"

he thought to himself. The traffic in Southern California was widely regarded as being the worst in the whole country and Angelenos spent more time stuck idling in their cars than other citizens of any other large city in the country.

He unfolded the map searching and finding the cross the he had marked on it a few days earlier. He looked out of the car window to try and get a bearing on where he was right now but he could not see any visible street signs. Just then two young teenagers were walking past his car carrying two skateboards. Tarik lowered the door window:

"Hi guys, Can you tell me where I am and how far I am from here"

and he pointed to the map in his hands. One of the teenagers sauntered towards the car window. He was wearing a baseball cap but the wrong way round and he was chewing gum noisily. He grasped the map and stared at it for a few seconds:

"Not far bud" he replied *"You're here* "and he stabbed a finger at the *map "and where you want to go is just a few blocks away but tell me why the hell do you want to go there? That is GuadaLahabra."*
"What do you mean" Tarik replied.
"Listen bud, La Habra is not bad. Like all neighbourhoods there are some better areas than others but where you are going is at the bottom of the pile."

Tarik was about to thank the youth but he was already wandering off down the sidewalk with his friend so he restarted the car's engine and moved back into the traffic following the route that had been pointed out to him on the map. He made a couple of mistakes but quickly realised it and carried out a U turn and got back on track. After about ten minutes he had arrived at his destination. The neighbourhood clearly had a very mixed ethnic population and old cars lined both sides of the street. Groups of kids were hanging out on the street and in the entrances of tall apartment blocks, smoking and drinking from cans and talking noisily above the loud hip hop music emanating from numerous boomboxes.

Tarik parked up the car and locked it. He wasn't that bothered about its security because it was a hire car he had rented at the airport and he had taken out the extra insurance so he had no excess liability to pay if anything was to happen to it. He looked up at one of the tall apartment blocks and saw the name on the front of the building in large but faded letters 'Brookdale Apartments.' He entered the lobby and walked to the bank of elevators. It was clean but scruffy with graffiti sprayed on nearly every available surface. He got into the elevator and selected the tenth floor. There was another couple in the lift with him and they were arguing noisily completely oblivious of his presence about whose turn it was to pay the rent which was due the following day and that there was no chance that they would be able to get another extension. Tarik exited at the tenth floor glad to be away from the noisy interchange which had got worse with the young woman starting to scream and thump her fists on the chest of the man who was accompanying her.

Tarik walked down the corridor following the numbers indicating the location of the apartments, he stopped outside a door with the numbers 1052 on it. He was about to press the bell when he saw that there were loose wires coming from it and that it was obviously not in service. So he knocked on the door hard twice. He was about to knock again when the door opened just a little and a face peered around it. It was clearly his college friend, Peter but he looked different to Tarik who had not seen him for over two years. He was drawn and pale with an almost yellowish complexion to his face and his eyes had large bags under them but he broke into a broad smile when he saw Tarik:

"Come in man," he said and opened the door wider.

Tarik stepped into the apartment and immediately detected a stale odour. He couldn't identify it but he suspected that it was a mixture of cigarette smoke, cooking fumes and lack of ventilation. They moved through into the lounge which was dark and dingy until Peter pulled open the Venetian blinds which had been closed. Tarik moved forward and shook his friend's hand vigorously:

"Good to see you. How are you doing? Tarik said breezily.
"Good thanks."

But Tarik was not convinced. His friend looked very thin and was wearing a sports shirt about two sizes too large for him which was covered with stains probably that of last night's take out given the remnants of the cartons that were littered across the coffee table in front of him next to an ash tray that was full of ends and overflowing on to the table.

"How is life back in Sarajevo"
"Very different from here and also very different from when I left but I am adjusting ok"
"Coffee?"
"Yeah that would be great" said Tarik *"White with no sugar"*
"Got no milk man"
"Ok black is fine with me"

Tarik sat on the sofa but first he had to move countless magazines - all of them computer related. Tarik lifted a few up and looked at the titles – *Maximum PC, PC Leisure PC Extreme, PC Mania and Planet PC.*

He thought for a moment. Actually he did not know that much about Peter Soberg. Yes he had been his friend at College, in fact Tarik was probably his only friend because he had never really seen him talking to anyone else and he had never seen him in a social context at any of the college events. He knew that he came from Abilene the son of a livestock farmer. He knew that he had an elder brother who was like his father, big and strong who was being groomed to take over the family homestead whilst Peter hated physical work, hated the animals and the outdoor life.

"Abilene is just a 'cow town' with nothing to do that remotely interests me" Peter had said to him once

He spent his time reading and it was clearly evident from an very early age that he was exceptionally good at mathematics always getting top grades and winning prizes and had taken like a 'duck to water' at the IT lessons at school. He stayed late every night practising on the desktop computers and he had learnt to write his

110

own programmes using MS Dos and then Windows. But despite his achievements he did not gain his father's approval. It was his mother who persuaded him to go into further education as she realised that it was probably better that he left home to pursue his interests and Peter had had little contact with them ever since.

"There's something different about you" Tarik said when Peter re-entered the lounge with two steaming mugs of black coffee.
"No glasses" replied Peter *"I got some contact lenses earlier this year which are much better"*

"I expected to see you at the reunion last weekend" Tarik suddenly said:

"It was a really great event and about eighty per cent of the year showed up. It is amazing to see what some of then are all doing now, Do you remember Steve Andrews? Well he is now an accountant and Jo Stilco is Manager of a large shopping mall."

"I couldn't be bothered to travel down" replied Peter *"Besides I never really knew those guys and they never bothered to get to know me. So what has brought you all this way to see me, I am sure it is not my coffee!"*

Tarik leaned back on the sofa and Peter was sat in the chair opposite him and he took out a cigarette from the crushproof pack on the table and lit it with a disposable lighter:

"Because I need your help" Tarik suddenly said quietly and directly.

"My help! How could I possibly help you" replied Peter
"Well I think you can for two reasons. One I think that you are probably the smartest guy I have ever known with computers and two, because you are the only one that I could trust with this."
"Shit man! It sounds heavy duty"

111

"Not really. It is not dangerous and I will pay you well but it will be very difficult and it is ultra personal and it may not be strictly legal.'

"Hmmn interesting! You'd better tell me about it then but wait a minute"

With that Peter disappeared back into the kitchen and returned with two cans of cold Budweiser beer and handed one to Tarik. For some time now Tarik had decided that he would allow himself to drink moderately. He had wanted to fit in with the social scene at college and whilst he respected his upbringing and religious beliefs he was happy to adapt them without compromising on the core beliefs. It was the same justification he had made to himself after sleeping with Kimberley. In any event if he had made a few compromises then they were between him and God and no one else.

Tarik talked to Peter for over two hours later telling him everything that had happened to him which he had never done during their time at college. At that time he had just told friends that he had come to the States to escape the war and to look after his seriously injured sister and had been lucky to get a place on the humanitarian relief programme. But now he relayed the events leading up to his father's murder and the family's fight for survival, his time in the forward trenches facing the enemy and the appalling atrocities that he had witnessed. But somehow he could not bring himself to explain what he had seen happen to his friend Afan as he had moved out of the shelter of a building to cross the road to get to the old brewery – perhaps he did not want to relive the images again voluntarily.

Peter had sat in silence not wanting to interrupt Tarik's monologue. He just nodded occasionally or screwed up his face. To be honest he had never heard anyone talk about experiences like this. After two hours when Tarik had finished Peter got out of his chair and stubbed out another cigarette:

"Let me show you something" and he led the way out of the lounge and into the smaller of the two bedrooms in the apartment.

"You are the first person to have seen this. This is where I really live" he exclaimed *"Not in your world but in the virtual world"*

Tarik was staring at banks of computers and screens that were all blinking bright green lights in the low light of the room and there was a dull hum and whirring of electrical machinery. He had never seen so much computer hardware in such a small space it was absolutely amazing. It reminded him of the TV footage of the Houston Control Centre for the NASA space missions.

"I don't go out very often. I make some money doing programming and stuff. Pretty run of the mill and boring but it pays the bills and enables me to keep up to date with everything I need."

It was clear to Tarik that Peter had completely withdrawn from society as he knew it. He wasn't sure what the *'virtual world'* was but suspected that it involved interacting though a keyboard rather than engaging in conversation in a coffee shop. He had become far more of a recluse than he had been at college and Tarik suspected that his friend was experiencing some mental health issues which had always been there but had now come to the fore.

"What time do you have to leave" Peter said turning to Tarik who had not said a word since entering the room:

"I am on the 17.30 flight back to Chicago this afternoon"
"Then you had better tell me everything I need to know"

They returned to the lounge and Peter asked a series of questions which Tarik answered in part but promised that he would respond more fully once he had returned to Bosnia in a few days time. Tarik looked at his watch and said "I'd better be heading back to the airport now:

"Can I just use the bathroom before I go"
"Sure man"

When Tarik came back out Peter was not in the lounge but he heard a movement coming from the second small bedroom so he entered the room. Peter was sitting in a large swivel chair in the half light staring at two screens at once and a cigarette was dangling from the corner of his mouth Tarik said nothing for a few moments but watched in awe as his friend's hands danced over the computer keyboard like an internationally acclaimed concert pianist playing the most difficult piece of the Russian composer, Dmitri Shostakovich. It was like he was in a trance; his hands moved so fast across the keys that Tarik could barely see them. Numbers and figures danced on to the screens in a bewildering array of constantly changing data.

Tarik took out his wallet from his back pocket and extracted ten $50 dollar notes and placed them besides Peter who didn't look away from the screens in front of him.

"For your initial expenses"
"Thanks man. Can you see yourself out? Be in touch in a few days. See you"

Tarik turned on his heels and left the apartment closing the door softly so as not to disturb the thin man with the stained sports shirt but now with new contact lenses in the small room so contentedly enveloped in his virtual bubble.

Chapter Twelve

A few weeks after Tarik had returned from his trip to America, Jelena began to grow more and more concerned about his behaviour and mood swings. He could switch from being a charming, gentle and caring individual into a persona that was withdrawn and irritable within minutes. Increasingly she felt that Tarik seemed to be 'in a different place' and somehow remote from her and those around him and yet he seemed to be in a state of vigilance, sometimes his eyes would dart around the room as if he was on some kind of constant alert. At times she would find him just staring into space, totally withdrawn and uncommunicative but still in this state of almost hyper vigilance as if waiting for something to happen.

Occasionally she had mentioned this to him enquiring *"Is anything the matter"* or *"What is troubling you Tarik?"*

and he would always reply tersely *"No. There is nothing the matter. It is just work or this or that."*

Jelena, however, was not convinced. She had also noticed that he was not sleeping well and that he would often wake during the night and get up and watch television or just sit on the sofa. After one such night she said to him over *breakfast:*

"Just what are you concerned about Tarik? Is it the wedding? Is it me or something that I have done?"

"No. Nothing! There is nothing wrong. OK?" he replied irritably and got up from the table and walked away across the room.

"You don't need to jump down my throat" she replied softly *"I am just concerned about you"*

Tarik turned around slowly and looked up at his fiancé, walked towards her slowly and then embraced her tightly, wrapping his arms around her and drawing her into him. His chest heaved and his eyes felt moist.

"I am sorry babe. I love you so much" he whispered. *"It is just that they won't go away. I still keep getting these flashbacks and I am back on the bridge and they are shooting at me and then I see my father lying in a pool of blood and then I can imagine the bastards up in the hills probably laughing and joking. It will pass, I have had this all before and maybe after the wedding things will all settle down again"*

"I hope so Tarik" Jelena replied quietly *"Maybe you should talk to a professional about this. It is not right to keep all of this stuff bottled up inside you."*

Tarik hugged her again and kissed her hair softly but inside he knew that whatever it was that was troubling him just simply would not go away. He could push it to the back of his mind but no matter how hard he tried he could not rid himself of these thoughts and the mood that they brought with them. Invasive and unwanted they certainly were but he could not shift them but the last thing he wanted to do was to talk to a stranger about all of this and how he felt.

The wedding had been planned for 21st July 2001. Tarik had discussed it at length with his mother and sister:

'What would papa have wanted me to do' he had asked
'What do you mean' his mother had replied
'Well would he have wanted me to get married in a mosque?'
'If you were marrying a Muslim girl then certainly – yes. But you are not. As you know we have brought both you and Minka up with your faith. We did our best to ensure that you both knew and followed the teachings of our religion. We always observed the most important days of the Islamic year but we were never fervent so in my heart I know that he would say the issue is between you and God

and you alone can have that conversation and make that decision. But I suggest that you take the advice of the Imam at the mosque. He has known you since you were a small boy.'

So a week or so later Tarik was sitting before the Imam. Tarik and his fellow Bosnians were largely of the Sunni denomination of Islam. The role of the Imam was largely in the form of a worship leader of the mosque and the local Muslim community. In this context, imams may lead Islamic worship services, serve as community leaders, and provide religious guidance.

After listening to Tarik for a while the old man spoke quietly but purposefully:

'Tarik. Listen to me. In Islam, going to a church or a mosque is not a condition for a valid marriage. A Muslim must seek blessings directly from God and only from God. If the woman that you wish to marry insists on doing so in a church and regards the marriage to be invalid otherwise then there is no problem with you going together to the church for that purpose. However, this is under the strict condition that you as a Muslim believe firmly in your heart that you're going there does not bring about the validity of the contract in any way and that this act on your part is solely that of carrying out a civil procedure that for you as a Muslim man has nothing to do with the lawfulness of the contract with God.'

Tarik offered his prayers, thanked the Imam and left with a lightness he had not felt before in his heart. He did not return to his apartment directly but took a detour on the tram to the cemetery and walked quickly and purposely until he arrived at the grave of his father. Kneeling he prayed softly:

'Papa. How I miss you. I miss your advice and guidance. I have tried so hard to get on with my life and support my mother and sister and now I have Jelena. I know that you would love her too papa and give us your blessings.'

Tarik spoke with Jelena's parents soon after this and was told them he was happy to agree that the wedding ceremony could be carried out at the church where Jelena had been baptised as a child. Adrijana was abosultely delighted and thanked Tarik profusely:

"It matters so much to me Tarik, Thank you so much. It is all the more important when you only have one child.'

'I have always regarded myself as a Muslim and that defines my identity and beliefs; Tarik explained to Jelena's father later on in the telephone call 'But I also regard myself as being what I describe as a 'Modern Muslim'' and that the communication an individual has directly with God is all that matters in my opinion. There will be many who disagree of course, but for me that is the basis of religion and spiritual well being – a one on one relationship with God."

Pavle thanked Tarik for his thoughtfulness and pragmatism but he also went on to say that in his opinion given the circumstances that they should keep the wedding ceremony very 'low key' and a very private affair so as to not attract any unnecessary and probably unwanted attention from any quarter. Belgrade was still a place coming to terms with what had occurred in the recent past and sensitivities were high. In the event, only immediate family attended the ceremony which was held in a small Serbian Orthodox Church.

Ružica Church is a small chapel tucked into the side of the Serbian Kalemegdan fortress and its name means 'little rose.' Its frescoed walls are lit by two chandeliers made entirely of spent bullet casing, swords, and cannon parts. It is a more fitting decoration than one might realise as the church was controlled at various times by the Serbs, Turks, Hungarians, and Austrians. Its small and dark interior had however, seen a lot of action and the space the church now occupied was, for over one hundred years, used by the Turks as a gunpowder magazine. The church had to be largely rebuilt after World War I. Though damaged by bombings, there was an upside to the devastation. While fighting alongside England and the US, Serbian soldiers on the front line had used their downtime to craft the incredible chandeliers from the materials that were available to them

- the spent shells and weaponry that lay strewn around the battlefield. So the instruments of war and destruction had been refashioned to form unique decorative items that would forever define this little church.

The wedding passed off perfectly and the small wedding party consisted only of the bride and groom, and on Tarik' side his mother and Aunt and his sister and her husband. On Jelena's side were just her parents, an aunt and uncle and a grandmother. Pavle had organised the wedding luncheon to take place at a restaurant in Zemun, an historic area of Belgrade located on the Danube river. With its large windows facing the river, the dining room needed little else but an arch of white flowers and simple centrepieces to create a festive scene. It had been a favourite of his and Adrijana's for many years and the proprietor had been delighted to close the restaurant for that day to take the private booking.

Jelena had only ever had one destination in mind for her honeymoon. Paris – the city of love and romance. She and Tarik flew from Belgrade to Charles de Gaulle airport the following day and took a taxi into the city. They had rented an apartment in the district of L'Opera just behind the magnificent upmarket department store of Galleries Lafayette. They spent a marvelous week visiting Notre Dame and the Louvre, dining in the Left Bank region at a restaurant overlooking the river Seine. They had been presented with a cascade of seafood set on coloured ice and Jelena and Tarik had the first oysters they had ever tasted in the lives that had come in from Cancale on the Normandy coast early that morning:

'The food of love' Tarik had remarked and laughed as they consumed the oysters washing them down with a glass of chilled Sancerre white wine.

They had also dined on board a restaurant riverboat with a glass roof down the Seine in the evening being serenaded by a violinist as they drifted past numerous famous landmarks of Paris that were all floodlit as they sipped chilled champagne and passed silently under the bridges spanning the river. Tarik found it all a bit of a surreal but

119

wonderful experience and he found it hard to believe that it was only five years ago that he had been running for his life every night with heavy water bottles strapped to his back dodging sniper's bullets as he zigzagged across bridges and dived from shadow to shadow but he simply refused to let his often recurring nightmares enter the bubble of these precious moments with his new bride. He raised his slightly frosted glass and watched the bubbles rising from the chilled champagne and he said quietly:

"To us and to our future together"

He smiled broadly and leant across the table to kiss his wife gently on the lips smudging her characteristic red glossy lip stick. She smiled back at him and reciprocated the toast:

"It is just so romantic here Tarik. I love everything about the city, the amazing architecture, walking arm-in-arm by the river Seine particularly at night, lingering in side street cafes and visiting museums and galleries and experiencing the romanticism of nineteenth century Paris and best of all candlelit dinners and champagne. We should stay here forever."

Tarik smiled and then laughed saying:

"It may be all of that but it is also very expensive. I cannot believe what we paid for just two cups of coffee in that cafe on the Avenue des Champs-Élysées this afternoon!"
"Don't spoil it" Jelena replied taking another sip of champagne and smiling as she reached for his hand across the table.

It had been nearly six months since Tarik had visited Peter in America. He had received numerous emails from him requesting information on this and that but no information of any substance. That was until today. As he turned on his computer and waited for it to boot up, he leaned back in his office chair and took a sip of the steaming black coffee that he had brought form the cafeteria in a styrene cup. He opened his mailbox and there it was. An email from

Peter marked *'Urgent.'* Tarik took another sip of coffee and opened the email and read:

"Hi Tarik

I hope you are well and that the wedding all went off ok. I am sorry that I have not accepted your invitation to come and stay with you and Jelena in Sarajevo but I am really busy at the moment and I don't even have a passport as I have never been out of the States and probably never will."

Tarik took another sip of the hot coffee and thought. Strange but true. He knew that only about ten percent of Americans held a valid passport and held no desire to travel beyond their borders; it was something that he regarded as being very odd. The United States was indeed a very large and diverse country but it did not compare to the excitement and stimulus of international travel. He read on:

"I won't bore you with the technical detail but I have accessed numerous databases, archives, registers and files. I have used software that I created to cross reference data and isolate data that only matched certain criteria and the parameters that I set and filter out the rest. This was an enormous task and hence the time lag since I have got back to you. It is a bit like the old gold miner back in the nineteenth century panning the streams for gold and after endless hours comes up with a life-changing nugget. Well here it is!

You were right. The pay records linked to an individual's service records and to the personal information of those individuals. It was like a hierarchy each with its own security levels which took me a time to break through but they were not that sophisticated. The trick was not to leave a 'footstep' or digital finger print so that no one knew that you had accessed these records and certainly could not see who it had been.

On the night of 25th November 1994 there were only two snipers on duty at the time of your father's death which was around 11.30pm."

121

Tarik took another sip of the coffee and put down the styrene cup, lent back in the chair and blew out a long breath:

"Clever boy" he whispered to himself.

Tarik did not know a lot about computer 'hacking' except what he had learned on his IT courses in the States. He had been taught that the origins of hacking went back a long way and originally were concerned with getting free access to telephone networks. It was in 1975, two decades earlier that two members of the Homebrew Computer Club of California begin making "blue boxes," devices based on an earlier discovery that generated different tones to help people hack into the phone system. Their names were Steve Wozniak and Steve Jobs, who would later go on to found a company called Apple Computers in 1977.

Hacking seemed to have entered the popular culture in the1980's when a number of films, novels and magazines emerged popularising the hacker and his belief systems. None more so than the release of the film *"War Games'* in 1983 which depicted the existence of hacking and the potential power associated with it. The publication of William Gibson's first hacking related novel *"Neuromancer"* which coined the term ' Cyberspace' in 1984 which had been requisite reading amongst Tarik's college friends. However, frequent high profile cases of hacking activity in the popular press alerted the growing band of computer users of their own susceptibility of attack and the loss of private data and information and so demanded tools to protect themselves. By the time that Tarik attended college, hacking had started to become the subject of scholarly research and major colleges and universities had started teaching about cyber culture and digital security and the romantic notion of a 'fringe' hacker was now clearly depicted being as a criminal and very damaging activity.

Whilst Tarik had had no more than an academic interest in the subject, his friend Peter was obsessed. He had been an avid reader of *'Wired'*, the monthly magazine which called itself the *'Rolling Stone'* of technology since its launch in 1993. He was a founder member of a number of user groups and hackerspaces exchanging information, knowledge and knowhow amongst its dedicated band of followers. In the few years since leaving college and Tarik's meeting in his apartment in La Habra, Peter had entered deeper and deeper into this parallel cyber world and his knowledge and abilities had developed exponentially. Peter, Tarik had come to realise relished his existence in this cyber world as an escape from a real world with which he could not fully engage. Social interaction was so much easier through a keyboard and a screen and Peter was a master of his own universe but Tarik was confident that his skills had never been applied to anything malicious, criminal or nihilistic.

Tarik continued to read Peter's email. His heart was banging in his chest and he noticed that his mouth was dry and his stomach had tightened but he was staring at the screen with an intensity that he had never really experienced before:

"The two individuals were both Bosnian Serbs. Borislav Paštrović and Ranko Bajić. *There is no updated record for Bajić but he came from Banja Luka. However, six months ago* Paštrović *updated his address and contact details presumably to ensure the future receipt of any pension that was due to him. As this was only six months ago I think it would be safe to assume that this is still current. The details are:*

Borislav Paštrović
144 Vlatka Vukovica
Kozarska Dubica
Republika Sprska

Tarik looked up from the screen and noticed that his colleagues were now at their desks so he moved the email into his personal folder and got up from his desk and walked to the toilet which was down the corridor. He lent over the sink basin and splashed some cold water over his face and took in a few deep breaths exhaling the air slowly through his mouth. His heart rate dropped and he dried his face on the towel and walked back to his desk calmly greeting a number of his colleagues as he went.

During the lunch break Tarik ate in the cafeteria with some of his friends discussing the baseball match that he was playing in that evening for the Dan Sarajevo Baseball Kluba which some of them were coming to watch and cheer him and the rest of the team on. With ten minutes left before he was due to restart work, Tarik made an excuse and returned to his desk. He reopened the email and then seeing that there was no one standing by the communal printer, he sent it to print and then sprinted over to the machine to receive it as soon as it printed out and entered the in-tray. He then walked back to his desk calmly, sat down and sent a quick 'Thank you' reply to Peter saying that he would be back in touch and then deleted both the incoming and outgoing emails. He looked down at the three sheets of paper in front of him and read on:

"I hope that this is what you are looking for Tarik. I do not know what you intend to do with the information but I would advise caution. These are not nice people. It may just be better to 'let sleeping dogs lie' but I know that that is not you. So just take care and if I can help out again let me know.

All the best
Peter

Tarik folded the sheets of paper and put them in the inside pocket of his jacket that was hanging over the back of his chair and returned to work but he found it hard to focus and a number of questions went round and round in his head:

"Should I tell Jelena?"
"What am I going to do now"
"I am not a detective and in the eyes of the Serbs no crime was committed anyway"
"Should I just report my findings to the Bosnian authorities and let any unlikely due legal process take its course?"

Tarik put all these thoughts to the back of his mind and refocused on his afternoon's tasks. He was due to meet Jelena after work and

124

walk to the stadium together and after the game they had booked a little restaurant which they had been to a few times and it had become a bit of a favourite of theirs. The food was great and had a really homemade feel about it and was reasonably priced.

'Maybe he would confide in her?'

Tarik's team had won. The coach had come into the dressing room afterwards congratulating them all but he clapped Tarik hard on the back:

"You were my man of the match".

Tarik however, declined to celebrate with his teammates saying that he had a dinner date with his wife and as he walked out of the changing room she was waiting for him and they embraced each other tightly:

"Careful" she says *"You nearly squeezed me to death"*
"Sorry. I thought you liked the bear hug!" he laughed

They walked hand in hand out of the stadium and waited ten minutes at the tram stop and took the tram into the city centre where they alighted and walked to the restaurant which was situated in the old town. They both loved the place for two reasons. The ambience was terrific with an ancient feel about the decor but mixed with a busy clientele of mostly younger Sarajevans. Secondly, the food was not only authentic and homemade and delightful but really inexpensive. They always opted for the same dish which they loved to share together. It was a traditional Sarajevski Sahan which consisted of hollowed-out vegetables stuffed with rice and various meats. Jelena loved this dish because it was based on vegetables; she considered it to be so much healthier than much of the other food on offer.

When they had sat down and ordered the food Tarik suddenly said:

"I've got something to tell you Jelena"

and for the next five minutes or so he poured out the story of how he had visited Peter and who he was and then the email that he had received today back from his old friend. Jelena just looked at him and slumped her elbows on the table and put her head in her hands:

"What are you doing Tarik? What possible good can come of this? I thought that you had decided that you could move on now and put the past behind you?"

"I just can't seem to let it rest Jelena. I need to have some sort of release"

"So what do you plan to do?" she said slightly mockingly *"Walk up to this guy and say heh you are the bastard who shot my father? What do you think he is going to say or do to you a Bosniak?"*

"I have not thought it through yet"

"Well you had better because you have responsibilities now. You are married and there is something else. I have been waiting for the right time to tell you so it may as well be now. I am pregnant."

Tarik leapt from his seat in joy and lent forward and kissed her passionately

"Sit down you idiot" she laughed *"Everyone will look at us"*

"Jelena I am so delighted. Have you told your parents?"

"No I wanted to tell you first"

Whilst they ate their food Tarik couldn't keep the smile off his face and they spent the rest of the meal and long afterwards having an endless discussion about names and when they would tell her parents and his mother and sister.

They left the restaurant and walked hand in hand to the tram stop and Jelena suddenly stopped, let go of Tarik's hand and looked up at him with a face full of concern and said:

"Tarik – you have got to drop all this nonsense about tracking down these Serbs. Only something really bad can come of it. You survived the war and now you have a wife and soon a family. You have a whole new life. You do not need to revisit a past that should be forgotten about. Let those evil men rot in hell."

They stepped on to the yellow tram and Tarik noticed that this one still bore scars and scorch marks from the war and he said:

"I will think about it" he said as he validated their tickets that he had bought from a kiosk previously.

Chapter Thirteen

A few weeks passed by but Tarik had never stopped thinking about Peter's email and the information that it contained. Every now and then he would research the areas on the internet that Peter had indicated where the two Serbians lived. Slowly a plan started to evolve in his mind. It was the only way he decided that he could finally lay to rest the ghost of his father and put all the horrors of his earlier years behind him so that he could get on with his new life in the new Sarajevo with his wife and his unborn child.

"Yes. This is the only way" he said to himself one lunchtime as he strolled through the park by his office before returning to his desk.

"I am not an avenger. This is not about revenge. I am not in an American movie. All I want is to know the truth, to confront the man who killed my father and to let him know the hurt and pain that he has inflicted on me and my family. I do not expect an apology. Neither do I expect that I can forgive but I hope that I may then be able to forget."

A few more weeks passed by and Tarik had firmed up his plan in his mind but for it to work he needed an accomplice. He could not do it on his own:

"But who?" he thought *"Who would want to go on such a crazy mission as this and why would they want to anyway?*

Then it came to him:

"Someone who was in the same situation as him. Someone with the same burning anger, motivation and probably the same desire to somehow even the score."

"Faris"

he said suddenly to himself as he sat on the tram returning home that evening. *"But I have not seen him since I left with Minka to go to America five years ago, I do not know if he even survived the war and I don't know how he will feel about me marrying Jelena and also not being invited to the wedding. A lot of issues there but I am going to find out."*

It took Tarik more than two weeks to track down his old friend Faris. Fortunately he had survived the war and he was still living in Sarajevo and they arranged to meet at a coffee house in Sebilj Square in the heart of Baščaršija, the old bazar and the historical and cultural centre of the city. This café situated in the pigeon-inhabited square looked out on to the main public fountain and had long been Tarik's favourites since he had been a small boy. The café culture is well established in Sarajevo and in the summertime everyone sits outside. The cafes ran together sometimes making it difficult to know which tables belonged to which establishment but it didn't really matter because they all offered the same ambience and service.

He recognised him immediately when he entered the café although he had changed significantly. The war had obviously taken its toll on him. He face was drawn and his eyes were slightly sunken and there were streaks of white in his dark brown hair even though he could only have been a few years older than Tarik. Faris scanned the room and caught sight of Tarik and they shook hands and embraced vigorously although Faris walked towards Tarik with a pronounced limp in his left leg.

"Took a round in the thigh a few months before the end of the war" Faris said pointing at his left leg as they made their way back to the table where Tarik had been sitting.

"Six years. Where has the time gone Tarik?"
Faris said as they sat at a table sipping the dark black Turkish coffee and nibbling at the jellied sweet rahatiokum that was served with it. The coffee was typically strong and dark and served Turkish-style in a copper pot with a tiny cup to pour into and sip slowly.

'Tell me everything that has happened to you Tarik. You look so well."

An hour passed quickly as they both related their stories of the last few years during which time Tarik noticed Faris had hardly had a cigarette out of his hand which was shaking gently all of the time.

"So we all have our scars" Tarik thought to himself *"Some visible and some concealed inside"*

Faris was now married to a fellow Sarajevan called Vildana and working in the office of a large timber and builders' merchants yard on the outskirts of the city. Business had been very good because of all the reconstruction that was going on. When Tarik told Faris about Jelena his friend's brow furrowed:

"A Serb Tarik that was brave"

"It was love" Tarik replied *"Come and meet her. Bring Vildana for dinner at our place."*

So they parted having agreed on a date the following week.

The dinner party went really well. Jelena had cooked a traditional Bosnian Ćevapi which was served on a large plate and cut into ten portions called Ćevapcici, or little Ćevapi. The grilled dish is a mix of two kinds of minced beef or lamb which are formed into finger-sized sausages and served with somun bread which is similar to pita. Raw, chopped onions and kaymak, a salty, creamy cheese, Ajvar, which is a creamy roasted red pepper paste and sour cream were served on the side and partnered perfectly with the slightly spicy meat.

Tarik was delighted to see that the two girls got on really well together and if there had been any hesitance about Jelena's nationality had been quickly dismissed. A couple of hours later Tarik was sitting at the table with Faris drinking coffee as the two girls were washing up in the kitchen. Tarik decided he would tell Faris about his plan and all of the information that he had received from Peter in America. Eventually Faris blew out a long breath:

"You are totally crazy man" he said *"You will probably get beaten to a pulp or worse. What on earth do you hope to achieve?"*

Tarik took a sip of coffee as Faris lit yet another cigarette:

"The same thing I think you want too Faris" he ventured
"And what on earth is that"
"Closure"

Tarik said simply and when he looked back across the table at his friend he saw there were tears in his eyes. Faris took a long drag of his cigarette and exhaled the smoke:

"Not a day goes by Tarik when I do not think of my mother and father and my brother. I feel guilty that I am alive and they are dead. Why was it that I was not killed in the apartment with them? Why was I out that evening collecting wood? Why did I survive and they did not? Before I met Vildana I had nothing. No one to confide in. You were the first friend that I had made after their death and then you left for America. I had never felt so alone and isolated. I just existed for the rest of that year until the end of the siege, I was not living. Probably at the time I did not really care that much about living anyway. There just didn't seem anything to live for any more. No family. No friends. No food or water. No real shelter. No end to the bombardment and the slaughter"

and Tarik just watched as the tears just rolled down his friend's cheeks.

Chapter Fourteen

Ever since the founding of Yugoslavia, two distinct nationalist policies had sought to achieve primacy, in the debate over the country's political future, Croatian separatism striving for an independent state and Serbian striving to preserve the Yugoslav state under its dominion. As communism collapsed, strategies in the different republics were determined by specific national interests and the opportunity to leave the communist system. Conflict was an inevitable result.

It is a well known and well understood social convention that members of all human groups share beliefs. Sharing beliefs is an integral part of group membership and group identity and provide meaning and direct or justify group actions. Conformity provides confidence and security from their similarity. The Serbian psyche in the late 1980's and early 1990's was dominated by a highly developed sense of victimisation. The key to the Serb-as-victim myth was the Battle of Kosovo, which the Serbs lost in 1389. Subsequent generations were taught it was the Serbs' finest hour and their noble attempt to save the continent from the Ottoman hordes was totally unappreciated by other Europeans. Vidovdan or "St. Vitus Day" is a Serbian national and religious holiday, a *slava* or feastday celebrated on June 28th (Gregorian Calendar), or June 15th according to the Julian calendar, in use by the Serbian Orthodox Church to venerate St. Vitus. The Serbian Church designates it as the Memorial Day to *Saint Prince Lazar and the Serbian holy martyrs* who fell during the epic Battle of Kosovo against the Ottoman Empire and it is a very important part of Serbian ethnic and national identity.

President Slobodan Milosevic understood the power of this myth well, using it to whip up Serb nationalist passions. Ranko Bajić was totally caught up in this nationalistic fervour. Milosovic embodied everything he had believed in all of his life: He had been born in 1972 in Banja Luka, the son of working class parents and had left school with no formal qualifications. He had not played sport either at school apart from kicking a football around but he was physically strong and intimidating and had belonged to a gang that regularly bullied and terrorised other weaker members of the school and local community. The members of the gang were all fanatical supporters of FK Borak Banja Luka, one of the most successful and popular football clubs in Bosnia and Herzegovina.

But Ranko and the other members of the gang however, were not just interested in the football itself. They used their support of the club to cover their greater interest which was to fight with and deliver as much violence as possible on the opposing supporters at all of the matches both at home or away. This ritualised male violence was related to a number of factors that included interacton, identity, legitimacy and power. After working as a mechanic's assistant in a local garage for a couple of years and then drifting in and out of other manual jobs he had joined the army in the autumn of 1992 at the age of twenty.

The Army of the Republika Srpska (VRS) was founded on 12th May 1992 from the remnants of the Yugoslav People's Army (JNA) of the former Socialist Federal Republic of Yugoslavia from which Bosnia and Herzegovina had seceded the same year. When the Bosnian War erupted, the JNA formally discharged eighty thousand Bosnian Serb troops. These troops, who were allowed to keep their heavy weapons, formed the backbone of the newly formed Army of the Republika Srpska

Ranko Bajić fitted into the new army like a hand in a glove. He took delight in the opportunity to share his world view with likeminded people and his confidence and swagger grew. He was popular amongst his comrades and because of his physical presence others seemed to gravitate towards him and listen to what he had to say. He would quote parts of speeches made by Radovan Karadzic, the Bosnian Serbian leader in particular the one that he made at the sixteenth session of the Bosnian Serb Assembly on 12th May 1992 which took place in Banja Luka some months before the start of the war which set out the strategic goals of the Serb people in Bosnia and Herzegovina which were then adopted by the Serb Assembly and became the official policy of Republika Sprska throughout t he war. Karadzic had stated that the first strategic priority was *"State delineation from the other two national communities."*

For Ranko Bajić this policy was clear, simple and straight forward. The Serb community should be separated from the Muslim and Croat communities which would lead to an 'ethnically clean' Serb state in Bosnian territory and if that meant the slaughter and displacement of thousands of men, women and children then so be it.

Bajić also displayed another critical element of the Serb psyche that of *inat'*, meaning "spite" which also included the idea of revenge no matter what the cost. Serbs themselves will sometimes engage in extended discussions when trying to define the concept of *'inat'*. Probably the least wordy English version of the word is "deliberately cutting off your nose to spite your face," although a more elegant definition is probably "defiance for the sake of defiance rather than to achieve a long-term goal." A common response among Serbs was to concede that *'inat'* was indeed an essential part of their culture, and that, yes; in consequence they would defy anyone who attempted to trample on their hard-won national rights. However, others observed that this was precisely the reaction that Slobodan Milosevic sought to provoke as a way of cranking up populist hysteria and further legitimising his undemocratic rule; in other words, that the ruling elite was consciously using language and cultural perception as an instrument of political control. This taste for revenge mixed with self-pity was a dangerous combination.

The Serbs were both proud and paranoiac at the same time. Their view of the world was totally Serb centric which was epitomised by Bajić who liked to tell the story of the Croat, the Muslim and two Serbs who found themselves on the moon. The Croat claimed it for Croats because he said its barren landscape resembled the mountains of Dalmatia. The Muslim claimed it for the Muslims because its shades of grey were exactly those of the hills and escarpments of central Bosnia. One of the Serbs then took out his gun and shot the other. *'Now the moon is Serbian'* he said *'for wherever a Serb has spilt blood or lies buried is forever Serbian territory.'*

Borislav Paštrović was thirty four years old. He had been brought up in the city of Prejida in the north west of the country on the banks of the Sana and Gomjenica rivers. His parents were farmers owning quite a substantial fruit farm and it had been expected that Borislav as the oldest son would join his father in running the farm once he had left school which he did. But Borislav hated the work. It involved long, arduous, physical and boring days and he decided that he did not want the life that his hardworking parents had lived. In the evenings he started to go into the town and drink heavily which in turn made the early starts even more difficult and the situation inevitably led to friction and conflict within the family with his father often complaining that he was not 'pulling his weight.'

Following the decision of Slovenia and Croatia to declare independence in June 1991 the situation in Prejida started to rapidly deteriorate. Bosniaks and Croats began to leave because of a growing sense of insecurity and fear amongst the population which was caused by increasingly visible Serb propaganda. The young Borislav became swept up in this atmosphere and started to repeat back at the farm the propagandist statements that he had heard in the bars in the town.

'This is absolute nonsense Borislav' said his father one night banging his fist on the large wooden table in the farmhouse kitchen as they all eat supper *'These people have lived here for years and years and they have just as much right to be here as we do.'*

But his words fell on deaf ears as far as Borislav was concerned and he began to read the local newspaper Kozarski Vjesnik avidly which had started to publish allegations against the non-Serb community. In addition the local radio station had started to propagandise the idea that the Serbs should arm themselves to protect their lives, properties and interests.

One evening Borislav returned to the farm after a heavy bout of drinking to see his father lying under one of the tractors in the main barn trying to fix something in the half light. His father called out to him to help but Borislav slurred his reply and just said that he was tired and was going to bed. His father was infuriated and came out of the barn to confront his son calling him *lazy and useless.* 'Without hesitation Borislav lashed out catching his father under the chin with a heavy blow from his right fist sending him sprawling backwards on to the dirt floor of the farmyard.

The following morning Borislav awoke to find both of his parents in his bedroom. His mother threw an old suitcase on the bed and told him to pack up his things and leave immediately and to not return until he had learned how to apologise, how to behave and how to respect and support his hard-working parents, So Borislav left later that morning and within a few weeks had joined up to the army.

Like Ranko Bajić, he too very quickly settled into the army surrounded by likeminded individuals. He had learnt how to shoot a rifle from a very young age by shooting rats around the farm and he graduated easily to military weaponry. He had a steady hand a very keen aim and was picked out early in his army career to join a sniper detachment using Yugolsav-made M76 sniper rifles. Two years later in April 1994 he had received a letter from his mother saying that his father had died of a heart attack and that he had left the farm to his younger brother. Borislav was welcome to return but he would not share in his brother's inheritance. He had never replied to the letter nor did he attend the funeral.

In 1994 two years into the siege of Sarajevo, Borislav Paštrović had met with Ranko Bajić. They were in the same sniper unit that was rotating on and off duty on the front line. There were hard long and boring shifts with fairly primitive conditions and bitterly cold in the winter time. Borislav got on with him fine but felt that he was very egotistical, short tempered and extremely violent. He seemed to actually enjoy the killing and in his role as a sniper he kept a personal count of his 'kills' in a way that completely dehumanised their targets. He realised that he too did this because perhaps it was the only way to rationalise what they were doing but not to the same extent as his colleague who just seemed to revel in it.

Ranko however, became disillusioned with life as a sniper. The shift rotas were long and boring and he craved more direct action so in January 1995 he applied and joined the elite special forces of the Republika Srpska Army, the so-called Red Berets. The purpose of the Red Berets was to fight alongside, as well as to arm, train and co-ordinate the activities of various Serbian paramilitary formations in Croatia and Bosnia-Herzegovina. However, many of these paramilitaries were run by gangland bosses and in the process of establishing and maintaining the Red Berets, the long-serving head of state security during the Milosevic era, Jovice Stanisc, managed to establish a degree of control over Serbia's expanding criminal underworld. But with the Red Berets recruiting many hardened criminals, the symbiotic relationship between Serbia's secret police and mafia bosses increasingly turned into an uncontrollable and unreliable force.

Ranko, however, fitted right into his new unit immediately and was completely comfortable with his new surroundings and comrades. He became fiercely proud of red beret and told many of his friends from Banja Luka:

'It's part of what defines me as a man.'

and he chastised himself that he had not made this decision a few years earlier. Almost nobody had not heard of the Red Berets, the two words bore a horrific resonance of war and death and they represented almost a license to kill and they became the most feared paramilitary unit of the Balkan wars. They were undoubtedly at the forefront of a number of violent ethnic cleansing campaigns. They executed civilians without mercy by shooting, knifing or just bludgeoning them to death with rifle butts. Ranko, however, would often recite the words of Serbian President, Slobodan Milosevic from the first days of the war to anyone who would listen:

'The government has an assignment to prepare additional groups which will make us safe and enable us to defend the interests of our republic, but also the interests of Serbs outside Serbia."

Within a few months of the war ending in December of 1995 Borislav Paštrović left the army and returned to the northern part of Bosnia and Herzegovina to the district around Kozarska Dubica. He like so many of his former comrades felt disillusioned and demoralised. Yes, they had created the Republika Srpska but they had not achieved their dream of a united Serbia within the country and many felt that they had given up so much for nothing whilst the men at the top had lined their pockets. Now penniless and hungry at times he felt bitter and a sense of personal betrayal had permeated his being.

Ranko, however, stayed with his unit and two years later ended up in Kosovo taking an active part in the attack on the village of Donji Prekaz in March 1998 when they wiped out the ethnic Albanian leader Adem Jashari and his family by firing mortars on houses and using snipers to shoot those who tried to flee. But in the days after the massacre as he watched a bulldozer digging a mass grave something changed within him.

"How many times had he witnessed scenes like this in the last few years?' he thought *'and what have we really achieved?'*

Suddenly a wave of fatigue seemed to wash over him. He was tired of the fighting and the endless killing. He felt no remorse whatsoever over his actions of the last few years:

'As a Serb, I was glad to have done it but I have just had enough' he often said to himself.

So that night under the cover of darkness he fled the unit and made his way back slowly on the five hundred mile journey back to Banja Luka careful to keep his Red Beret concealed in a kit bag.

Chapter Fifteen

"But just what do you hope to achieve Tarik? What is your endgame?" Faris asked as they sat drinking coffee back in the café in Sebilj Square. Tarik looked past Faris and out into the square towards the fountain and it was a few moments before he spoke:

'*I have been thinking about that for a long time. This is not about revenge Faris. What has happened has happened. I cannot turn back the clock and bring my father back so that he will be able to see his grandchild. I have come to the conclusion that this is about me.*'

'*What do you mean?*' Faris enquired

'*Both of us are still relatively young but we have both suffered terrible loss. You even more than me. But it is not just the loss of our family members it is the loss of our teenage years. It is the loss of a normal life. We have both seen and done things that will haunt us for the rest of our lives. Our city will never be quite the same again. Yes they will reconstruct the destroyed buildings but can we rebuild people's hearts and minds? Can we rebuild the trust, confidence and friendship that existed here before the war? I am not so sure – certainly not for a generation or two at least.*'

Tarik took another sip of his coffee and reached out for one of the jellied sweet rahatiokum whilst Faris lit another cigarette.

'*When I was in America they call these Turkish Delight*' Tarik said with smile as put the sweet into his mouth.

'*So how does confronting these two ex-Serbian soldiers solve any of that?*' Faris asked with a puzzled frown.

'*I need to move on Faris. I am married now and soon to be a father. I have a good job and responsibilities. I owe a debt to those who have trusted in me and protected me. I have to set things right in my head.*'

For the next hour he told his friend everything about his recurring nightmares, panic attacks, constant anxiety and vigilance and severe mood swings.

"I was there watching when Afan had his head blown to pieces and I just cannot forget it."

'You are not alone Tarik. Look at my hand' and Faris stretched out his hand which was clutching a half smoked cigarette across the table towards Tarik. It was shaking constantly making the cigarette smoke spiral upwards in a haphazard fashion. There was a long silence again between them until Faris eventually said:

'So what is the plan to set things right in your head?'

Tarik looked left and right to make sure that he could not be overheard.

'I want to confront them both. I want to know which one killed my father.'
'And then what' Faris pressed
'I am not sure'
That does not seem much of a plan to me" Faris replied dismissingly

He then blew out a long column of smoke and stubbed out his cigarette in the ash tray in the centre of the table.
'And you want me to come with you?'
'Yes'

Tarik took another rahatiokum from the plate in front of him and as he did so Faris got up from the table and walked with the pronounced limp towards the fountain in the middle of the square scattering pigeons that took flight as he walked. The fountain had long been a significant city landmark and the original fountain had been intended for the refreshment of horses who plied the trade route from Istanbul in the east all the way to Venice in the west. He stared at the cascading water and lit another cigarette. The sunlight was illuminating the water spray as it descended creating a kaleidoscope of colours that lasted for a few seconds disappeared and then reappeared again.

'*So the cycle of life goes on*' he said to himself

and he flicked the cigarette butt across the cobble stones of the square. He shoved his hands in his pockets and slumped his shoulders and just stared around him but away from the Café where Tarik was sitting. People were going about their daily lives, a businessman with a briefcase was walking quickly and purposely across the square obviously late for an appointment and he sent dozens of birds into the air as he strode along at pace. A mother was remonstrating with two young children who would not keep up with her and kept running off to chase the pigeons and two old men were sitting on a bench talking and smoking. The cafes were all about half full and there was a low background drone of a hundred conversations.

'*Ok you crazy idiot*' he said as he returned to the table '*I owe you one anyway.*'

"*That's great. Thank you Faris it means a huge amount to me. What did you mean that you probably owe me one?*" Tarik said looking directly at his friend.

"*That night in the trenches when you picked up that rifle of our dead counter sniper and fired it. That Serbian bastard in the raiding party almost certainly had me in his sights next.*"

Tarik cast his mind back and recollected the scene. It had been another bitterly cold Sarajevan winter's evening and he remembered retching in the trench at the sight of his dead comrade whose head had just been reduced to a bloody mess beside him and then the anger welling up inside him that he had never experienced before. It all came back so easily. Too easily he thought. Like it was yesterday. He did not like the thought that he had killed someone but he had not realised until now that he had probably saved the life of his best friend.

Tarik parted company from Faris after agreeing to be back in touch in a couple of days' time. He walked out of the Square and into Kazandziluk Street which was one of the oldest and most beautiful streets in Sarajevo and dated back to the sixteenth century and had once been part of the larger Kazandziluk Bazaar. Kazandziluk means coppersmith in keeping with the tradition of naming streets after the wares being sold and produced. Traditional copper items were still being crafted here using a special technique called filigree. Tarik paused for a moment at number four in the street which under a huge elaborate silver pot was the name 'Stari Bazar' which according to a sign had been making traditional copper crafts for two hundred and twenty years and as he stood reading a young lady came out and asked him in English:

"My name is Azra and I am the only female coppersmith in the city. Would you like to see our museum in the basement?"

Tarik replied in English saying:

"Thank you for the offer but I am short of time today but maybe another day as it is absolutely fascinating."

Tarik was amazed to see the resourcefulness and entrepreneurship of the coppersmiths who were fashioning decorative items from the vast quantities of left over shell casings and cartridges to sell to the tourists.

"So life and commerce goes on here as it has always done so throughout the ages" thought Tarik as he passed by.

Meeting again a few days later Tarik and Faris had checked their diaries and it was agreed they would both take a week's holiday from work. They would hire a van and tell Jelena and Vildana that they were going on a trip together to look up old friends who were scattered around Bosnia and Herzegovina and maybe even do a bit of fishing. Jelena had thought it was a good idea:

'It will do you good Tarik to have a break and Faris is a good friend. Do not worry about me as I will spend the week visiting my parents. Things are a little different now in Belgrade."

Tarik knew that just over eighteen months ago on 5th October 2000, Slobodan Milošević had been overthrown as President. Milošević's overthrow was reported as a spontaneous revolution. However, there had been a year-long battle involving thousands of Serbs in a strategy to strip the leader of his legitimacy, turn his security forces against him, and force him to call for elections, the result of which he would not acknowledge. Prior to this, Milošević had been cracking down on opposition, non-government organisations and the independent media but now change had come to Belgrade.. Vojislav Kostunica was to be the new President, the last of the Federal Republic of Yugoslavia.

Chapter Sixteen

Tarik and Faris had decided that they would try to track down Borislav Paštrović first because the information that they had received from Peter in America was that he had updated his address within the last six months so there was still a good chance that he would still be living there.

Kozarska Dubica was originally known as Bosanska Dubica and it lay in the northern part of Bosnia and Herzegovina and is administratively part of the Republika Srpska entity. *Dubica*, for short, is situated in the eastern part of Bosanska Krajina region and was situated about sixteen miles from the Zagreb to Belgrade highway. The population had been about thirty thousand but during the war some six thousand Bosniaks were driven out from their homes through the Serbian drive for 'ethnic cleansing' and they were replaced by Serbs who arrived from Croatia, many of whom settled in the homes that had belonged to the expelled Bosniaks.

The distance from Sarajevo to Kozarska Dubica was around one hundred and sixty five miles with a drive time of just over four hours. Tarik had rented a plain white Volkswagen courier van with two opening rear doors for the week. He had loaded in sleeping bags, cooking equipment, clothes and various bags. He had also rented a small cottage a few miles out of the town in a forested region by a fast running stream that cascaded down from the towering Mount Prosara above. He had used Jelena's maiden name in case there had been any resistance to renting the cottage to a man with a Muslim name.

The Inter-Entity Boundary Line or IEBL for short, divided Bosnia and Herzegovina into two entities, the Republika Srpska and the Federation of Bosnia and Herzegovina. The IEBL and the political divisions of Bosnia and Herzegovina had been agreed upon as part of the General Framework Agreement for Peace concluded at the Dayton peace conference at the end of the war. By now the IEBL was no longer controlled by the military and was not even policed. There were no border controls and crossing the IEBL was like crossing a US state or a Schengen state boundary in the European Union so Tarik and Faris entered the Republika Srpska without any problems. Freedom of movement between the entities had also been improved by the introduction of standardised car licence plates. Registration plates after the war clearly stated which entity one was from which had often led to harassment or random acts of violence against the vehicle's occupants. Tarik and Faris were now protected from that and could remain anonymous in their rental van.

After returning home when the war was over and he had left the army, Borislav Paštrović had made a living by being a hunting guide in the shooting season. The area around Kozarska Dubica designated for hunting was large at nearly two hundred square miles. Much of it was rich with coniferous forests and was full of deer and wild boar. His training as a sniper meant that he was a crack shot and was sought after by shooting parties as both an instructor and as a guide. However, recently he had noticed that the hunting parties had started to decline.

Bosnia and Herzegovina was once the home to one of the largest bear populations in the world and had thriving wolf, deer, wild boar and wild goat communities. However, these populations of wild animals suffered severely from the war. Throughout the conflict many of the frontlines were in the high mountain regions and they had become exposed to heavy gun and artillery fire as well as being hunted for food by soldiers.

He got by ok but it was hard, physical work, often walking and climbing in thickly wooded mountainous regions for hours on end. He received a fixed daily rate for his efforts and relied on the generosity of his guests at the end of trip tip to make any real difference to his income. This as always depended on how successful the shooting team had been and even if he had successfully tracked quarry for them if they could not hit the targets that he had presented they would go home disgruntled and his pockets would be empty. It was an uncertain occupation but it was all he had.

Tarik had chosen the cottage well from the rental web site. They found the entrance easily enough because there was a clearly placed sign with the house name on the side of the road. They made a left turn off the main road through an old set of wide wooden gates that were left open and drove through, up a steep and lengthy gravel driveway and into a cobbled courtyard. They parked up the van in front of the house, got out and walked round. There was a large garden at the back which extended further than they could see and from there was a magnificent view up towards the summit of Mount Prosara. The cobbled courtyard was bordered on one side with a number of outhouse buildings which Tarik inspected one by one. Some were in complete disrepair with the roof fallen in but he then found what he was looking for. It was an old wood shed which was only about a quarter full of logs which were neatly stacked up against the rear wall. The tiled roof was intact and it had a stout planked wooden door with peeling pale blue paint and the door was secured by a large rusty sliding bolt which moved easily with only a little pressure applied to it. There were two old wooden chairs left in there but apart from them and the small pile of logs the shed was empty.

Tarik and Faris unloaded all of their gear from the van and chose a bedroom each. They had bought some supplies from a shop in the town before finding the cottage and Faris went about making some coffee and slicing some bread in the kitchen whilst Tarik was studying a street map of the town that they had also purchased at the store. He drew a large cross on the street that had been identified by Peter as being the address of Borislav Paštrović which was situated on the western outskirts of the town.

"I just hope that he hasn't moved' he thought *'because that will make things a lot more difficult as we do not even know what he looks like."*

Faris joined Tarik at the kitchen table with two cups of coffee and some thickly cut ham sandwiches which they both devoured greedily

146

as it had been a long drive from Sarajevo. It was now two in the afternoon. *'This is the plan of action'* Tarik then said as he sipped the coffee:

"We need to find Borislav's address and then park the van close by but move it every hour so that it does not draw too much attention. One of us will stay in the van and the other will walk around the nearby streets checking out shops and bars and any other likely places that he may visit as part of his daily routine. We do not know if he is working at the moment or indeed what he does for a living but we have to try and build up some kind of pattern over the next few days and unfortunately we are thin on both resources and time."

Faris then made some more sandwiches of ham and cheese and a thermos of coffee. It was going to be a long and boring few hours. Tarik drove the van on the twenty minute journey back into the town. As Tarik drove, Faris was studying the street map that they had bought. They were on the main M14 road and Faris said take the next right into a road called Skendera Kulenovica and then bear right into Vlatka Vukovica.

They then drove slowly up the street looking for the house numbers.

"There it is on the left – number 144" called out Faris

and they parked the van across the street and about twenty yards down from the house but facing towards it so that it gave whoever was sitting in the driver's seat of the van a clear view of the front door of the quite substantial property and of who was coming in or out. Faris got out of the van and walked past the property on the opposite side but deliberately not looking left at it so as to show no interest whatsoever to anyone who may have been watching him. He returned, however, about thirty minutes later on the opposite side of the road and stood for a few moments outside the front door looking at a row of bell pushes which they had not seen from the van. Number 144 had obviously been divided into four flats but unfortunately they only had the numbers of the flats on the bell pushes and not the names of the current occupants.

"Damn it" thought Faris *"I suppose that would have been just too easy!"*

Four hours had gone passed and they had swopped over a couple of times with Tarik walking and Faris sitting in the van and vice versa. It was now six in the evening and during that time two people had entered the building, an elderly lady whom Faris had established had gone into flat number one because as he had slowly walked by he had watched her open the door and then use her key to open the letter box for flat number one which was in a row of four just inside the lobby behind the front door. A second lady in her mid forties and quite smartly dressed had then entered the apartment block and then left again only to reappear about ten minutes later with two carrier bags of shopping after visiting the small local supermarket further up the street. She too, checked her letterbox and Faris was able to see that she was the occupant of flat number two.

A half an hour later at six thirty a short stocky man with broad shoulders and a short haircut with a stubbly beard and casually dressed in old clothing left the building. He obviously did not care much about his appearance thought Tarik as he watched him from the parked van which he had just moved to a different vantage point on the street. On this first night of their stakeout they watched him return about four hours later with the mobile phone once more pressed against his ear but it was clear to them that his gait was unsteady and that he was wavering as he crossed the street. It took him some time to open the front door of the apartment block as he tried to juggle his keys, mobile phone and a lit cigarette but eventually he stumbled through.

'He's drunk' Faris suddenly said involuntarily.
'What do you think' Faris said to Tarik as they drove back to the cottage

'I think that he could be our man but we need more information to be sure' Tarik replied.

The following day they observed the short stocky man come and go out of the apartment block a number of times during the day. Each time they saw him he had his mobile phone to his ear and he seemed to be talking animatedly but neither Tarik nor Faris had got close enough to him to ever hear anything of what he had been saying. He seemed to be repeating the pattern of the day before and at about six thirty he left the apartment block again and made his way across and up the street.

'I have got a hunch about him' said Tarik as they watched the target of their surveillance enter the bar as on the previous evening.

Tarik and Faris drove off in the van and passed the entrance to the bar without looking in that direction and turned right and then right again behind the bar and the small parade of shops. They parked up the van in a space which was used during the day for unloading deliveries. After a while they walked back around the corner and onto the street and went into the bar that their target had entered about an hour earlier. The bar was larger than it looked from the outside, quite narrow but extended back a long way and it appeared to be about half full. It was darker in the bar towards the rear and there were clouds of cigarette smoke hanging in the stale air. Tarik sat at a table near the entrance and Faris went to the bar and ordered two beers and came and sat back down with Tarik. The beer was the golden coloured *Lav Pivo*.

'It was strange' thought Faris *'Even beer and their advertising umbrellas now defined the regional and ethnic differences in post war Bosnia and Herzegovina. In Sarajevo the majority of the beer that he drank was Sarajevsko with the distinctive green umbrellas advertising the beer over the tables outside the bars and cafés. If the umbrellas were white and red then they were advertising Karlovačko which meant that you were most probably drinking in one of the Croatian areas of the country and if the umbrellas were yellow they*

were advertisng Lav and you had entered into the Republika Srpska, where the majority of the Serbian population lived.'

As they drank their beers both Tarik and Faris tried to scan the bar without making it obvious what they were doing. After a while they had both identified the stocky man from the apartment block across the road. He was seated at the rear of the bar with six or seven other men and they all appeared to be drinking heavily and talking noisily and animatedly. Above them a television was showing a football match but no one was paying it any particular attention but the commentary added to the overall background noise level and general ambience of the bar.

Occasionally one of the group would go to the bar and return with a tray of small glasses full of a colourless liquid which Tarik presumed would be rakija and probably sljivovica which was made from plums. They all lifted a glass and saluted one another and then drained the liquid it contained in one. Tarik knew that rakija was one of the most popular alcoholic drinks amongst Serbs. It was their national drink and was internationally identified with their culture. Serbia is the world's largest rakija producer and drinks more per capita than any other country. Personally Tarik hated the taste and the high alcohol content of these fruit brandies and he shuddered as he saw the group of men down another round just as another tray of glasses arrived to be met with much noise and boisterousness.

Faris and Tarik drained the last of their beer and Faris lit a cigarette and wandered out of the bar whilst Tarik decided to visit the toilet which was situated at the rear of the bar and to get there he had to go past the group of men that they had been studying but they paid him no attention as he walked by. As Tarik came out of the toilet and re-entered the bar he was certain that he heard one of the group of men say loudly:

'Yes. You are right Borislav.........'

and then the stocky man started to address the group with a very animated speech in which he waved his arms around constantly but

Tarik could not hear the rest of the conversation and just walked quickly past.

Ten minutes later he was sitting with Faris in the parked van behind the parade of shops and then they drove around and parked on the street about twenty yards away from the front door of the apartment block. At about ten thirty the stocky man came out of the bar with another man who he slapped on the back and then disappeared away up the street. Their target crossed over the street and pulled out the keys from his pocket but as per the previous evening it again took him a while to open the door as he kept putting the wrong key in the lock.

'*It has to be him*' Faris said
'*I agree but we need to be sure*' Tarik replied as they drove back to the cottage.

The following morning they got the confirmation they were seeking. At about nine in the morning a smartly dressed businessman with a briefcase left the apartment block. They had not seen him before but Faris seized upon the opportunity and approached him from the other side of the street where he had been once again strolling slowly by:

'*Excuse me sir but I am looking for someone who lives around here somewhere. His name is Borislav Paštrović. Do you know whereabouts he lives?*'
'*Yes I know him. He lives in Flat number four next to me. He is a right nuisance, being drunk most of the time and very noisy when he comes in at night.*' And with that he just walked on without another word being spoken.

"*Bingo*" said Faris as he climbed into the front passenger seat of the van and told Tarik.
Tarik blew out his cheeks and said:

"*We are not the FBI. We really need a six man team on permanent rotation to really build a proper pattern but we just do not have either the resources or the time. The risk will be that he is either accompanied or we will be observed. We will have to be very vigilant and very careful."*

So they decided to put their plan into action that third night. Borislav repeated the pattern of the previous two nights. At about 10.30pm he reappeared from the bar with his mobile phone attached to his ear as usual and a cigarette dangling from his mouth. Once again he was wavering slightly and as he approached the front door he put the mobile back in his pocket and searched for his keys. On the other side of the road Faris checked the street in both directions. As on the previous two evenings there was no passing traffic and no pedestrians and the only sound was that coming from the bar up the street from where Borislav had just come from so he gave a thumbs up sign to Tarik who just at that moment rounded the corner. He walked towards Borislav who was still fumbling for his keys and swearing to himself. He had got one of Faris' cigarettes in his mouth and on approaching Borislav he said:

"Have you got a light?"
"Yeah sure" came the slurred reply and he started to fish in his other pocket for his lighter with his shoulders slumped. Meanwhile Faris had silently crossed the street and crept up behind him and got down on all fours and in that instant Tarik pushed Borislav hard in the chest with two flat hands and he tumbled over the back of his crouched friend and onto the pavement. To anyone who had observed this sequence of events it would have looked like a pantomime trick but it was extremely effective. As soon as Borislav hit the ground Faris hit him hard in the face with his fist and then as he started to try and get up he kicked him in the side of the head.

Borislav began to cry out but he was slurring his words and Faris had already pulled the hessian sack that he had been carrying out and over his head and was tying the draw strings around his neck. Borislav was struggling hard now and flailing out punches to targets that he could not see. However, the last thing Tarik wanted was a noisy commotion so he hit him on the side of the head hard with a piece of metal tubing that he had found in one of the sheds at the cottage and had been concealing behind his back under his shirt and tucked into the waist band of his jeans. Borislav slumped and Tarik and Faris put an arm each under his and half frogmarched and half dragged him across the street and threw him into the rear of the van. Faris got in the back with him and Tarik got into the driver's seat and quickly started the engine and pulled away but not too quickly so as to draw attention to themselves. As Tarik drove out of the town and back towards the cottage Faris bound Borislav's hands and feet with some stout rope that they had brought with them from Sarajevo and which they had left in the back of the van.

Twenty minutes later they were back in the courtyard of the cottage. Tarik ran to the cottage door and opened it and turned on the outside lights. He then went to the rear of the van and unlocked it and Faris jumped out. Borislav was moving now and moaning and groaning and starting to cry out in a drunken rage. They both dragged him out and once again frogmarched him across the courtyard and into the wood shed which Tarik had left open. They seated him on the chair and then bound his already tied arms to the back of the chair and his ankles to the front chair legs. They then pulled on the stockinged masks from their pockets and Faris undid the knots tying the hessian sack around Borislav's neck and withdrew it.

Immediately he started shouting and swearing but he could not move.

'Where am I here and who the hell are you?' he half shouted and half groaned.
"You are here because we want some information from you" Tarik replied.
"What information?" he slurred.
"We'll discuss that in the morning."
"Like hell we will" and Borislav started to shout at the top of his voice:
"Kidnap!! Help! Help me!"
'Shut up" replied Faris.

"I forgot to tell you" Tarik said purposely *"We are five miles out of town and the nearest house is three miles away so you can shout all you like but no one is going to hear you."*

With that both he and Faris turned and walked out leaving Borislav in the dark with just a few shafts of light streaking through the gaps under and above the wooden planked door. Then he heard the rusty old bolt being slid into place.

Wherever he was it was going to be a very long and uncomfortable night.

Chapter Seventeen

"Why am I here? Why have you bastards imprisoned me?" Borislav said to Tarik as he slid back the bolt and opened the door in the morning. *"Let me go immediately. My friends will know where I am and then we are going to kill you for this!"*

"No one knows where you are Borislav"

"How do you know my name?"

'We know a lot about you' Tarik replied coldly *'You are here because you killed an unarmed man in cold blood"*

"What the hell are you talking about you crazy bastard" said Borislav to the man in the stockinged mask standing in front of him. *"Just let me go and we will forget all about it."*

Tarik sat down on the spare wooden chair and faced his captive and said slowly:

"On the night of 25th November 1994 you were with other Serbian forces on Mount Trebovic overlooking Sarajevo and you were one of two snipers on duty that night. Your role was to take out counter snipers but to relieve your boredom you decided to take pot shots at anything and anyone who moved whether they were armed or not, whether they were a combatant or not. You shot and killed an unarmed man who was fetching water for his family so that they could survive for another few days. He didn't stand a chance as he could not even see you."

'You are talking a load of bollocks'

"Am I? I don't think so. We'll talk again tonight" and with that Tarik got up and closed the door and slid the lock back into place and then peeled off his mask and walked across the courtyard and back into the cottage.

That evening the conversation continued and after Tarik had repeated the same accusation, Borislav replied:

"During that period a lot of Bosniaks were shot in the city. It was my job; it was what I was ordered to do."

"Is that what you joined the army for, to shoot at defenceless and unarmed men, women and children who were collecting food, water or firewood just to survive your persecution?"

"It was my job and I was ordered to do it and I was proud to serve in our forces. Why are you so concerned about this one particular man on this one particular night?"

There was a long pause in the conversation and then Tarik suddenly got up from the chair and walked towards the door but before he left the shed he turned back to the bound captive:

"Because he was my father'"

and with that he closed the door and slid the bolt back into place once more.

Alone in the half light with just the moonlight seeping through the gap at the top and bottom of the door and through the cracks in the door's planking, Borislav blew out a long breath. It was going to be another long night as he looked down and saw a group of rats scurrying across the floor and around his bound feet. He thought back to over the last few years to his time at Sarajevo. He had done a number of assignments. They had been very hard shifts. Two weeks on and two weeks off and the conditions were primitive. It had been cold and damp on the mountainside and above all it had been tediously boring. Endless hours of staring through a rifle scope at the darkened city below.

"You talk to me about Sarajevo and Srebrenica'" Borislav said on one of the 'interrogation' sessions that Tarik and Faris had with him the following day *"But what about Krajina?"* he spat out with real venom in his voice. *'Why has Srebrenica been everywhere, yet Krajina barely gets a mention in any reporting about the war? It is as it always has been that us Serbs stand on our own. It is as Karadzic once said 'We have no friends but God."*

"You are so misguided Borislav.' retorted Tarik. *'Your isolation was of your own doing. It was your pride and paranoia which was your undoing. Even your masters in Belgrade eventually turned their back on the Bosnian Serbs. Yes, atrocities were committed by all sides in the war but it was you, the Serbs who systematically decided to dehumanise the conflict by introducing the nonsense of 'ethnic cleansing' and destroying the trust and friendship that had existed in my city for centuries. I have heard enough"*

and with that Tarik left closing the door and sliding the rusty bolt behind him.

As he walked back into the cottage he thought of the conversation that they had just had. He was aware of what had been reported to have happened in Krajina.

The Republic of Serbian Krajina, was a self-proclaimed Serb parastate within the territory of the Republic of Croatia during the Croatian War of Independence. It had been established in 1991, but was not recognised internationally. It formally existed from 1991 to 1995, having been initiated a year earlier via smaller separatist regions. The name *Krajina* ("Frontier") was adopted from the historical borderland, the Military Frontier, of the Austro-Hungarian Empire, which existed up to the 19th century. Its separatist government engaged in a war for ethnic Serb independence from the Republic of Croatia, within and out of Yugoslavia, once Croatian borders had been recognised by foreign states in August 1991 and February 1992.

Under *Operation Storm*, the Croatians won the last and most significant battle in their fight for independence when it attacked across a three hundred and ninety mile front against the Republic of Serbian Krajina. There were numerous reports of widespread abuse by Croatian forces including looting, arson, murder and other war crimes. The Croatian authorities knew that an attack on this scale would force the mass exodus of Serbian civilians, an outcome that they regarded as being not only inevitable but probably desirable which could also be described as an act of 'ethnic cleansing.'

157

Although they had left accessible escape routes, columns of feeling refugees were reported to have been shelled, attacked by aircraft and subjected to various sorts of harassment and military assaults. As he re-entered the cottage Tarik thought for a moment. In war there are no winners and there is no moral supremacy and the biggest loser of them all is always basic humanity.

Later that evening, Tarik looked at the Blackberry mobile phone which they had taken off their captive and was now lying on the table in front of him. It was an 850 model which had been in Borislav's jacket pocket when they had searched him and Tarik had immediately switched it off.

"Where did you get the money to buy this Borislav?" Tarik asked him later that evening.
"I need it to run my business'"
"What business is that?"
"None of yours'" Borislav snorted

Tarik looked at the Blackberry and switched it on and accessed the email account. There was nothing of interest. Communications between drinking friends and it would appear that he visited a few local prostitutes on a fairly regular basis. Then it dawned on him Borislav wasn't just a punter he was their pimp or controller. He probably provided a level of security and protection in case of abusive or rough punters.

'Takes all sorts Borislav. I am not judging.'
'Just fuck off'

Tarik had no problem reading these messages or indeed communicating here in Republika Spraska as the languages of the Balkans were all very similar. When Bosniaks, Croats and Serbs talk amongst each other, the other speakers usually understand them completely, save for the odd word, and quite often, they will know what that means much as with British and American English speakers.

Nevertheless, when communicating with each other, there is a habit to use terms that are familiar to everyone, with the intent to avoid not being understood and/or confusion. For example, to avoid confusion with the names of the months, they can be referred to as the "first month", "second month" and so on, or the Latin-derived names can be used if "first month" itself is ambiguous, which makes it perfectly understandable for everyone. Although the languages all come from the same Slavic base, they have some noticeable differences in vocabulary. Bosnia, with its Muslim community, tends to have more lasting linguistic influence from the Ottoman Turks, as exemplified by the use of the greeting "merhaba", which is the same as the standard greeting in Turkish. Serbian tends towards Slavicisms, and Croatian has more Germanic and Italian influence from its time as part of the Austro-Hungarian Empire. Additionally, during the break-up of Yugoslavia, Croatia and Serbia both changed their standard languages to try to distance themselves from each other which often meant reviving rare, archaic, or words affected by dialect.

Tarik rose from the chair that he was sitting on facing his captive, walked over to him and tilted his head back and drained some water down his throat from a plastic bottle that he was carrying and then closed the door and slid back the rusty bolt just as dusk was settling in once more.

"I hope you are ready to talk in the morning Borislav" Tarik shouted through the door after taking off his stocking mask once more.

"Just fuck off" came the familiar reply. However, Tarik noticed the rebuke was not as determined as previously. *"Was he weakening? Was he getting to the point of having had enough?"*

Alone in the half darkness. Borislav Paštrović was tired and hungry and every muscle in his body now ached uncontrollably and the binds were cutting through his wrists and ankles. On the back of his head was a large swelling caused by being hit with something hard when they had jumped him from behind and threw that sack over his head and it hurt like hell, sometimes throbbing for hours on

159

end. Moreover he stank. He could not avoid the pungent smell of stale urine and faeces that filled his trousers and had now leaked on to the floor of the shed in a growing pile of excrement. It was revolting and he felt disgusting and every now and then he thought that he would vomit because of the smell and on a few occasions he did which just added to the mess all over his clothes and on the floor and to the overall stench of the small enclosed space.

"I don't need all this grief. I didn't kill that Bosniak bastard back in Sarajevo that he keeps going on about" he said to himself. *"I have protected my comrade enough. I didn't think so at first. I didn't think that he would have the stomach for it but this bastard is crazy enough to let me die here. It was his father after all."*

As Tarik walked across the courtyard back into the cottage he turned the mobile device over in his hand an idea came to him *'I wonder if?'*

He walked into the kitchen where Faris was making some coffee.
"Faris. I have had an idea. Tomorrow I'm going to that internet café in town to send my friend Peter in America an email."
"Ok replied" Faris. Then he suddenly turned towards Tarik and said:

"I have been wondering. Are we doing the right thing here? We have captured and imprisoned a man in pretty miserable conditions for three days and nights are we not stooping to the same level as those who imprisoned us?"

"It has been bothering me too Faris but I think we should persevere but we are right to question ourselves all of the time."

"But what are we going to do if he admits that he was the one that shot your father?'' Faris persisted.

"I don't honestly know"' Tarik replied quite genuinely and his shoulders slumped: *"We have no right to judge. He will be judged by God but I just want to do what is right for my father."'*

160

"Well you had better know what to do soon because we could be facing that situation in the morning and quite frankly although he is a bastard if we kill him we are no better than they were and it is really starting to bother me."

And with that he walked out of the cottage and stood in the garden at the back staring up at Mount Prosara that soared above them and lit a cigarette. He inhaled deeply and at that moment he thought of his own family that he had lost. He hung his head and rubbed his eyes with one hand and he blew out a long plume of smoke that curled upwards in the evening air. He stubbed out the cigarette on the courtyard, sighed and walked back into the cottage.

"We'll talk again in the morning Tarik" he said ' *'I am going to get some sleep now"*

"Ok 'Tarik replied *"I can absolutely assure you Faris that we are not going to kill him. We are not cold-blooded murderers. If we do not get what we want then we will just have to think again or abandon the whole thing."*

But Tarik did not retire. He sat up thinking and then after a while he did something that he had not done in a long while. He got down on his knees and prayed:

The following morning when Faris pressed him again on what they were going to do Tarik replied:

"When the time comes I am sure that I will know what to do"

Then leaving Faris to have the morning 'chat' with Borislav, Tarik drove the van into the town and walked into the small internet café and bought a coffee and thirty minutes of time on one of the old computers in the shop. It was an ageing IBM desktop which had clearly seen better days and it was hooked up to an old monitor with a green screen. Tarik had not seen one of these for years and he laughed to himself as he thought his friend Peter whom he was about to email would wonder where you put the coal into it! Twenty minutes later after sending and then deleting the email he left the cafe and bought the items they needed in a local shop and headed back to the cottage.

As the van drew up he switched off the engine. Borislav cried out from inside the wood shed:

"Let me out"
"Are you ready to tell us what we want to know" replied Tarik
"Fuck off balija"

Tarik resisted the urge to retaliate either verbally or physically. He had not heard that racial slur for a long time. The term was derived from the description of descendants of Turks of the Ottoman Empire in the Balkans but it had entered the Serb slang vocabulary as a derogatory word to describe anyone who was a Bosnian Muslim.

That afternoon Tarik and Faris sat in the back garden of the cottage. It was a large garden and had clearly been a 'labour of love' for a previous owner for many years, It had established borders full of plants and shrubs which led on to a small orchard of plum and apple trees which then opened out into a huge vegetable garden which was surrounded by a crisscross of low brick walling which was now covered in moss and ivy. The vegetable garden had long since 'gone to seed' and was overgrown with weeds but it was still a place of tranquility and beauty and all the time overlooked by the mountain and the high ground.

Faris and Tarik were drinking coffee sitting in an old gazebo half way up the garden on the edge of the orchard and Faris held a ubiquitous cigarette in his hand which Tarik noticed was still shaking slightly causing the smoke to spiral upwards. Breaking the silence between them Tarik suddenly said:

"Tell me about your family Faris. You have never really told me about your background and what happened to them."

Faris took a long drag of his cigarette and then blew out the smoke in a long exhalation of breath and then stubbed out the butt on the ground with his foot.

"Ok"

He had been born Faris Sidran to Muslim parents in Sarajevo. He was about twelve months older than Tarik. His father had worked at a local light engineering factory as a lathe operator and his mother had worked part time as an assistant in a nursery school. He had a brother called Eman but on mentioning his name Faris suddenly broke down in tears:

"He was my twin. We were not only brothers but we part of the same being. We had been inseparable since birth. We did everything together. We liked the same things whether it was food, what programmes to watch on television or what games to play. Other people had best friends we had each other."

Faris wiped his face with his hands and reached for another cigarette and continued. *"When the war started we were still living in the apartment block where I had grown up. A few months later my father's engineering factory had taken a direct hit from a Serbian artillery shell but fortunately it was in the evening and there had only been a skeleton maintenance team inside or so it had been thought."*

Faris took another cigarette from the packet and lit it with his disposable lighter. Tarik said nothing and waited for his friend to continue:

"However, my father and two other workmates had volunteered to continue machining some parts that were urgently required to fulfill a government contract in return for the promise of a packet of precious fresh coffee for each of them. The building had all but been destroyed and two maintenance men and my father's two fellow machinists had been killed. My father had survived but he had lost the lower part of his right leg and from then on had to hobble round on crutches. Looking back I suspect that the firm had been making

parts for the government to bring back into service old communist era heavy military equipment and the Serbs probably thought this too."

Faris continued his narrative and Tarik learnt that the next two years of the war had passed for him much like his own life. The family were surviving on minimal food and water and without electricity or gas. But his brother Eman had had severe asthma since being a young child and suffered particularly badly in the winter months. Now with the cold Sarajevan winters setting in with no proper means of keeping warm he was suffering more and more and to make matters worse despite the best efforts of his parents they had not been able to get him a replacement canister of Salbutamol for his inhaler which he desperately needed.

Faris regularly went out at night on scavenging missions because his father was not able to do so on his crutches to find firewood or anything to burn and Eman had initially accompanied him. However, the acrid fumes from hundreds of homemade domestic stoves burning plastic, rubber, foam or many other kinds of toxic combustible materials had made his asthma far worse if he stepped outside the apartment so Faris had started to make the regular forays on his own. He was returning from one such trip in October 1994 and as he turned the corner of his street he saw flames and smoke belching out of the apartment block where he lived. He dropped the bundle of strips of wooden fencing that he had been carrying and ran towards the building but was prevented from getting any nearer than fifty yards away by soldiers, firefighters and rescue workers.

"Stay away" one shouted *"They may very well strike again at the same target."*

It was clear to Faris that the building had taken a direct hit form a very large shell probably fired from a tank or large artillery piece.

"But I live on the third floor and my family are in there" he had shouted back

"The third and fourth floors have been almost completely destroyed'" said the rescue worker without thinking what he was saying and what the implications meant for the young teenager.

As he related this part of the story Faris stood up in silence and just walked away from the gazebo where they had both been sitting for some time and into the middle of the small orchard of fruit trees. Tarik watched him walk away, his own head full of sadness and memories and he knew what his friend must be thinking.

Faris returned to the gazebo where Tarik was still sitting in silence about ten minutes later. He took out a cigarette from the near empty packet in his pocket and lit it.

"Tell me the rest another time '" Tarik encouraged

"No it is good to talk. I want to tell you now. I have never really had this opportunity to talk to anyone about it before."

Faris had spent the rest of that night sitting on the pavement opposite his apartment block watching the frantic efforts of the firefighters to quell the belching flames and smoke and all of them frequently looking up to the hills above the city half expecting another shell to come raining down on them at any moment. He must have fallen asleep for a few hours because when he woke up he was freezing and rigid with cold and dawn was breaking over the city. He could see the apartment block clearly now. His face was covered in dirt and dust and stained by smoke with streaks where floods of tears had flowed uncontrollably. The fire was out but columns of smoke were still rising from great gaping holes in the structure but not as intensely as a few hours before, the side of the building was charred black and it was not long before bodies covered in blankets or bed linen were being carried out of the front door of the wrecked building.

On being discovered, Faris had been taken by the rescue workers to a local sports hall that had been turned into a makeshift mortuary. He had been asked if he was prepared to identify the bodies of his family but if he was not up to it other relatives would be found. Faris had not flinched from the task but it was only when the sheet was pulled back to reveal the corpse of his brother did he completely breakdown and collapsed on the floor with utter despair, fatigue and desperation. A few moments later he stood up and walked to his brother's unmoving body and bent down and kissed him on the forehead:

"We are one Eman. We always have been. We always will be."

He then carefully removed the silver chain which was around his brother's neck and put it around his own to match the one that was already there. They had been a present from their parents on the boys reaching thirteen, the start of their teenage years.

He replaced the sheet gently back over his brother's face, turned and silently walked out of the sports hall and into the winter sunlight outside. After a few moments he looked up at hills and said quietly:

"I will do whatever I can to hurt you as you have hurt me."

As he said this Faris put his hand inside his shirt and felt the reassuring touch of the two silver chains around his neck and then he continued relating the events. He had been taken in by his uncle, his father's brother who lived alone in a small apartment in another district of the city.

Tarik had met Faris there months later in January 1995, a few weeks after he had started to do logistical support for the Bosnian defence forces in the city which Faris had been already been doing since moving in with his uncle. They had become friends. Tarik was probably the first friend that Faris had had since the death of his twin brother and his parents and probably his first ever real friend because that role had always been played by his brother Eman.

Night after night they ran up and down the trenches carrying and distributing food, water and ammunition to the soldiers on the front lines. They became immune to the whistle of high velocity rounds whizzing over their heads or spitting up dirt near their feet. The bitter winter nights turned into hot long summer ones and then round again in a seasonal cycle of never ending violence, destruction and suffering.

Faris had been very sad to see Tarik leave for America with his sister Minka. He had put a very brave face on it as he had embraced him saying *'goodbye and good luck'* that morning outside the hospital as he watched his friend and his sister climb into the armoured car and speed off towards the airport.

"Doviđenja Tarik. I hope that we will be able to meet again when all this insanity is over"

He turned and walked away but after a few moments he looked back to see Tarik's mother Jasmina hugging and embracing her sister Jela. He had never felt so utterly alone and despondent in his life. No father, no mother, no twin brother and now no best friend. The tears just rolled down his face as he walked back across the city to his uncle's apartment to get some sleep before the crazy nightly ritual began all over again because that was all there was.

Chapter Eighteen

The following morning Tarik and Faris visited their captive as usual. They replaced the stocking masks that Tarik had made by cutting up some of Jelena's tights. He looked at Faris. It was amazing how this simple disguise completely distorted his face and made him unrecognisable. As they slid back the rusty bolt the stench hit them. Borislav's trousers were clearly wet with urine and he had obviously soiled himself again as well. His unshaven face looked even rougher than before and his eyes had dark lines under them.

"I'm going to fucking kill you bastards for this" he said but without conviction.
'You have kept me here for three days without food and just a little water. You are just fucking animals. I know you are Bosniaks but who are you?"

"A few days" Tarik scoffed *"You imprisoned and starved us for over three years. Now do you have anything to tell us?"*

"Fuck off"' came the familiar terse reply.

Neither Faris nor Tarik said anything and Tarik just pulled Borislav's head back roughly and Faris poured some water down his throat from a plastic bottle that he was carrying and then they left sliding the bolt back into place once more. An hour later Tarik made the trip into the town to the internet café as he had done the day before. He bought a coffee and another thirty minutes on the old IBM PC. He typed in the URL of his email account and waited for it to open. There it was a reply from Peter. Tarik opened it:

Hi Tarik

A model 850? That's fairly new kit. I wonder how he got hold of that? Yes I think I can do what you want. I can send him an email

which contains a Trojan and if he is dumb enough to open it – then bingo!
Rgds
Peter

Tarik did not have a clue what Peter was talking about so he minimised that window and typed in phising and then trojan into the search engine and he read quickly what he could find:

'In the world of computing a Trojan horse, or Trojan, is any malicious computer programme which is used to hack into a computer or mobile device by misleading users of its true intent. The term is derived from the Ancient Greek story of the wooden horse that was used to help Greek troops invade the city of Troy by stealth.

Trojans are generally spread by some form of social manipulation, for example where a user is duped into executing an e-mail attachment disguised to be unsuspicious. Although their payload can be anything, many modern forms act as a backdoor contacting a controller which can then have unauthorised access to the affected computer or device.'

Tarik typed in *'backdoor in computing'*
'Backdoor is a method, often secret, of bypassing normal authentication in a product or computer system and are often used for securing unauthorised remote access to a computer or other device.'

"Bloody hell Peter" Tarik thought.

Early that evening as Tarik put on his stocking mask, took a deep breath and slid back the rusty bolt and opened the door to the wood shed he knew that something had changed. Borislav was slumped in the chair as far as his restraints would allow him to be and his head was on his chest. He raised his head as Tarik walked in but Tarik could see that much of the fight had gone out of his eyes. There was no doubt the hatred was still there but the determination was gone.

"Give me some water" he rasped at Tarik.

After giving him a drink Tarik had to leave the shed because of the appalling smell, ripped off his stocking mask and then immediately vomited in the courtyard. Five minutes later he re-entered the shed.

"Come on Paštrović. *Haven't you had enough? We will let you die here – you know that don't you?"*

In fact both Tarik and Faris had discussed this increasingly on a number of occasions and had not yet decided what they would do if their captor refused to break and release the information that they sought but they had absolutely agreed they would not kill him and If that meant they had failed in their quest then so be it. Tarik was growing more and more uneasy about the whole situation and he knew that Faris was probably further down the line than he was but neither of them had let their feelings show to their captive in the slightest.

"It wasn't me who shot your father in Sarajevo that night. It was my colleague. There were two snipers on duty at any one time."

'How can you remember this and how can I know that it was not you?' Tarik demanded but in a softer tone now.

"Because it cost me an expensive packet of American cigarettes which I bet him because I thought that he would miss as I believed that the shot was too difficult."

Tarik swallowed hard and went out of the shed and was immediately sick again and walked across to the far side of the courtyard away from the cottage and stared up at the mountain.

"So these bastards bet a packet of cigarettes on the life of my father! It is beyond belief. Can a human life have such little value? They had discussed hitting a target as if they were at a fairground shooting range. Do they know what they have done and the pain that they have caused?"

Tarik slid to the floor outside the shed and the tears just rolled down his face and he broke down into a fit of uncontrollable sobbing which is how Faris found him thirty minutes later and he looked at his friend's red eyes and wet face.

"What is it Tarik"' he enquired softly.

So Tarik quietly and slowly related the conversation he had had earlier with Borislav.

Faris didn't say anything and just sat down next to Tarik on the stone floor of the courtyard. He took out a cigarette from a packet in his pocket and lit it with his lighter. It was only when he had finished the cigarette and had flicked the butt across the courtyard that he blew out his cheeks and said:

"I didn't think that after everything we have experienced during the war that anything could shock or surprise me anymore but I just don't know what to say. It is just beyond belief. So what is the name of his colleague?"

"I don't know I didn't ask as I had to leave at that point."

"Well let's find out shall we?" and he got up and outstretched his hand and pulled Tarik to his feet.

Together they walked back across the courtyard to the wood shed where the door had been left open which made the air inside slightly less rancid. They both pulled out their stocking masks from their pockets, put them on and went inside.

Borislav opened his eyes when he saw them enter. There were dark rims around his eyes and his lips were bloated and blistered. His unshaven face was streaked with sweat, dirt and vomit.

Tarik sat down once more on the chair in front of him and Faris stood behind him:

*"What is the name of your colleague who shot my father Borislav?"'*Tarik asked quietly. He expected the obligatory refusal

peppered with unsavoury adjectives but the crumpled man in front of him just uttered two words:

"Ranko Bajić."

Tarik and Faris both left the shed and Tarik said:

"Go and get that large can of disinfectant that we bought. It is still in the back of the van."

Whilst Faris walked off Tarik went back to the cottage and unreeled the large coil of garden hose that was stored there that had obviously been used for watering the vegetable patch at the top of the garden in the past. He turned on the tap and reeled out the gushing hose back to the shed across the courtyard. Without saying anything he entered the shed and just aimed the hose at the sitting captive until he was absolutely drenched and then he turned the hose on the floor. Faris returned with the disinfectant and a stiff old yard brush and started sweeping out the shed floor as Tarik hosed it.

"Right. Let's get rid of him" Tarik suddenly said

"Not before time" replied Faris and with that they both walked back to the cottage.

"Perhaps the bastards do intend to kill me after all"
'Borislav thought to himself as he was once more alone in the shed which had been his prison cell for the past few days and nights. However, the two of them returned five minutes later and Tarik had a small rucksack over his shoulder. Faris bent down and cut the ankle ropes that were binding Borislav to the chair and then the binds of his hands that were behind his back but still leaving his hands bound but free from the chair. The two of them put their arms under Borislav and lifted the soaking wet and stinking captive to his feet where he stood unsteadily. They then frogmarched him, half dragging him to the back of the van and threw him in and locked the door.

Tarik got in the driver's seat and Faris into the front passenger seat and they set off but remembering to take off their masks before they exited the grounds of the cottage. Tarik drove in silence for about five miles higher up the mountain. It was now half light and he pulled off the road into a small clearing within the thickly forested mountainside. He switched off the engine and they both reapplied their masks and then got out of the van and opened the rear doors.

They pulled the exhausted and disorientated Serbian out of the back and then cut all his remaining ties, half expecting him to charge at them but he just stood there unsteadily and then sat down. Tarik took out the small rucksack from the van and threw it at him.

"In there you will find a towel, torch, cigarettes, matches, bottle of water and some bread and cheese and your jacket and here is your Blackberry' and he threw him the mobile device which he had had in his pocket. *"Perhaps one of your business associates will come and pick you up."*

With that they both turned away, shut the rear van doors and Faris got into the front passenger seat. Just before Tarik closed his door, Borislav shouted at him with a smirk across his face:

"I would take care Bosniak. Ranko is a very violent man and probably a psychopath. Not that I care if he puts a bullet in you."

Borislav pushed himself up and leant against a large rock and watched the van drive away. He was in a real mess and he absolutely stank and he was starving. He reached out for the small rucksack that Tariq had thrown at him and he opened it and took out the towel and the bottle of water. He took a long drink from the bottle and then poured the rest over his head and let it run down his face for a few moments and then he dried his hair and face with the towel. It had not done much good in cleaning him up but it had made him feel a bit better. He reached in for the food and tore off a hunk of bread and some cheese and stuffed it into his mouth eagerly. After two quick mouthfuls he looked at the Blackberry in his hand and he turned it on.

"Great! I've got a signal" he cried.

He opened his email box and saw a number of unread emails he had received over the last few days. All of them were from friends or associates except one:

'Sexy girl. Free photo of my big breasts'

Borislav could not read English but he got the gist of the message so he maneuvered the central black button of his Blackberry until it was positioned over the attachment and then he clicked it. After a few seconds an image appeared of a blonde haired girl with impossibly large breasts which she was cupping with one hand and rubbing in some foam with the other. Though his lips hurt he smiled. He would show it to his friends in the bar the following day when he had recovered from his ordeal. However, unknown to him, inside his device the malware carried by the Trojan was now released and primed and ready to perform its clandestine pre-programmed tasks.

Borislav then made a call to one of his friends back in Korsaka Dubica who he knew had a car. The problem was that he wasn't exactly sure where he was. It was going to be another long night.

Tarik and Faris wasted no time. They sped back to the cottage and parked up the van. They then set about clearing out the cottage and completely cleaned out the wood shed leaving the door open to air it. If asked they would say that they had kept some hunting dogs in there at night and then disinfected it afterwards. They left the keys in the place where they had found them under a large plant pot and drove off in the middle of the night heading back to Sarajevo.

For about an hour neither of them spoke. They were both physically and mentally exhausted. Despite his fatigue Tarik's mind was racing, with the events of the last few days going round and round in his head. He looked across at Faris and saw that he had fallen asleep with a cigarette dangling from his fingers which he took off him and threw out of the window.

"Who the hell is Ranko Bajić? How do I find him and what do I do if I do? Will Borislav and a number of his thug friends be able to track me down?

He dismissed this last thought as unnecessary worry because both Faris and himself had never used their names nor showed their faces but he really did not know what to do now. It was time to go home.

Tarik drove the hundred and sixty five miles back to Sarajevo in silence with just his thoughts as company and they entered the city just as the dawn was breaking. He dropped off Faris at his apartment and then drove back to his own. He entered quietly so as not to wake Jelena but he opened the bedroom door and gently kissed her exposed cheek on the pillow. She stirred.

"Are you ok?"
"Yes. I'm fine. We had a great trip. I will tell you about it in the morning"

He left the bedroom and had a shower and then made a coffee and sat on the sofa once again lost in his thoughts. Tomorrow he would have to return the van and recontact work because he had been away one day longer than he had said and they would be concerned about him. He also decided that he would visit his mother and sister. Not that he would tell them anything of what had happened but if he could just hold them then some of the pain of what he had just learnt might just fade away.

After a half hour or so he got up with a long sigh and crawled into the bed next to his sleeping wife.

Chapter Nineteen

Just over a week later six thousand miles away in the city of La Habra in the suburbs of Los Angeles, a computer 'geek' sitting in his 'cyber cave' suddenly shouted *'bingo!'*

He had accessed Borislav Paštrović's Blackberry regularly for the last few days thanks to the 'backdoor' facility installed by the Trojan that had been hidden in the email attachment that he had sent him anonymously a week before. He was staring at a text message which had been sent the previous evening to another mobile phone which read:

"Hello old friend. I hope that you are keeping and doing well. I must warn you that a crazy Bosniak is looking for you. He does not mean well. Take care comrade. Regards Borislav."

He then saw the reply and a chill ran down the back of his spine:

"Thanks old friend. Do not worry. If he comes to me I will put a bullet between his eyes like we did with so many of the other balija scum."

Peter copied the two text messages and sent them in an email to Tarik together with the mobile telephone number that it was sent to. He also added a caution that perhaps Tarik should not go any further with his quest as this individual could cause him serious harm and what was the point now anyway? He took out a cigarette from the crushproof packet lying next to his keyboard and lit it with a disposable lighter. He blew out a plume of smoke into the already stale atmosphere. He looked at the clock in the corner of one of his monitors it was four am but Peter did not live by ordinary time any more. It simply did not matter to him. With him because of the passion over what he loves to do, it was not surprising to find himself achieving 'flow', the state of mind when he felt fully engaged in what he was doing and consequently lost track of time. Eventually, that feeling of euphoria from the flow had become an addiction and a way of life.

Peter knew that he was different, that he may well be socially awkward and reclusive but he that he had his own attributes. He had an undying commitment to what he loved, a fanatical obsession. Many people were interested in computers and programming as a hobby or as a pastime but to him it was the reason that he existed. It quite simply defined who he was. He only sought the company of those who demonstrated the same passion as he did. It was tight knit group who thought the same way, used the same language with their own terms, acronyms and slang which only they understood anyway. You had to earn your acceptance through demonstration of your knowledge and expertise – it was not possible to just 'gate crash' your way in.

The only difference with Peter's peer group was that they had never met physically or spoken face to face. They existed in the cyber or virtual world and the medium of communication was using a keyboard and not the mouth. To outsiders it was surreal but to Peter and his likeminded group it was very much reality and something that consumed him every waking hour.

Peter thought for a moment about Tarik and how different they were but he had been a good friend at college, The only one he had had and he now felt that he had repaid that loyalty, He had probably done as much as he could do and besides he had his reputation to consider, he had entered the backdoor on Borislav's Blackberry on a number of occasions now and even though he had been very careful about covering his tracks there were other smart guys out there who might be able to find a trace. It was time to close this particular door forever. Tarik was on his own now.

A few days later Tarik met up with Faris again at their usual café on Sebilj Square. Faris had called him earlier that day to suggest that they meet up. As he approached the table Tarik saw that he was limping much more than usual.

"Are you ok" he said as they shook hands pointing at his left leg.

"Yes I am fine. It is just hurting at the moment. The night that we captured Paštrović I had to kick him hard when he was on the ground to try and subdue him a bit and I have really aggravated the muscles in my thigh where the bullet went through but it will be ok. Thanks for asking."

"I have been thinking very carefully Tarik" Faris said after lighting a cigarette and taking a sip of coffee. Tarik could see that he was nervous and that he had slipped the hand that was not holding his cigarette between the buttons of his shirt and was fiddling with the two silver chains that hung round his neck as if for comfort or support.

"I cannot help you anymore Tarik. You now know who killed your father. You should leave it at that now. There is nothing to be gained and everything to lose if you pursue this man Ranko Bajić. He is clearly a violent and possibly psychopathic man and we now know that he has been warned that you are looking for him. It is insanity to continue. We were lucky with the kidnapping of Borislav Paštrović. It could have gone horribly wrong. I really think that you should draw a line under all of this now Tarik."

Tarik stared across the table at his friend. Eventually he said:

"That is fine Faris. You have been a true and loyal friend. I will take your words of advice and think things over very carefully but whatever happens I cannot thank you enough for your support. It is something that we will share together forever but not with anyone else"

They both stood up from the table and shook hands firmly and walked off in different directions across the square scattering pigeons as they went and Tarik glanced at the fountain. As always the sunlight was shining through the water spray creating a transient rainbow that appeared briefly and then was gone.

It was September 2002.and Jelena was now nearly seven months pregnant and starting to feel more and more uncomfortable. Tarik had thrown himself both back into his work and his domestic life with enthusiasm much to Jelena's relief that he was seeming to be more 'normal again. But in reality nothing had changed. Tarik was still having anxiety and panic attacks and still waking up at night sweating and reliving the same old sequences over and over again. He had just got better at concealing it from the outside world and keeping it inside.

Both he and Jelena had decorated the small spare room in their apartment and created a nursery room for their unborn child. Because they did not know the sex of the baby they had opted for neutral colours and Jasmina had bought a cot and Minka had brought round a baby mobile which was now dangling from the ceiling. It featured circus-themed characters and played a tune every time it moved in the air. Tarik adored it and would often sit for a few quiet moments in the room feeling pleased with their efforts and listening to the comforting tune of the lullaby that the mobile was playing.

It was five months now since he and Faris had kidnapped Borislav Paštrović and the thought of Ranko Bajić had once again started to gnaw at his soul.

"I have to sort this out one way or another," he said to himself one evening on the tram on his way back to work. As he looked out of the window he saw that he was passing the Vijećnica, the destroyed National Library which was now in its second stage of reconstruction following the award of a grant from the European Commission.

"But it cannot be what it was' thought Tarik *'The constitutional background in Bosnia has now frozen us into compulsory ethnic identity lines. This building always represented the plurality of Balkan voices throughout the ages. I have to move on. I cannot keep thinking like this. I have to live my life in the modern Sarajevo and accept the Real Politik of our current situation. This is my future and that of my unborn child."*

179

In that moment Tarik realised what he must do. He had to exorcise this ghost that was still haunting him after all these years once and for all. He would track down and confront Ranko Bajić. Whatever would happen in that confrontation he did not know. He would just pray that in the process of that confrontation he would achieve some form of catharsis and at the age of twenty four he could finally say 'goodbye' to his father and the demons of his past that had caused him so much pain and look forward with optimism and hope surrounded by the love of his family.

As the tram rattled on towards his stop Tarik thought to himself:

"Am I being reckless? Am I being irresponsible and reneging on my responsibilities as a husband and a potential father?"

He decided that he could answer *'yes'* to all of those questions but he could see no other way

A few months ago he had been sitting at his desk in the office eating a sandwich and surfing the internet as usual. For some reason he had started to read an online article about ex American and British servicemen who had served in the Gulf War in what had been called 'Operation Desert Shield.' Since returning home many had started to show similar physical and mental symptoms as they struggled to reintegrate back into civilian life. It was called post traumatic stress disorder or PTSD for short. The condition affected different people in different ways – for some it was a short lived experience and was over in a few months but for others it could go on if left untreated for years. However it affected you the symptoms were the same – flashbacks, nightmares, repetitive and distressing images or sensations and physical sensations such as pain, sweating, nausea or trembling. The article went on to say that the condition was not limited to ex-servicemen but to anyone who has had a traumatic experience that has either affected them directly or someone close to them. The traumatic experience had undermined their sense of security and makes it vividly clear that death can occur at any time.

Tarik 'bookmarked' the page and leant back in his chair and blew out his cheeks.

"So I have not being going crazy all these years' he thought *'and it has a name – PTSD'"*

In some ways he felt a slight burden lifting off his shoulders. He no longer felt so alone. Other people and by the sound of it many other people had suffered the same experiences that he had for the last few years. Then he recalled something Paul Stanton, his American foster parent had said to him a couple of years ago when he had introduced Jelena to him and his wife Christine before returning to Sarajevo:

"After our son Joel was killed in Vietnam many of his old army buddies used to call in on us from time to time and some of them took a long time to adjust back into normal life, they just couldn't forget, let go and move on. Many had taken to alcohol and drugs to try and mitigate their feelings of grief, anger, depression or guilt as a result of their survival when someone else close to them didn't or as a result of what they had seen or done."

As Tarik stepped off the tram and walked the short distance to his apartment block he knew that this was the only way that he could deal with this situation. He would be on his own as he had always been. Therapy sessions were not for him. But if it didn't work then with Jelena's support he would seek external help for her sake and the sake of his unborn child – they would have the husband and father that they deserved.

A week Later Jelena announced at breakfast that she was going to spend two weeks in Belgrade with her parents as she had now finished at work and was on maternity leave and she was wanting to ask her mother a whole list of baby-related questions that were troubling her.

"It was now or never" thought Tarik as he travelled to work that morning. On arriving at his office desk he switched on his computer

and while he waited for it to 'boot up' he walked to the coffee machine chatting with colleagues as he went. When he returned and sat down he opened his email box as usual and there to his surprise was an email from Peter in America. He quickly opened it and took a sip of the lukewarm coffee. *'It was never that good from that machine'* he thought.

Hi Tarik.

I hope that you are ok.
I know that you will not have listened to my advice and probably that of others around you that you have confided in because you are what you are and that is what makes you the person that you are

Tarik wasn't sure what he was getting at here but he read on:

So if you haven't started on your crazy mission already I can offer you two things:

1. My best wishes that you find what you are looking for and can finally lay any ghosts to rest and stay safe

and

2. The attached may prove to be very useful to you

Regards
Peter

Tarik eagerly clicked on the attachment, a JPEG file which opened slowly. A few agonising seconds later he was looking at some sort of military document. He could not tell what because staring back at him was a 'passport type' photograph, the head and shoulders of a man that had been enlarged in size. Despite the official looking stamp over the photograph the face was plainly visible. Underneath the photograph was the name of the face – *Ranko Bajić.*

"Thank God for geeks" Tarik exclaimed a little too loudly because his colleague at the next desk said:

"What did you say Tarik?"

"Oh nothing" I am just rambling on' he replied.

Tarik looked back at the image on the screen. The man was in military uniform with a very short hair cut. He had a large head with a cold, hard looking face with an olive complexion and dark eyes but one thing about him stood out above everything else. On the right side of his neck, plainly visible above the collar of the uniform jacket was a large tattoo of what looked to Tarik like some kind of Serbian nationalistic emblem. He could clearly make out the Serbian Cross.which was based on the *tetragramme*, a Byzantine symbol, and is believed to have been adopted at least by the 14th century. It consists of a Greek cross and four firesteels pointing outwards. It is alleged that the firesteels are acronyms for *'Only Unity Saves the Serbs.'*

"Well done Peter" Tarik thought again. *"There would be no difficulty in identifying this man. The visible tattoo was like having a neon sign above his head with his name on it.'*

He downloaded the image on to a new USB flash drive that he had bought recently and was on the key ring in his pocket. He then deleted the image, sent back a 'thank you' email to Peter promising to update him in the near future and then deleted both the incoming and outgoing emails. Later that day he booked ten days leave for when Jelena was going to be away staying with her parents.

Over the next few days he started to formulate his plan. He would hire a car in Sarajevo and then drive up to Banja Luka.

Chapter Twenty

It would have been clear to any trained therapist that Tarik's mind was not thinking clearly. He was trying to rationalise his behaviour in a way that would have been seen as being bizarre, chaotic and confused to any trained third party. He kept asking himself after the last meeting with Faris:

"Think logically Tarik. What do I want to achieve from this confrontation? The guy could easily kill me and for what? In fact he had already threatened to do just that in the email that he had sent to Borislav Paštrović that had been intercepted by my friend Peter in America. What would my father want me to do now? What about Jelena and my unborn child?"

The thoughts raced around his head but they always ended at the same point which was obviously created by the PTSD that he was still suffering from.

"I just want this whole thing to end. I want him to feel some pain, some remorse, some understanding of the enormity of what he had done and to take some responsibility for it. Above everything else I just want to be released from this dark cloud that has been hanging over me for all these years."

To have this confrontation, was in his mind, the only way to achieve this catharsis that he craved but to any outsider it was pure madness and foolishness which is how his friend Faris had tried to argue it with him in the café in Sebilj Square.

Tarik rented a white Volkswagen Golf car in Sarajevo on the Saturday morning after Jelena had departed for Belgrade to visit her parents. He loaded the car with spare clothes, a sleeping bag and various other items that he thought that he might need. He had downloaded a street map of Banja Luka from the internet and printed it out at work. He set out to drive the one hundred and eighteen miles to Banja Luka which he estimated would take him about three hours.

The journey was quite spectacular with views of high and lush mountains and there were long stretches of road where it was possible to do the maximum speed limit allowed. Tarik was careful to remain on the main roads as he had read warnings of the dangers of the minor roads with sharp hairpin bends and treacherous and terrifying mountain passes. He arrived in Banja Luka which was situated at the head of the winding valley of the river Vrbas and is the capital of the Republika Sprska; the strange creation of a state within a state. It was just after lunchtime and he checked into the budget hotel that he had pre-booked online before leaving Sarajevo which was located the closest to the last known address of Ranko Bajić that Peter had sourced for him.

Sitting having a coffee and a sandwich in the hotel lounge he studied the street map and estimated it was about a fifteen minute walk to the address that he had been given. So he set off in the early warm afternoon walking slowly so as to remain completely anonymous. The city was well known for having numerous tree-lined avenues, boulevards, gardens and parks. Nearly all of Banja Luka's Croats and Bosniaks had been expelled during the war and all of the city's sixteen mosques including the Ferhat Pasha Mosque were destroyed. Tarik was only too aware of a very nasty incident that occurred here in May last year, about eighteen months ago, which had been well reported in Sarajevo at the time.

Angered by plans to rebuild a mosque in their city, a Bosnian Serb crowd attacked dozens of Muslims and forced United Nations and other Western officials to take refuge inside an Islamic centre.
More than one thousand Serbs broke through a police cordon and attacked people at a ceremony to begin the reconstruction of the mosque, which Serbs had destroyed in 1993. Five buses had been set ablaze as was a bakery and protesters chanted, *"This is Serbia"* and, *"We don't want a mosque."*

About one thousand Muslims who had lived in Banja Luka had been bussed in for the ceremony after Bosnian Serb leaders had grudgingly agreed to the reconstruction as part of international officials' efforts to return refugees to their houses across the country. However, the Serbs beat up the visitors and set Muslim prayer rugs on fire. About two hundred and fifty of the Muslims had been trapped in the building along with the head of the United Nations in Bosnia, Jacques Klein; the British, Swedish and Pakistani ambassadors; and other international and local officials at the ceremony. In addition there had unfortunately been indications of local police collaboration with the Serbian protesters.

As Tarik began to near the district in which he hoped that Ranko Bajić still lived he noticed that the area was starting to decline. The houses were less well maintained, many had peeling paint on the doors and windows and old cars lined both sides of the street. He walked on and then turned left into what he hoped was Ranko's street. It was even more run down then the one he had just exited and many of the houses had old household items such as refrigerators and washing machines that had been discarded still left outside. He was looking for number 182 which he realised must be on the other side of the road because the houses on this side were all odd numbers so he crossed over slowly and without indicating any particular purpose or destination.

He was at number 120 so he carried on past another twenty six very similar houses and then he passed 182 but he did not turn to glance at it and instead looked at the street and walked past an old dark blue Peugeot 309 that was parked there and he noticed that the near side front tyre was bald because the cord was showing through the rubber. He passed a parade of shops and a launderette and about four hundred yards further on the other side of the road was a large bar with some people sitting outside at small tables drinking beer and coffee. Tarik entered the half full bar and immediately the light dimmed and the air smelt strongly of stale cigarette smoke. The walls looked stained and there were a few loose electrical wires dangling from one of them. At the far end some men were playing Pool and talking animatedly. A large television was located above the bar which was draped with a scarf of the local football team of FK Borak Banja Luka.

Tarik walked slowly up to the bar and placed an unlit cigarette in his mouth from a packet that he had bought earlier and just pointed at the beer tap of Nektar Pivo, the pale lager beer that was brewed in the city by the local brewery Banjalučka Pivara so he didn't have to speak which would have revealed his slightly Americanised Sarajevo accent. He paid for the beer and sat down at an empty table and unfolded a copy of the local newspaper that he had bought en route from the hotel. He pretended to be engrossed in the paper but all of the time he was listening to other conversations and permitting himself the odd glance around the room at the other clientele.

Suddenly he was aware of movement close to him in the corner of his eye and he looked up and a man was standing by his table who had clearly already had a few drinks:

"Can I have one of your cigarettes?" he said pointing at the packet on the table in front of Tarik.

Tarik nodded his head and made an open-handed gesture of ok so that once again he didn't have to speak unnecessarily as the last thing he wanted was to get into a conversation with this person which could lead to all sorts of difficulties.

After about a half an hour he had scanned the whole room and Ranko was clearly not here. Perhaps he no longer lived in the area. There had been no corroboration of the address on the web site that his friend Peter had uncovered for some years. He would have to establish this one way or the other in the next twenty four hours otherwise he was wasting his time and worse still he would be back to square one.

"Maybe I could get a lead on where he had relocated to"

he thought but that was very wishful thinking and could not be easily achieved and would most certainly cause suspicion.

"No this was not going to be easy at all."

He drained the last of his beer and got up from the table and walked towards the exit deciding that he would return later in the evening. He was just about to reach for the door handle when the door swung open forcefully and if he had not put his hand up to protect himself, it would have hit him hard in the face. A man walked through the open door. He was about six inches shorter than Tarik and far more stockily built with very short hair, dark eyes and an olive complexion and with a stubbly unshaven face. He ignored Tarik and pushed roughly past him but as he did so Tarik could not avoid noticing that he had a large tattoo on the right side of his neck. The tattoo was plainly visible above his navy blue T shirt and was unmistakable. It was a Serbian Cross.

Chapter Twenty One

Tarik waited for over an hour in the bricked recess in the wall behind the parade of shops sharing the space with two or three large refuse bins that were overflowing with rubbish. He didn't know what smelt worse, the rotting rubbish or the stench of stale urine because the place had obviously been used regularly as a public urinal. He had decided that he would not wear a mask like Faris and he had done previously when they had abducted Borislav Paštrović. He wanted Ranko to look into his eyes and he into his. He knew that Ranko did not even know his name and he doubted very much that he had the skills to track him down.

"If he sticks to his normal routine that he has followed for the last two days then he will come out soon" he thought.

Ten minutes later he felt his heart rate quicken and his stomach tighten as he saw a man turning the corner and entering the dimly lit car park. The red glow of a cigarette clearly illuminating his face and the distinctive tattoo on the right side of his neck. It was Ranko.

Tarik stepped out of the shadows and stood straight in front of the man walking slightly unsteadily towards an old dark blue Peugeot 309 car that was parked in the dimly lit car park behind the parade of shops that contained the bar where Ranko had been drinking.

Without hesitating Tarik said firmly:

"You are the low life who shot my unarmed father in cold blood for the price of a packet of cigarettes."

For a second Ranko was taken aback and then a broad smile came across his face:

"Ah the crazy Bosniak. I have been expecting you. It has been a while since I heard that you were looking for me and so I thought that you didn't have the stomach to face me. I have been keeping something for you'"

and with surprising speed he swung a vicious punch which crashed into the side of Tarik's head and sent him staggering backwards:

"So according to an old comrade I killed your father well now I'll finish you balija scumbag'"

and he lurched forward. The veins bulged in his neck distorting the very visible tattoo and his dark eyes were fixed and staring as if they were on fire. Tarik saw something burning in those eyes that he had never seen before and never wanted to see again – pure hatred.

Tarik had never been in a serious fight before. But he just visualised that he was going to pitch the hardest and fastest baseball of his life. He was at least four inches taller than Ranko and stone cold sober and he had a much longer reach and as his opponent lurched at him he smashed his fist into the man's face splitting flesh and bone. Almost instinctively he did the same with his left fist which hit an undefended and unsteady target sending Ranko reeling back against one of the large rubbish bins.

However, far from flailing. He stood up again quickly and grinned a blooded smile and said:

"Ok Bosniak so you want a real fight do you"

Ranko had been a thug and a bully all his life and he was well used to street fighting. He may have taken a couple of hits and he may have had a bit to drink but he was far from finished and he knew that he was more than a match for his taller but inexperienced opponent. He sprang forward quickly catching Tarik slightly unawares spinning him by his shoulder turning him round and with his other fist delivered a hammer blow into his lower back dropping him to his knees in excruciating pain and as he did so Ranko lifted his right leg and smashed it viciously into Tarik's face smashing his nose and loosening a front tooth.

Ranko stood over his opponent watching the blood pour down his face:

"Why did you come here Bosniak? What do you want?"

Tarik spat out blood and saliva as he replied:

"I wanted you to know what you had done and the pain and hurt that you have caused. You destroyed my family. I wanted to confront you with your crime and to tell you that you will not go unpunished. Your Day of Judgement will come."

"You are so fucking naïve you stupid Bosniak. Did you think that I would capitulate in front of you in some kind of 'mea culpa' moment? I did my job and it was hard and boring duty"

"But you killed an unarmed man"

"I killed many men, armed and unarmed. So what? They were just a target. Besides they deserved it. As Karadzic said it was a fight to the finish, a fight for living space. We should have trashed you all."

Tarik was taken aback by the blatant racism, hatred and violence and the complete contempt and dehumanising way in which this man described his victims. As he spoke Ranko backed off a little and Tarik struggled back on to his feet. He had now realised that there would be no rationalising with this man. He was one dimensional, secure in his ideological fanaticism and his myopic view of history and what he regarded as the Serbian national destiny.

"Well your Day of Judgement has come early Bosniak"'

and he reached into his pocket and withdrew a large flick knife and Tarik saw the blade spring out and glisten in the moonlight. He knew that he was no match for Ranko in a fight and that this psychopath had every intention of killing or seriously injuring him and wouldn't even give it a second thought and that he would probably even enjoy it. There was only one option open to him.

Taking his opponent by surprise Tarik suddenly darted to his left and raced around the corner of the car park and into the street. He was fitter and in far better condition than Ranko who no doubt had also consumed a number of liters of beer and was struggling to keep up. Tarik with adrenaline pumping through his bloodstream ran as hard as he could despite the beating that he had just taken until he was about fifteen yards away from where he had parked his rented white Volkswagen Golf car. He reached into his pocket for the key fob and pressed the open door button as he continued running and up ahead he was pleased to see the telltale flash of the two amber indicator lights which told him that the car was now unlocked.

As soon as he reached the parked car he jumped in and started the engine but Ranko had caught up now and had prevented him from closing the door. He was shouting and swearing at Tarik in a very loud voice and people were starting to come towards the scene of the confrontation. Tarik tried to hold onto the door handle with his right hand and with his left put the car in gear and let out the clutch. The car surged forward forcing Ranko to let go of his grip on the door. Tarik sped off leaving Ranko now joined by two or three other men who had come out of the bar shouting and swearing at the rapidly departing car. Then just before he got out of sight, Tarik could see in his rear view mirror that Ranko had gone back to the car park. He was most certainly not going to give up this fight.

Tarik had never had much of a plan but whatever he had intended was now of no use. Not for the first time in his life he was in a serious situation for which he had no plan.

"The first thing I must do' he said to himself *'is maintain my anonymity."*

So two miles up the road he pulled into a side street and turned off the engine and switched off the lights. He quickly opened the boot, wiped the blood that was pouring from his shattered nose and took out a roll of duct tape that he had brought with him and taped over the rear number plate and some of the front one as well. Just as he got back into the car he saw a car travelling at speed pass by the entrance to the side street, It could only be Ranko as there was such little other traffic on the road at this time of the evening.

"It won't take him long to know that I have stopped" he thought *"and he will double back"*

Tarik set off again going in the same direction as his pursuer had taken a few minutes before and as he did so rain started to fall slowly at first and then with increasing intensity so much so that within a few minutes it had become a deluge and his windscreen wipers were struggling to cope even on their fastest speed. He was now out of the town and the road was dark and narrow and curvy with numerous sharp bends appearing quickly with little warning other than the indicative black and white road signs. He was ascending sharply up the mountainside but this was a typical Bosnian road with numerous pot holes and he was also aware that everyone drove far too fast here often not bothering about crossing a solid white line and overtaking wherever they wanted to. His senses were on full alert as he stared through the windscreen just focusing on the line in the middle of the road picked out by his headlights. There were no cat's eyes here. He was completely on his own.

All of a sudden a car came speeding around the bend in the opposite direction but in the middle of the road and Tarik had to swerve to the right to avoid hitting him head on. It was an old dark coloured Peugeot 309 with a single occupant:

"It could only be Ranko" Tarik said out loud to himself as he had not seen another car on the road since he had left the town. He put his foot on the accelerator and sped on. He had no idea where he was going he just had to put some distance between himself and this crazy psychopath who was pursuing him with a vengeance that he

had just not imagined. He was scared now but he didn't have time to think about it as the adrenaline was pumping through his blood stream. It was fight or flight the automatic psychological human response to a perceived threat to survival or harmful situations. Unknown to Tarik was the fact that people already suffering from PTSD would demonstrate symptoms of hyperarousal in these situations which would serve him well for a while but it was not a state that he would be able to maintain for very long without collapsing.

As he accelerated around a bend he was immediately aware of un-dimmed headlights shining directly into his mirror which momentarily disorientated him as he tried to maintain focus on the road ahead.

"How the hell did he catch up with me so quickly in that old car" he once again said out loud.

But Ranko was now obsessed. He knew these roads like the back of his hand and was used to driving at speed along them and at night and after he had been drinking. He had a rage inside of him, fuelled by alcohol and years of blind indoctrinated hatred. He felt like he was back with the Red Berets patrolling the borders of Muslim held areas. He remembered that it was like a cat-and-mouse hunt but with the Muslims always greatly outnumbered he was the hunter and they were the prey. He reached for a packet of cigarettes from the dashboard and pulled one out keeping one hand tight on the steering wheel and pushed in the car's cigarette lighter and a few seconds later lifted the glowing lighter to the cigarette dangling from his lips. He sat up straight and shook his head to clear some of the fogginess from the night's drinking and then accelerated again.

"Right you bastard I've got you now"

he said as he narrowed the distance to the back of Tarik's Volkswagen. He was on a mission and he was not going to fail. Minutes later he was literally on Tarik's rear bumper and then he accelerated again and nudged the Volkswagen hard forward. Tarik fought the steering wheel to try and maintain control and not spin off the narrow road and over into the dark wooded ravines that lined the road on both sides. For the next ten minutes Tarik felt like he was back in a theme park in America riding a roller coaster. His car had taken numerous bangs and shunts from the rear but he had managed to keep control but only just. He glanced at the speedometer they were going even faster now. The slightest mistake could prove fatal and still he could not shake off the dogged pursuer on his rear bumper.

He glanced up into the mirror and then he saw them. It was another set of headlights right behind Ranko's car and travelling equally quickly and dangerously. It could not be just another motorist not driving at that speed and in that fashion and in these conditions. It had to be Ranko's friend or friends from the bar who had decided to join in the pursuit and possible death of a person they considered to be not just an enemy but someone to be eradicated in a sinister blood sport chase.

Just as Tarik thought that things could not get worse there was a howl of engine revs and a screech of brakes and as he glanced to his left Ranko's dark blue Peugeot was suddenly right beside him on the narrow road and Tarik could see him glaring at him through his open window. As they approached a right hand bend Ranko suddenly turned his car sharply in and banged into the side of Tarik's door lurching the Volkswagen violently to the right and heading off the road into the dark abyss below. Tarik had clearly intended to shunt him right off the road and down the embankment. Tarik slammed on the brakes and fought the steering wheel causing the car to pitch and swerve dangerously close to the edge but he managed to gain some traction on the edge of the road and just get it back away from the edge but in doing so Ranko had leapfrogged him and he was now sandwiched between the two cars that were now hunting as a pack.

Ranko leant to his right and opened the glovebox and fumbled about for a few seconds and then withdrew an object and slammed the glovebox closed again.

He was applying the brakes slowly but deliberately. Tarik could see the brake lights glow so vividly in the dark but the offside one was not working and neither was his nearside tail light. Ranko's car was not n particularly good condition but that was of no consequence now. He was only too well aware that if they managed to force him to stop now he would be finished. Thoughts of Jelena and their unborn child flashed through his mind and his heart started to beat faster and his throat and mouth were bone dry:

"You stupid selfish fool" he cried out loud. *"How the hell have I got into this mess. It is all of my own making. I have confronted the devil and now he has unleashed his demons against me"*

and the tears began to well in his eyes but he brushed them away quickly so that he could focus on the car right in front of him. The rain was still coming down very heavily and bouncing off the surface of the road and his headlights were struggling to pierce the gloom to light up the road ahead. There was no way that they could pick out a pot hole. If he was unlucky enough to hit one at this speed he would either wreck the car's steering or lose control altogether.

A sudden loud noise, 'crack' pierced the night air easily overcoming the noise of the three car engines and the windscreen on the passenger side of Tarik's car shattered and the rain started to pour in. The screen had cracked and splintered but remained intact on the driver's side but the wipers were now scraping against glass fragments and making a screeching sound which added to the cacophony of noise. In that split second the awful realism slammed into Tarik's brain with the same force that the bullet had penetrated his windscreen – Ranko had a gun and he was intent on using it.

On leaving the army Ranko had not surrendered his side arm. He believed that the weapon together with his red beret had been fought for and were rightfully his and he was not going to let them go. It was a Zastava CZ 99, a semi-automatic pistol developed to replace the M57 in the Yugoslavian military and police.

Tarik kept focusing on the road and the Peugeot in front of him and swallowed hard. There was no doubting it now, this could only end one of two ways – either he would get away or he was going to die on this dark, isolated and wet mountain road. Rain now slammed through the shattered windscreen on the near side and Tarik continued to slow as Ranko braked and baulked him in the middle of the road swerving from side to side to prevent him from passing him. Within a few minutes the cars were virtually at a stop but Tarik had deliberately left a gap between his and Ranko's car in front. It was a surreal situation. Three cars were now stationary in the middle of a dark, narrow mountain road with rain drumming down with even greater intensity. Tarik felt his heart racing in his chest but he took three deep breaths exhaling the air slowly out of his mouth. His mind momentarily drifted to when he was standing on the mound about to deliver his final pitch. Almost in slow motion the passenger door of the dark blue Peugeot opened in front of him and Ranko who had turned off his engine stepped out of the car and was about to walk towards the white Volkswagen Golf behind him when Tarik selected first gear and floored the accelerator turning the steering wheel violently to the left and then to the right as he sped past the motionless Ranko and his stationary Peugeot 309. With the front wheels spinning and the tyres skidding on the soaking road surface Tarik accelerated away but as he did so he heard another 'crack crack' and the thump of another two rounds slamming into his car's bodywork somewhere behind him.

Ranko was apoplectic with rage. He swore and cursed loudly and tossed the cigarette that was in his mouth to the ground. He leapt back into the car and shouted at his friends behind him to follow him. He turned the ignition key but the car did not start so he kept pumping the accelerator madly and turning the key again and again. Eventually after a few moments the car restarted with a huge cloud of blue smoke blowing out of the exhaust and the two cars sped off into the darkness in pursuit of the fleeing Volkswagen Golf.

Tarik estimated he was about two minutes ahead of the two chase cars but based on his earlier experiences he didn't expect this gap to exist for long. He drove on fast for about another five miles and then as he rounded yet another sharp bend in the road he saw a lay by ahead in the beam of his headlights. He swerved to the right into it and slammed on the brakes skidding on the gravel at the side of the road. He switched off the engine and the lights, withdrew the ignition key and scrambled out of the car and over the top of the embankment at the side of the road unaware where he was heading but now simply running for his life. He found himself on a densely wooded escarpment that descended sharply and he fought through soaking wet undergrowth as the rain relentlessly poured down onto his already sodden clothes. Brushing away branches and undergrowth he lurched downwards in the pitch darkness stumbling and flailing his arms wildly just to get away. Then he looked back and saw the headlights of two cars pull up and stop above him on the ridge by the side of the road, there was the sound of shouting and commotion and eventually a loud voice boomed:

"No we're not going down there Ranko. It is dark and wet and dangerous. Let's go back and have another drink. He isn't worth it!"

There was some more shouting and swearing and then one of the cars started up and put on its lights and drove away and then there was only total darkness and the sound of the rain bouncing off the leaves and other foliage. Tarik walked on, slower this time so as to try and not make a sound. It was a cloudy night and there was very little moonlight to guide him through the sodden shrubbery and once or twice he banged into an overhanging branch or scratched his face on tall brambles and tripped over tree roots and rolled around in the dark hoping that he had not broken or sprained an ankle. After descending another hundred yards or so he saw an old large tree and wiping the rain out of his eyes and face he could see as he approached it that it had a hollow trunk. He squeezed himself inside and waited catching his breath, every sense on hyper alert.

Ranko was now like a man possessed. Nothing else mattered to him other than catching this man who had had the audacity to confront him. That was his mission and it was now a matter of honour and more than that patriotism; it was his duty that he should hunt him down and deal with him. He walked slowly down the slope with the gun extended in his right hand out in front of him, the rain slamming into his already soaked clothing but Ranko was oblivious to his surroundings. He just kept on moving forwards and down the slope.

Tarik stood inside the relative protection of the hollow tree trunk grateful that the penetrating rain was not able to affect him so much in here. He listened and then listened again but he could hear nothing other than the rain. He suddenly felt a sense of *déjà vu* that once again in his life he was hiding from a Serbian gunman who wanted to kill him. His mind drifted back to the dark night streets of Sarajevo. He was once again running from a place of safety to another taking refuge in the shadows, just another ghostly silhouette running through the night with his sister's headscarf tied around his face and the sound of explosions all around him and the flashes of tracer fire lighting up the night sky.

The sound of a snapped twig suddenly broke his reverie and he was instantly alert. Walking slowly with his right hand extended out in front of him carrying a gun, Tarik could make out the shape of Ranko Bajić moving stealthily through the undergrowth about ten yards away from where he was hiding. He tried to shrink further down inside the hollow tree trunk to gain some extra concealment and he remained absolutely rigid taking shallow breaths and not making a sound. His heart was beating so hard in his chest that he thought that the sound or vibration would betray his position. His nerves were alert and tingling, every muscle tense in his body. He had no idea what he was going to do but he would be ready for any opportunity that came his way. Once again he thought of Jelena but he pushed the image out of his mind. He had to focus. He was no match for Ranko physically and now that his opponent was armed and determined it would be a one way fight that would be over very quickly indeed. As in a previous life, stealth and living in the shadows was his friend and would be his only means of survival.

It soon became clear that Ranko had not seen him as he was continuing on his slow descent down the embankment swearing and cursing to himself under his breath. Tarik waited five very long agonising minutes. He wondered how long Ranko would keep going before he decided to retrace his route and search for a hidden foe. Each second was more agonising than the last but he waited silently and completely motionless. He listened, Nothing. Not a sound. Even the rain was starting to ease up a bit now and the water falling now was just dripping off the sodden foliage overhead.

Cautiously Tarik stepped out of his hiding place and very slowly started to reclimb the embankment taking each step very gingerly as if he was walking on hot coals. After about ten minutes he reached the top of the ridge and the roadside. He thought about disabling Ranko's car but it was locked and he had no knife to slash a tyre and in any event he intended to be absolutely silent until he had no option. He opened the door to his car as quietly as he could hoping that the double flash of the amber indicator lights would go unseen and he immediately extinguished the vanity light when it came on. He put the key in the ignition and took a deep breath and as he exhaled he turned the key and the engine started immediately. He slammed the door shut unconcerned about noise now, turned on the lights and accelerated hard out of the lay by with the front wheels skidding and spinning on the gravel by the side of the road.

From about fifty yards below in the middle of the dense woodland came a scream of obscenities and Tarik heard the distinct 'crack' of a gun shot as he drove away into the night. Ranko had now lost any remaining reason. He charged like a maniac back up the escarpment, tripping and falling and pushing branches out of the way, he half ran back up to the ridge. He ripped open the door of the Peugeot and unlike previously it started first time. He gunned the engine which howled in response and he catapulted himself up the road in pursuit of the Volkswagen which was now about five minutes in front of him. For Ranko this was now ultra personal. This Bosniak would not deceive him and make a fool of him again. He stamped on the accelerator pedal until it was flat against the floor of the car. He pressed his face which was contorted in rage forwards almost touching the windscreen and he just swung the car through the corners sliding across the road completely ignoring the potential of oncoming traffic which if there had been any would have hit him head on.

In front Tarik suspected this. Ranko knew the road and although his car was more modern and superior he did not believe that he could out run him. So once again he looked for an exit off the road. Ten miles further on and Tarik could make out headlights coming into the bend behind him just as he was leaving it; his foe was not far behind. As he focused on the road ahead he remembered a 1971 American movie directed by Steven Spielberg that he had watched when he was at college. It was called 'Duel' and it was about a middle-aged salesman who became entangled in a life and death struggle on a remote and lonely California highway with a grimy tanker truck and its unseen mysterious driver. Tarik remembered that it was bravery and ingenuity and not brawn that had won the day then and that it would be his only option now.

Five minutes later and the dark blue Peugeot was only a few hundred yards behind him. His eyes frantically searched ahead in the light provided by his mainbeam headlights for an exit or turning off the road and just as he exited another tight left hand bend he saw a side road going off to the left about a hundred yards ahead. He didn't have time to see if there were any signposts and just turned in as quickly as he could. He didn't know if Ranko had seen him turn but he suspected that the lights of his car would betray his position and he was right as he soon detected the headlights in his rear view mirror once more.

As soon as Tarik had turned into this narrow side road he was not sure that he had made the right decision.

"Why was there a narrow, tarmacked road leading into the dense forest at this desolate point?"

A few minutes later his headlights illuminated something that did indeed confirm that this had been a bad decision and answered his question about the road. Up ahead he could clearly see a large crane and other heavy lifting equipment and stacks of large logs ready for transportation. This was obviously a depot for timber that had been felled in the forests and was awaiting loading and collection by heavy transport lorries.

What was worse was that Tarik very quickly realised that it was also a dead end.

Chapter Twenty Two

Apart from the light projected by his main beam headlights it was pitch black as Tarik slowed as he neared to the entrance of the huge timber yard. Ranko could only be just over a minute behind him. He had to think now and think fast as if he decided to get out and run Ranko would hunt him down and very likely shoot him and he thought it improbable that he could evade detection a second time.

He was now absolutely exhausted after the anticipation of the confrontation, the fight and then this horrendous life or death chase through the mountains. Every muscle ached and he just wanted to slump down and sleep. But in the final stages of his state of hyperarousal something strange happened. He started to act as if he was on auto pilot as if someone else was guiding his hand and things began to happen fast and without thinking.

He put the Volkswagen in second gear and moved forward slowly till the headlights behind him were only about a hundred yards away and then he accelerated sharply whilst turning the steering wheel very quickly at the same time but before he did so he applied a slight flick of the wheel the opposite way before turning it back in the direction that he wanted to go; in what was called a 'Scandinavian flick.' The Volkswagen responded perfectly on the wet tarmacked surface entering a controlled skid and ending up facing in the opposite direction with Ranko's headlights bearing down on him. The dark blue Peugeot had to brake sharply to avoid a head on collision and Tarik accelerated again and swerved past it and raced back up the narrow forest road.

When Tarik had first gone to America after being evacuated with his sister Minka, he had been keen to make friends with as many people at High School as possible so that he could settle in quickly, be accepted and learn and improve his English as fast as possible. One group he had initially started to hang out with were not at the

School but were on the periphery of some of those who were. Tarik had been introduced to them through someone in his year group and he had met up with them at weekends on occasions. It was one such Sunday afternoon and he was with the group on the open top roof level of a huge mostly empty multi storey car park. There were four of them and two had arrived in a fairly new red Honda Civic which they started to race up and down the car park roof space, burning the clutch to spin the wheels and skidding and swerving by pulling on the handbrake as they turned. It was certainly not doing the car much good but it was great fun.

"Hey Tarik. I'll teach you to do a bootlegger" said one of the guys who had brought the car with them.
*"What's that "*replied Tarik
"Get in and I'll show you. It is quite easy really" he continued as Tarik got in the passenger seat. *"The idea is to reverse the direction of travel of the car by one hundred and eighty degrees in the minimum amount of time whilst staying within the width of a two lane road."*

After a couple of solo attempts, Tarik had perfected the maneuver and soon after the group had dispersed because they suspected that sooner or later the noise would attract the attention of the local police.

"Why is it called a bootlegger" Tarik asked as he and his friend descended the stairs of the car park quickly because of the stale stench of urine.
"I am not sure but I think the term originated from the Prohibition era of the United States when bootleggers transporting illegal liquor would use the maneuver to escape from police officers in high speed chases"

What Tarik did not know at the time was that the car had been stolen but fortunately for him over the next few weeks, he drifted away from the group and potential trouble as other friends took their place.

Ranko Bajić smashed his fist on the top of his dashboard as Tarik's Volkswagen sped past him. He had been outwitted again and he was not used to this humiliation. He did not care what happened to him now, he would hunt this Bosniak down and if he died with him then so be it. He turned the car around and drove as fast as he could back up the tree lined narrow road. When he got to the junction he could not see Tarik's lights but he suspected that he would have turned left and not return back towards Banja Luka. He drove the old car like a mad man. The engine was squealing and howling as it over revved through all of the gears, he slid round corners and once or twice the rear end fish-tailed and slid dangerously close to the edge of the road and the steep embankment beyond it but Ranko was impervious to danger and just kept his foot on the accelerator in the dogged pursuit of his prey.

The rain had now returned and was sweeping across the dark mountain road making driving even more treacherous. Tarik's windscreen was deteriorating further and the rain and wind were now penetrating the car with real force. Five minutes later and Ranko spotted Tarik about a mile ahead as the road straightened out and he floored the accelerator pedal once again whilst Tarik was forced to slow because the windscreen wipers were becoming ineffective on the rapidly diminishing glass. He was also tiring, the adrenaline that had kept him so pumped was now ebbing away leaving him completely exhausted and washed up. He felt the fight going out of him:

"Should he stop and try and reason with Ranko saying it was all a big mistake?"

Whilst he was having these thoughts the old dark blue Peugeot had once more closed right up behind him and was just yards off his rear bumper. Tarik accelerated again but then he saw some red road signs illuminated in his headlights which indicated a series of very tight hair pin bends together with a very sharp descent in the road and warning notices advising motorists to select a low gear and proceed with caution.

He dropped a gear and turned into the sharp left hander looking for the maximum grip on the outside of the road and immediately he flicked the wheel to negotiate the tight hand bend that followed it and as he did so he switched off the ignition just for a few seconds and pushed in the clutch and the Volkswagen responded perfectly but in complete darkness as all of the lights had been extinguished. This was a do or die move and Tarik just held on and hoped. Ranko however, had not seen the warning signs and was purely focused on the rear of the car in front of him and he had also taken one hand off the wheel to feel for the Zastava pistol which he had left on the passenger seat beside him. The Peugeot negotiated the left hand bend but then suddenly there was pitch darkness in front of him and the Volkswagen was nowhere to be seen which completely took him by surprise and he was just not set up for the sharp right hand bend that followed it. Blinded he tried to turn in but it was far too late and with the road soaking wet and with bald tyres on the Peugeot through complete lack of care and maintenance the car did not turn in at all but just careered straight ahead aquaplaning off the road and smashed head on into a large oak tree. From the moment that the car had exited the left hand bend Ranko had become a mere passenger and was no longer the driver as events moved completely out of his control. The windscreen shattered, the headlights went out and the bonnet crumpled under the severe impact and steam hissed out of the radiator grille into the dark wet night air. Ranko was propelled forward and his head hit the steering wheel and then bounced back before he slumped, collapsed over the wheel once more.

After just a few seconds Tarik switched the ignition on once more and let out the clutch to bump start the car and with the lights back on he slowed right down conscious that there were no headlights following him anymore. Either Ranko had suddenly given up the chase or he had crashed but Tarik suspected the latter was the case.

Chapter Twenty Three

Tarik brought the Volkswagen to an abrupt stop and parked on the side of the road leaving the hazard lights flashing. He got out of the car and the rain lashed at him once more. He walked back about fifty metres to where he could see the Peugeot had crashed head-on into a large oak tree. The front of the car was all smashed in, the bonnet crumpled up and the windscreen shattered. There were no headlights working but the rear lights were still on which gave him some background light in which to see.

He approached very slowly and cautiously. He half expected to hear the 'crack' of a gun shot at any second so he tried to keep himself in the shadows and not make a sound. But as he neared the car he could see that he need not have worried as he could make out the shape of the driver slumped down over the steering wheel and completely motionless. He peered in through the window and he could plainly see a large tattoo of a Serbian cross on the right side of his neck – it was definitely Ranko Bajić.

Tarik pulled open the damaged driver's door and stepped back. He could not see the pistol but he was not going to take any chances. Ranko lifted his head from the steering wheel just a few inches and stared at Tarik. His face was battered and blooded:

"Urgh! balija! I should have shot you straight away when I had the chance like I did your father and....."

But before he could finish the sentence something just snapped inside Tarik's head. The mental and physical exhaustion of the life and death chase, the confrontation and fight and the strain of having his life hang in the balance and the possibility of not seeing his beloved Jelena again or their unborn child had suddenly taken their toll and had finally exploded within him.

In that split second he thought of his father Sejo lying face down on the cold cobblestones with the heavy water bottles strapped to his back and his life blood ebbing away cut down by a bullet from this monster in front of him for the sake of a cheap bet. He thought of his aunt Jela slaughtered with many others in the Markela marketplace as they sought to buy vegetables. He thought of his sister Minka who was now scarred and maimed for life and he thought of his friend Afan crossing the road on the way to the old brewery and his head suddenly exploding in a red spray that shot upwards in to the air. He thought of all the hundreds and hundreds of others and all of the misery, deprivation and destruction that he had seen and witnessed and he thought of the loss of his way of life, the carefree existence that he had enjoyed until it was cruelly taken away from him at the age of just thirteen.

Ranko pushed his right hand over towards the passenger seat frantically searching for the Zastava pistol which he knew was there somewhere and as he did so all of that rage and emotion that had been bottled up inside Tarik for so many years just exploded like a champagne cork out of a bottle and he hit Ranko in the side of his head with his fist and then again and again. Ranko rocked back in his seat and Tarik grabbed a packet of cigarettes that were on the dashboard recognising the familiar branding of Marlboro; an irony that was not lost on him.

"As you sow so shall you reap" Tarik shouted out loud.

He tore open the top and took out a handful of cigarettes which he stuffed forcefully into Ranko's open mouth and then he clamped both of his hands over the Serb's nose and mouth and held them there in a vice-like grip. He could feel Ranko struggle and writhe beneath him but he clamped his hands even tighter in their grip and then gradually in the dim light he saw his hunter's veins in his neck start to bulge and the giant tattoo distort and his face start to turn blue.

Then something happened. Time seemed to stand still. Tarik's heart stopped racing. He took three deep breaths and expelled the air though his mouth and said out loud:

"No this is not the way of my faith. This is not what my father would want. This is not the way of the future. I will find a more appropriate way of punishing you for what you have done."

and once again the words of Martin Luther King once again came to mind:

"The old law of an eye for an eye leaves everyone blind."

So he released his grip and removed his hands from Ranko's face who immediately started coughing and spitting out bits of cigarettes in between gasping for breath. Tarik stepped back and left him to it and walked to the other side of the car and ripped open the passenger door. He saw the pistol lying in the floor well together with a mobile phone so he picked them both up. He put the phone in his pocket and threw the pistol over the edge of the road and down the steep embankment. He walked back round the car to see that Ranko was trying to sit up in the driver's seat but he was struggling and holding his chest. He had probably broken or badly bruised some of his ribs and he could also see that his right leg was protruding at a strange angle below the knee and was undoubtedly broken. Ranko was staring at him with an expressionless face that looked like he had gone fifteen rounds with a heavy weight professional boxer and was probably wondering what Tarik was going to do next but he uttered no words and just kept on sporadically spitting out tobacco, saliva and blood.

Tarik looked down on the ground and picked up the discarded pack of cigarettes and took out two leaving just one in the packet which he replaced on the dashboard and picked up the disposable lighter that was lying there, he put both cigarettes in his mouth at once and lit them both handing one of them to Ranko who reached out to take it without saying anything. Tarik took a few steps backwards and sat on the grass verge and although he had never smoked in his life he took two long pulls of the cigarette, exhaled the smoke and stubbed out the rest. He looked back at Ranko and his battered face who was still just staring at him and he said quietly:

"Bajić you belong to the past and not to the future. You do not have one shred of humanity or compassion within you and you may find it strange but I actually find myself feeling sorry for you. But whatever may or may not happen in the future then you just remember that you had it coming to you."

And without saying another word he took the mobile phone out of his pocket and threw it into the car and turned and walked back to the white Volkswagen parked fifty metres up the road with its bright orange flashing hazard lights piercing the dark of the night. It had completely stopped raining now and wrapping his hand in a towel from the boot he punched out the remains of the windscreen, started the engine and switched on the lights. He turned the car round and proceeded to drive back down the mountain road up which he had raced up not long before without glancing at the wrecked Peugeot as he passed by. He drove slowly not just to minimise the wind that was streaming through the open windscreen frame but also because he was lost in a myriad of thoughts, a kaleidoscope of mixed emotions. He drove on for about an hour and then decided to pull off the road, conceal the car and try to get a few hours sleep.

He awoke a few hours later to see the pink light of dawn on the horizon above the trees and he restarted the car and drove on stopping at a village about ten miles outside of Banja Luka. He found what he was looking for, a public telephone box so he parked up. There was no one around in the village square at that time but the telephone kiosk had a single light bulb in it which burned brightly. He dialled the number for the police emergency services and told the operator that he had been carjacked late last night by two men as he parked by a bar in Banja Luka – the one in which he had seen Ranko Bajic where he had also had a beer so if the police checked and gave his description the bar man should remember that he had been there. He relayed to them that he had been knocked unconscious in the car park behind the parade of shops and driven out of Banja Luka and dumped somewhere in the woods at the side of the road. He had awoken a couple of hours ago and had walked to the village to make this call. He was given a crime number and told to make a statement at a police station when he returned to Sarajevo which would be sent to the police in Banja Luka. However, they were not confident of catching the criminals because they said that Tarik's description of his assailants was not specific enough and there was a lot of crime in that area with rival criminal gangs fighting each other in some kind of turf war and this kind of incident was not uncommon. However, Tarik also strongly suspected that once again his name had revealed his ethnicity and that here in the heart of the Republika Sprska they were not overly concerned about spending a lot of time and effort over something that had occurred to a Bosnian Muslim from Sarajevo. Tarik then phoned the hire car company in Sarajevo and retold his story and gave them the crime number that he had been issued with.

A half hour later he walked back to the car. It was getting lighter now and it was the first time that Tarik had been able to take a good look at it clearly. The white Golf looked in a real mess. Its rear was all caved in from the repeated shunts incurred by the Peugeot on the mountain road the night before. It was dirty and covered with mud and the windscreen was missing with fragments of glass still clinging to the edges of the frame and shards of glass littered the interior. But most disturbing of all were three clear bullet holes in the bodywork, one that had penetrated the boot space and two in the centre of the offside rear passenger door. Tarik felt a distinct chill run up his spine. Here was a vivid and graphic sign of how close he had come to disaster the night before. He decided to leave the village quickly before the car was seen and people started to ask questions.

He drove out of the village and abandoned the car about a half mile down a side track that led into the forest. He removed all of his few possessions that were in the car and took the towel and dipped it in the ditch to make it wet and wiped down the steering wheel, gear knob and door handles and then walked back to the road and waked on until he came to a bus stop and he waited for the first bus to take him into central Banja Luka. He made his way quickly to the train station, bought a cup of coffee and a sandwich and caught the first train back to Sarajevo.

He had three days before Jelena would return so he made an appointment at the dentist to fix his loose front tooth which he explained had occurred when he had been in the changing room before a match and someone was practicing a swing of the bat without realising that he was behind them and he was caught full in the face which also accounted for the bruising on his face and nose. He finally felt free. He felt lighter than he had in years as if a heavy burden had suddenly been lifted from his shoulders. A large dark cloud that seemed to have been permanently hanging over him had suddenly parted and he could feel the warmth of the sun on his face once again. It had been a long time coming.

There were five things that he had to do, attend prayers at the local Mosque, visit his father's grave, have dinner with his mother and Minka, arrange to meet Faris at the café in Sebilj Square and email Peter Soberg in America.

Sitting by his father's grave on the hillside above Sarajevo he stared at the white stele in front of him. It was quiet and tranquil up here. There was a gentle breeze blowing and he was the only person in the cemetery at the time. Tarik just sat there saying nothing and breathing slowly and shallowly. He let the peace of the situation just wash over him. For the first time in years he felt at ease with himself, his life and everything that had happened. Once again as so often in the past he reflected on the words of Martin Luther King but this time it was a quote from the American Civil Rights leader's wife, Coretta Scott King that came into his mind and just stayed there whilst he gazed back down the hillside towards the city that he loved so much:

"Hate is too great a burden to bear. It injures the hater more than it injures the hated."

Chapter Twenty Four

Three days later Jelena returned from Belgrade and was delighted to find Tarik in such fine spirits. He explained that he had played a lot of baseball while she had been away and he explained away the bruising on his face and nose caused by the punches inflicted on him by Ranko during their initial confrontation in Banja Luka which were now starting to fade.

Tarik and Jelena were now attending ante natal classes and awaiting the birth of their first child. Tarik had started to forget about the whole episode that had occurred in the Republika Sprska the previous week and he was concentrating almost entirely on domestic issues and once again throwing himself into his work determined to build his career.

But there was one thing left for him to do and he hoped that he could then have complete closure on all of this for the rest of his life. Ranko Bajić had never apologised for murdering his father nor had he tried to explain it away as being an action carried out in the 'fog of war.' Quite the reverse. He had celebrated the fact that he had shot him and many other unarmed Sarajevans as they had struggled to survive whilst the city was under siege. Tarik was also in no doubt that had things turned out differently on the mountain road that night he would have had no hesitation in killing him too.

A few days later Tarik stayed late at work to both catch up on what he had missed while he was away and also to write a long email to Peter in Los Angeles. He had not wanted to involve Peter again in his troubles but he could see no other option. He explained in detail what he wanted to do and whether it was possible and what could he possibly do to return all the favours that Peter had done for him. He also realised what he was asking Peter to do was most probably illegal and that if he did not want to do it that was fine by him as he had helped him so much already. Tarik was careful to delete the email once it had been sent.

However, he needn't have had any concerns though because the following morning when he booted up his computer at his office desk there was an email from Peter;

Hi Tarik

No problem I can do that. It will be a pleasure and I will relish the challenge.

I cannot believe what happened to you. You are very lucky not to have been killed. That guy has it coming anyway. Don't worry I will leave no trace and it will all be completely anonymous and it will boost my reputation and credibility in the right quarters.

However, Tarik this is the end of it. I will not undertake any more tasks for you. Not because I do not want to but because I believe that you have to draw a line under this now, accept your new responsibilities and move on.

By the way thanks for the money that you transferred by Western Union the other day. I am going to buy myself a new piece of kit that has just become available. I will be back in touch in a few days.

Rgds
Peter

Just over a week later following another email from Peter:

Hi Tarik

All done. Not sure how long it will last but that doesn't matter. This particular chapter in our lives is now closed.

Best
Peter

Tarik typed in the URL for the Republika Srpska web site into the browser of his computer and clicked .He waited whilst the computer searched for the site and he felt his mouth go dry and his heart rate quicken. Then all of a sudden the home page of the site opened but almost immediately a large white box filled most of the screen and he was staring at two photos of Ranko Bajić. One was in his military uniform which Peter had downloaded from the Service Record site and the other was one taken by Tarik on his mobile phone when Ranko had been motionless in the car after hitting the oak tree.

Above the photos was a banner headline in both Serbian and English:

'Murderer' *and* **'Убица.'**

'This man is called Ranko Bajić. On the 25th November 1994 he shot an unarmed man in cold blood for the price of a packet of American cigarettes. The man he killed was a loving husband and father of two children who was desperately trying to fend for his family to prevent them being starved to death during the long siege of Sarajevo.

Ranko Bajić still thinks that life is cheap. The life of a Bosniak particularly so. If on reading this you feel moved to offer him a light for his cigarettes then please find his contact details below.'

The web site was eventually taken down 'for maintenance' it said a couple of hours later but not before it had been visited by just over one thousand people from around the world. Most of these had been encouraged to do so by the posts and links left by Peter on numerous bulletin boards, activist web sites and hacker spaces. Ranko Bajić was very likely to have a number of visitors both in the cyber world and possibly in the real world too. Perhaps for a while the hunter would now become the hunted.

Tarik just smiled and whispered to himself:
'Then *so be it.'*

Chapter Twenty Five

The red taxi pulled up outside Tarik and Jelena's apartment block and honked its horn loudly twice. Minutes later Tarik, Faris, Vildana and Jelena who was pushing a buggy with six week old Mak Sejo Tanović came out of the front door of the block and got into the taxi after folding the buggy and placing it in the boot. Tarik got into the front passenger seat and gave instructions to the driver and then put some sun glasses on and sat back in the seat.

The journey out of the city did not take long and then they started climbing steadily. No one had said a word throughout the journey and even baby Mak was content wrapped in a blanket in his mother's arms. Each of them were absorbed in their own thoughts as they looked out of the windows of the taxi. A little while later they were awoken from their reverie by Tarik saying to the driver:

"This will be fine here. Please wait and we will be back in about fifteen minutes."

They all got out of the taxi and took the buggy out of the boot and walked slowly following the lead that Tarik was taking. Five minutes later he stopped at the edge of the ridge near the summit of Mount Trebović. He stretched out his arms to the city that was laid out below before them. The sun was just starting to set and was casting long shadows across the city but many of the iconic buildings were still clearly identifiable bellow them were bathed in a soft glowing light. From their vantage point they could make out Sarajevo's Old Orthodox Church, Sarajevo Cathedral, Gazi Husrev-beg Mosque, the City Hall, the Latin Bridge and the construction site that was being created around the ruins of the National Library to restore it to its former glory.

Tarik turned his head back to the group and smiled and then faced forward once more and keeping his arms outstretched before him he said in a loud voice:

"City of hope. City of faith and resolve, City of friendship. Our Jerusalem."

Epilogue

In March 2014 it was estimated by Bosnian Federation entity, The Veterans' Affairs Ministry that around two thousand children could have fought in the 1992-95 war, sometimes in horrific conditions on the frontlines but nobody really knows for certain:

"We have no data on how many of them there are, what really are their problems and needs are," Federation veterans' affairs minister Zukan Helez said.

A total of six hundred and sixty one soldiers between the ages of ten and eighteen were killed during the conflict, according to data collected by the Research and Documentation Centre in Sarajevo:

"Of those who survived, many suffer seriously from post-traumatic stress disorder" Helez said.

Twelve years later Tarik was reading the newspaper at breakfast with Jelena and his thirteen year old son, Mak Sejo and ten year old daughter, Ana Jela in their new apartment and as he read the headlines a broad smile came over his face and he whispered to himself *"There is a universal justice."*

International News 24th March 2016

Radovan Karadžić jailed for Bosnia War genocide.

Former Bosnian Serb leader Radovan Karadžić has been convicted of genocide and war crimes in the 1992-95 Bosnian War and sentenced to forty years in jail.

UN judges found him guilty of ten of the eleven charges, including genocide over the 1995 Srebrenica massacre and the campaign of sniping and shelling against the civilian population of Sarajevo with the aim of spreading terror amongst them.

Prosecutors said that Karadzic, as political and commander-in-chief of the Serb forces in Bosnia, was responsible for some of the worst acts of brutality during the war, including the forty four month deadly siege of Sarajevo and the 1995 massacre of more than eight thousand Bosnian men and boys in the Srebrenica enclave.

Speaking after the verdicts, Serge Brammertz, the tribunal's chief prosecutor said:

"Moments like this should remind us that in innumerable conflicts around the world today, millions of victims are now waiting for their own justice. This judgement shows that it is possible to deliver it."

Also by Tony Barnard:

The Sheffield Avengers

A story of supreme courage.

Two boys who grew up together in the district of Tinsley in Sheffield against a backdrop of the declining fortunes of the once world-beating steel industry. One indebted to the other from an early age and both with powerful ambitions. *The Sheffield Avengers* is the story of their development, their personal relationships with their families and their lovers, acts of supreme courage and the restoration of pride. 'Made in Sheffield' is a global endorsement of quality, strength and consistency that can apply to its people, products and a warship that carried its name.

Fast paced and international in its breadth and reach. The Sheffield Avengers is a meticulously researched and compelling 'what if' story of the skill and courage of Britain's Special Forces during the Falkland's War in 1982.

Paperback: 212 pages
Publisher: lulu.com (9 Jan. 2015)
ISBN-10: 1326080865
ISBN-13: 978-1326080860

Printed in Great Britain
by Amazon